PRAISE FOR DIANE KELLY'S
PAW ENFORCEMENT SERIES

"Kelly's writing is smart and laugh-out-loud funny."
—Kristan Higgins, *New York Times* bestselling author

"Humor, romance, and surprising LOL moments. What more can you ask for?" —*Romance and Beyond*

"Fabulously fun and funny!" —*Book Babe*

"An engaging read that I could not put down. I look forward to the next adventure of Megan and Brigit!"
—*SOS Aloha*

"Sparkling with surprises. Just like a tequila sunrise. You never know which way is up or out!"
—*Romance Junkies*

ENFORCING THE
PAW

Diane Kelly

St. Martin's Paperbacks

This is a work of fiction. All of the characters, organizations, and events portrayed in this novel are either products of the author's imagination or are used fictitiously.

ENFORCING THE PAW

Copyright © 2017 by Diane Kelly.

For information address St. Martin's Press, 175 Fifth Avenue, New York, NY 10010.

ISBN: 978-1-250-09486-5

Our books may be purchased in bulk for promotional, educational, or business use. Please contact your local bookseller or the Macmillan Corporate and Premium Sales Department at 1-800-221-7945, ext. 5442, or by e-mail at MacmillanSpecialMarkets@macmillan.com.

Printed in the United States of America

St. Martin's Paperbacks edition / July 2017

St. Martin's Paperbacks are published by St. Martin's Press, 175 Fifth Avenue, New York, NY 10010.

10 9 8 7 6 5 4 3 2 1

ACKNOWLEDGMENTS

An author is just one of the many people who get books from an idea bouncing around in a brain to a printed or digital reality. Thanks to everyone who played a part in getting this story out of my gray matter and into the world!

As always, many thanks to my top-notch editor, Holly Ingraham, who is insightful and patient and keeps me on a loose leash.

Thanks to Sarah Melnyck, Paul Hochman, Jennie Conway, Allison Ziegler, and the rest of the team at St. Martin's for all of your work in getting this book to readers.

Thanks to Danielle Christopher and Jennifer Taylor for creating such fun book covers for this series.

Thanks to my agent, Helen Breitwieser, for your efforts in furthering my writing career.

Thanks to the creative and professional Liz Bemis and the staff of Bemis Promotions for my great Web site and newsletters.

Thanks to authors Angela Cavener, Christie Craig, DD Ayres, and Susan Muller for your input and suggestions on my work, and for acting as sounding boards for me. I couldn't do this without you, and I feel privileged to call you friends.

Thanks to Lis for your generous donation to the Richardson Adult Literacy Center at the annual Buns & Roses Romance Tea for Literacy. It was fun getting to feature your furry little girl Maya in the book!

And finally, thanks to you fabulous readers who picked up this book! I hope you enjoy this latest adventure with Megan and Brigit.

ENFORCING THE
PAW

ONE
SHATTERED

The Devoted One

The brick felt as heavy and hard and cold as the broken heart in the Devoted One's chest.

Perfect.

Launching it into the air provided a sense of power and control the Devoted One hadn't felt in a long time.

CRASH!

The back window of the house exploded into a dozen shards that tinkled as they fell to the concrete patio and the wood floor inside. *Safety glass, my ass.*

The brick might just be a rectangle of baked clay, but it would send a clear message. *We're not over.*

TWO
TINKLE

Fort Worth Police Officer Megan Luz

On a Monday night in early August, my shepherd-mix partner Brigit and I were out on patrol, working the night shift. Well, at least *I* was working. Brigit snoozed away on the carpeted platform in the back of our specially equipped K-9 cruiser. A human officer would have been fired for sleeping on the job, but K-9s? They could get away with it. *Lucky dog.* She wasn't quiet about it either, snoring loud enough to wake the dead. *Way to rub it in.*

Her snooze came to an abrupt end when a vandalism call came in over the radio. She snuffled and raised her head from the comfy cushion I'd bought her, casting me a bleary-eyed look that said she was none too happy about her sweet dreams being interrupted.

"We've got a report of a broken window," the dispatcher said. "The victim reports she believes her ex-boyfriend tried to break into her home."

Ugh. Domestic violence is the worst.

The victim's address was on College Avenue in the

southern part of the Fairmount neighborhood, only a few of blocks from our current location. Brigit's unique K-9 skills could be especially helpful in a situation like this, where the perpetrator would have left a scent trail.

I grabbed the microphone from my dashboard and responded to the call. "Officers Luz and Brigit on our way." I slid the mic back into its holder and punched the gas. *Off we go!*

Three turns and less than thirty-eight seconds later, my cruiser rolled to a stop in front of the address. While the historic Fairmount neighborhood boasted some beautifully restored homes, many of which were quite large, this single-story white house was among its more modest dwellings. My eyes took in the place, while the brain behind them performed some quick computations of its own accord, estimating the home to be approximately twelve hundred square feet given its width and depth.

White oleander bushes flanked the front porch and spanned the width of the house. *Hmm.* You'd have thought the owner might have planted pink oleanders to add some color, but who was I to judge? There was no garage. The house had been built long before cars were common and the owner had apparently decided not to add one, though there was a short paved driveway in which a beige Hyundai Accent was parked. The porch light was on, as were lights inside the front room, the glow visible around the edges of the slatted wood blinds in the windows. *The broken window must be around back.*

I climbed out of my car and opened the back door to let Brigit out. After allowing her to take a quick tinkle in the grass, I clipped her leash onto her collar and led her up the single step to the front door. While many of the other houses in the area sported cheery floral wreaths on their front doors, a large sign that read NO SOLICITING was plastered across this door. Even the welcome mat wasn't very welcoming. Instead of greeting visitors with a simple WELCOME or funny phrase—the one at our house read WIPE YOUR PAWS—it looked more like a torture device, all stiff and bristly.

I raised my hand and knocked. *Rap-rap-rap!* A moment later the door was answered by a pretty, petite Latina woman. Being of both Mexican and Irish descent, my skin, like this woman's, was slightly darker than that of most Caucasians, though mine bore a scattering of freckles while hers was more uniform in color. She appeared to be in her early thirties, giving her a six or seven-year lead on me. She stood a couple inches shorter than my five feet five inches, putting her around five three. As long as we were talking in numbers, I'd put her around an 8 on the attractiveness scale. As for myself, I'd let others be the judge of that. The number I was more interested in was my IQ, which was above average, thank you very much.

The woman wore a drab gray bathrobe over pajamas, no makeup, and a strained expression. Her dark hair was messy from sleep, loose curls playing about her head, much unlike the taut bun into which I'd pulled my dark locks. Her eyes flickered down to Brigit, who was sniffing at something through the wooden boards of the porch, and she took what appeared to be an involuntary step backward. Not unusual. Many people found police dogs intimidating. Rightfully so. Brigit could just as easily rip a person's throat out as lick him or her to death.

"He's at it again," the woman said, gazing downward and speaking so softly I could barely hear her.

I pulled out my notepad. "I understand someone attempted to break into your home?"

"Not *someone*," she said, a little louder now, her gaze moving up to my badge. "My ex-boyfriend."

She could very well be right. But she could also be jumping to conclusions. I'd learned early on in my law enforcement career not to take everything at face value. "What's your name, ma'am?"

"Adriana Valdez."

I noted her name on my pad. "What happened exactly?"

"I was in bed sleeping a few minutes ago," she said, gesturing back into the house behind her, "when a loud crash woke me up. I turned on my lamp and found one of my bedroom windows broken and a brick lying on the floor."

"Did you see anyone?"

She shook her head. "No. I didn't try to look. I was too freaked out. I grabbed my phone and took it into the closet and called 911 as fast as I could."

"What makes you think it was your ex?"

"It *had* to be him," Adriana said, her feeble voice finally wielding some force as her gaze met mine for the first time. "Nobody else would have a reason to do something like that."

Juvenile delinquents did things like this all the time without a reason, but no sense arguing with her. "Can you show us?"

"Us?" She glanced down at Brigit again. "The dog's coming with you?"

"I'd planned on bringing her inside, yes." She was my partner, after all.

Adriana's lips pursed and her nose twitched. "Does she shed?"

Brigit was a furry, hundred-pound shepherd with approximately eighty billion active hair follicles. She shed enough hair each day to stuff a sofa. So, naturally, I said, "Not much."

Adriana looked skeptical, but stepped back to let me and Brigit inside, gesturing to the door mat. "Wipe your feet, please."

Well, all righty then.

Once I'd scrubbed my feet across the bristly mat, she said, "The bedroom's back here."

I stepped into the house, Brigit alongside me. The place had been built in a shotgun style, the rooms in a single row from front to back. Brigit and I followed her through a tidy combination living and dining room decorated in colors that hardly qualified as such. Muted beiges and ivories with no accents. Oddly, the living room featured only a love seat, no couch or occasional chairs. Ms. Valdez must not have people over much. The throw pillows on the love seat were perfectly positioned in the corners, and the books on the bookshelves were arranged fastidiously by height, each row precisely level. Not a speck of dust appeared atop any of the furniture surfaces.

The door at the opposite end led into a small kitchen with a butcher-block island. A circular rack of pots and pans hung over the island, while a wooden white bistro set sat in the back corner. The place gleamed and smelled strongly of disinfectant, as if she'd recently cleaned.

As we passed through, I took a quick glance around. A set of herb pots sat on the windowsill next to a metal baker's rack loaded down with more cookbooks than I'd ever seen outside of a bookstore's shelves. There were a dozen books on dieting, too, everything from the raw food craze to books with titles suggesting hormones, blood sugar, and renal function could all be controlled via food intake. A toaster and pasta maker stood on the counter to the left of the stove, a blender, a juicer, and a sparkling top-of-the-line silver Cuisinart food processor to the right. From the looks of it, Adriana could slice, dice, and perform brain surgery with the complicated thing. A carving knife and a long meat fork with two pointy prongs lay drying in a dish rack, along with a single plate and glass.

No coffeepot was in sight. How anyone could survive without caffeine was beyond me. I'd never get through my night shifts without a thermos or two of the stuff. A large rack mounted on the back wall was loaded with a combination of cooking spices and vitamins arranged in alphabetical order, the vitamin B_{12} tablets coming just before bay leaf.

We exited the kitchen into a small bedroom being used as a home office. Like the other rooms, this one was perfectly tidy, a place for everything and everything in its place, looking like a model home where people only pretended to live. The door on the opposite end led to a hallway with a bathroom to the side. A shelving unit in the bath was loaded down with every cleaning product on the market, from antibacterial wipes to citrus-scented degreaser to wood floor cleaner.

A second, larger bedroom spanned the back of the house. The overhead light was on, illuminating the interior of the master bedroom. Two narrow windows flanked the queen-sized bed, which was covered in a plain ivory spread. The window on the left was indeed shattered, the damaged wooden miniblind hanging cockeyed, the slats splayed. Broken glass littered the night table and the floor below the window.

I'd need to take a closer look, but I didn't want to risk Brigit cutting her paw on the shards. "Sit," I ordered my partner, giving her a scratch behind the ear and a "good girl" when she obeyed. I eased around the bed and spotted an orange brick lying amid the glass, the word ACME imprinted on the end. I glanced out the window and, noting the backyard was not well lit, pulled out my Maglite. When I switched it on and shined it around the patio, a pair of big, round eyes stared back out of the darkness.

"Holy crap!" I shrieked, jumping back in surprise. "He's still back there!" My heart pounded so hard it was a wonder we couldn't hear my rib cage rattle.

Adriana sent a disdainful look in my general direction. "That's not my ex. That's a garden gnome."

A gnome? Sure enough, when I shined the light out the window again, I saw a foot-high garden gnome with round, unblinking eyes. He wore blue overalls, a yellow hat, and a smile so creepy I was tempted to whip out my pepper spray and douse him.

Taking the beam off the tiny man and playing it about, I saw a wide slab of concrete and a narrow vegetable garden situated along the perimeter of the yard. A dozen gnomes of various ages, genders, and occupations stood among the plants. A white-haired female gnome with a pink dress and a basket of apples. A dark-haired male gnome pushing a wheelbarrow full of rocks. A young, blond girl gnome scattering food to the flock of ceramic chickens at her feet. My light moved from the gnomes to the plants. They were loaded down, bending under the weight of their produce. Looked like Adriana had raised a bumper crop of tomatoes and zucchini. She must have a green thumb.

While I aspired to become a detective one day and had been working hard to develop my investigative skills, this situation required little analysis. Someone threw the brick through the glass. This woman assumed that someone was her ex. She could very well be right. People who once loved each other could be capable of doing some very spiteful things. But if I were going to accuse the guy and arrest him, I needed to get my ducks in a row first, collect some evidence. "Mind if my partner and I take a look out back?"

"I'd appreciate it," Adriana said. "There's a door from the kitchen."

Brigit trotted along as I followed Adriana back to the kitchen, where she opened a side door adorned with a set of café curtains. The porch light mounted next to the door provided some illumination, but the light didn't go far. I used my flashlight to light the way along the narrow flagstone path that ran between the house and the privacy fence.

"Stay where you are," I told Adriana, as I stopped at the edge of the concrete patio and shined my flashlight about, looking for evidence. At first all I saw were the questioning eyes of the gnomes peering at me from among the plants.

Nothing over here.

Nothing over there.

Nothing by the house.

But then, *bingo!*

At the back edge of the concrete was a man-sized footprint next to a small, half-ripe tomato that appeared to have been knocked off the vine. The muddy print showed a clear waffle pattern. I carefully circled closer for a better look, crouching down to look among the tomato plants. The beam of my flashlight revealed another footprint between two plants. Looked like whoever had thrown the brick must have veered off the path in the dark.

I glanced back toward the side gate, which hung open a few inches. "You don't keep a lock on your gate?"

"No," Adriana replied, seemingly focused on something over my left shoulder. "I use a mowing service and the gas meter is on the wall behind the fence so I have to keep it unlocked for the meter reader, too. Besides, the latch is off-kilter and doesn't catch. I've reported it to my landlord, but you know how they are."

I knew exactly how landlords could be. Dismissive. Unconcerned. Miserly. The guy who owned the studio apartment where Brigit and I used to live had refused to replace the air-conditioning unit until it went up in smoke and threatened to take the entire building with it. *Cheap son of a bitch.* Thank goodness I didn't live in that rat-infested hellhole anymore.

I stepped over to the gate to take a closer look. Sure

enough, the latch needed to be repaired. "Did your ex-boyfriend know the latch was broken?"

"Yes. He said he'd fix it for me but you can tell how good he was at keeping his word."

Not at all, it seemed. "So he's taken a look at the gate before?"

"Yes."

The fact that he'd touched the hardware in the past meant that if his prints were found on the latch it would not conclusively prove he'd been the one who'd come into the backyard and thrown the brick. "What about the brick?" I asked Adriana. "Did that come from your yard?"

"No. I have no idea where it came from."

In other words, if the ex's prints were on the brick, it would link him to the crime. Of course he might have been smart enough to wear gloves, and if he didn't have a record his prints wouldn't be in the database anyway, but it was worth a shot.

"I'd suggest you have the latch fixed right away," I told her. "Call a handyman if you have to. And put a lock on the gate. You can give the lawn care company a key. The gas company can tell you what day your meter is going to be read so you can plan ahead and remove the lock for that day only. You might want to add some more outdoor lighting, too. Maybe something with a motion sensor. Those types of lights tend to act as a deterrent."

I'd given the same advice to people in the Berkeley Place neighborhood recently when a Peeping Tom had been creeping around the area, spying on women. Criminals tended to like dark, shadowy spots where they could hide. Shine a light on them, though, and they scattered like cockroaches.

I snapped a few photos of the footprints with my phone, returned it to my pocket, and pulled out my notepad. "I have some questions for you. But let's g-go back inside." No sense waking the neighbors if the crashing glass hadn't already.

Once we were back in the kitchen, I readied my pen. "What's your ex's name?"

"Ryan Downey."

I jotted the name down. "You said earlier you hoped we could put a stop to things 'this time.' Has there been a history of this type of incident?"

"History?" She scoffed. "There's enough history to fill a textbook. It's been one thing after another since I broke up with him a month ago. He was putting too much pressure on me, wanting to get too serious too fast. To be honest, I just wasn't that in to him. We're too different. At first he tried to get me back. He came by here every day for a week, sometimes more than once. When I stopped answering the door he left flowers and gifts on the porch. He's the one who gave me the gnomes. If they weren't so cute I'd get rid of them."

Hmm. If I had a beef with an ex and something around my house reminded me of him, I probably would have gotten rid of it, cute or not. But I knew not everyone thinks the same way, so I accepted her explanation.

She opened a drawer and pulled out a stack of greeting cards. "These are the cards he left after I dumped him."

She held them out to me. I took them from her and

quickly looked them over. Each of them was a typical, vague "thinking of you" type of card. He'd scrawled handwritten messages on each one.

You should be with someone who deserves you.

Your soul mate is out there. Don't keep him waiting.

You won't be alone much longer. Someone's going to snatch you up!

Ryan's words could be seen as encouraging. Then again, they could be taken as veiled threats.

I handed the cards back to her. "Hang on to those."

"You think they're important?"

"They could be." It was too soon to tell.

She nodded and returned the cards to the drawer before turning back to me. She seemed to be addressing my earlobe. "The last time Ryan came by, I told him in no uncertain terms that we'd never get back together. After that he started doing mean, vengeful things. He stole my mail and poured salt in my garden to try to kill the plants. He's also driven by late at night several times and thrown tennis balls at my car to set off the alarm. My neighbors have complained to me about the noise. It's a nightmare."

"Did you see him do these things? Pouring the salt and stealing your mail and throwing the tennis balls?"

She frowned. "No. But like I said, there's no reason for anyone else to be doing things like this to me."

Again, she could be right. But she could also be wrong. It was my job to gather facts and explore all potential leads. Could the brick be the result of a petty sibling squabble? Brothers and sisters could do some pretty mean things to each other under the right circumstances.

I'd once broken up a fight between two brothers, but not before one gave the other a bloody nose. "Do you get along with your family?"

"As well as anyone does, I guess. We're not exactly close, but there's no animosity between us."

"Do they live here in town?"

"No. My parents live down in Waco where I grew up, and my brother is in graduate school in Austin."

Looked like the immediate family could be ruled out. "What about your friends?" I asked. "Have you had a falling-out with anyone?" Women could be petty, too. One wrong look at another's boyfriend and a woman could find *Whore!* scribbled across her windshield in red lipstick.

"No. I haven't had any problems with friends."

"How about coworkers?" I asked. "Do you get along with everyone at the office?"

"I don't work in an office," she corrected, a hint of impatience in her voice. "I work at a rehabilitation center. My work is pretty solitary. I mostly just interact with patients, and even then it's not often. Only two or three times a day."

"What do you do?"

"I'm a clinical dietitian."

That explained all the tomes on diet and cooking. "Your n-neighbors," I said, noticing her gaze went to my mouth when my stutter manifested again. "How are your relationships with them?"

"Fine, I suppose. We say hello if we happen to pass each other on the street or see each other getting the mail, but other than them complaining about my car alarm, that's been the extent of our interactions."

She didn't appear to have a dog that might be barking and annoying anyone, and I hadn't heard any noisy wind chimes dinging and donging in the breeze. Still, in these types of situations the culprit was sometimes a neighbor who'd reached the end of their rope. I told her as much. "Do you have a noisy hobby or play music loud in the backyard? Maybe have an outdoor cat that uses someone's flower bed for a litter box?"

"I know what you're getting at, but no. I don't have any pets and I'm quiet and I keep to myself. The perfect neighbor." She threw her hands in the air, her voice growing shaky and high with emotion. "The cop who came out before asked me virtually the same questions. I'm telling you the same thing I told him. Ryan is behind this. I know it!"

I raised a palm. "I'm not saying I don't believe you, Ms. Valdez. It's my job to ask questions and rule out other possibilities."

She crossed her arms loosely over her chest. "I understand." Though her words said she knew where I was coming from, her tone told me she didn't like it.

"Do you recall the name of the officer who came out before?" It couldn't hurt to have a chat with him or her, compare notes.

"Mackey," Adriana snapped without hesitation. "Tall, redheaded guy. No offense, but he was useless. Do you know him?"

Hell, yeah, I knew Officer Derek Mackey. Derek, a.k.a. the Big Dick, had been my training partner. He was an asshole of epic proportions. He'd once sent me out into a monsoon to buy him a bag of chips at the convenience store, then locked the doors on me and cackled when I yanked on the handle and banged on the glass, trying to get back in the squad car. There was an inch of water in my shoes by the time he let me in. He passed gas in the cruiser on multiple occasions and held the button down so I couldn't unroll my window. He never asked where I wanted to eat lunch, stopping once or twice a week for meals at Hooters or a topless bar, claiming a regular police presence was a help at the latter due to the crime associated with sexually oriented businesses. *Yeah, right.* He'd just wanted a cheap lunch and cheap thrills. I'd learned to pack a lunch box and eat in the car by myself.

"Sure, I know Officer Mackey." I hoped my distaste for my former partner wasn't evident in my voice. "He and I were partners a while back."

Adriana gave me a pointed look. "I hope you'll do more than he did. He took my statement but that was it. He said that since there was no property damage and no witnesses, it would be a waste of time to talk to Ryan or take the tennis ball in to be checked for prints."

Though I didn't exactly feel inclined to defend the bastard who'd made my life miserable for months, I did feel the need to defend the integrity of the Fort Worth Police Department. I also felt the need to make this woman feel safe again. "Officers have to make case-by-case judgment calls," I said. "Officer Mackey must've thought it would be futile to check with Ryan because people rarely admit their crimes. As for the tennis ball, it's virtually impossible to lift prints off them due to the texture of the covering. But I'll speak with your ex. If he's behind these acts, he might back off if a police officer shows up."

"Tell him he needs to move on," she said. "I already have. I'm dating one of the doctors from work now."

"Good," I said. "It's nice to have a special someone."

I had a special someone of my own. *Seth*. While my life had seemed full enough before him, he added something I hadn't realized I'd been missing. Romance. Companionship. A pair of ears to listen and broad shoulders to lean on.

I held my pen at the ready. "What's Ryan's address?"

She rattled off the name of an apartment complex on Hulen Street, which sat at the western edge of the W1 Division, my usual beat.

"He lives in apartment 206."

"Got it." I also asked if she knew his middle name, which she did.

"Michael. Why?"

"I'll need to run his name through the system. See if he has a record of any sort."

"He never mentioned having one."

"Most people who have a criminal record don't speak of it." Especially if they wanted to get close to someone, to be trusted. "I'll be right back." I returned to my car with Brigit trotting along behind me. After retrieving latex gloves and a plastic evidence bag from my trunk, my furry partner and I went back to the kitchen. I ordered Brigit to stay put while I ventured again to the bedroom, picked up the brick, and dropped it into the evidence bag. Why the guy had thrown a brick instead of a garden gnome was beyond me. But maybe he didn't want to end an innocent little life.

Adriana stood in the doorway, watching as I collected the evidence. "I appreciate you taking this seriously. I guess because you're a woman you understand how scary something like this can be."

"It would certainly be unsettling," I agreed. Still, a brick through a window was child's play compared to a sociopath strapping a bomb to your chest, gang members aiming guns at your face at point-blank range, and a stranger slamming his SUV into you on the highway, running you off the road into a construction zone, and opening fire when you were trapped in your car. But no sense one-upping her with my dangerous on-the-job exploits. Besides, a stalker could pose a real threat. It was never clear how far a stalker would go. Some merely exacted a bit of petty revenge and moved on. Others escalated their threatening behavior, doing more and more dangerous things until they were either caught and jailed, or until they killed their victims. I had no idea what type Ryan Michael Downey would prove to be but, for everyone's sake, I was hoping he was the petty type.

I tucked the bagged brick under my arm, removed the gloves, and tossed them into Adriana's trash can. After obtaining her cell phone number, I slid my pen and notepad back into my pocket. "I'll let you know how it goes."

"Thanks, Officer Luz." She blinked several times, as if holding back tears. "I really hope you can put a stop to this. I just . . ." Her breath hitched. "I just want it to be over."

THREE
THIS MAKES SCENTS

Fort Worth PD K-9 Sergeant Brigit

Outside, Megan led Brigit to the gate and ordered her to find a scent and trail the disturbance. The dog obliged, sniffing around, but the only disturbance she smelled was in the backyard where they'd just been, and along this fence. She stretched up, putting her paws on the boards and looking over at Megan, trying to communicate that there was no trail to the front yard.

Megan wasn't showing any teeth. *Darn.* When Megan showed her teeth, she was more likely to give Brigit a liver treat. But it never hurt to ask, right?

Still propped on the fence, Brigit emitted a soft, insistent *woof.* Translation: *Pay me, or I quit.*

Megan shined her flashlight over the top of the fence and stood on tiptoe to look over it before reaching into her pocket and pulling out a treat. "Here you go, girl."

Brigit wolfed the treat down. *Yum!*

They left the backyard. Megan stepped over to the fence next door and tried to open the gate, but it didn't move. Back into the car they went.

A few minutes later, Megan let Brigit out of her enclosure at an apartment complex. As they went up a set of outdoor stairs, Brigit's nose picked up two familiar scents. The first was the aroma of squashed tomato. The second was the faint smell of a human male that she'd scented coming from the brick Megan had bagged.

She put her nose down to seek the sources, moving faster as she hit the landing and scurried over to a pair of shoes lying tucked behind a folded lawn chair leaning against the outer wall. The shoes smelled like both the tomatoes and the man. She sat and looked up at Megan, giving her passive alert. Megan hadn't asked her to look for a tomato or the man, but Brigit sensed it might be important and could earn her another liver treat. It was worth a try, right?

Megan shined her flashlight on the shoes, whispered, "Good girl!", and tossed her another goodie.

This was turning out to be a darn good shift!

FOUR
LOVE LESSONS

The Devoted One

Tonight's lesson had been short and simple, just a pop quiz in what would be a complete course in love and respect.

> Question 1: Was it right to treat me the way you did? To end things between us for no good reason?
> Correct answer: No, it was not.
> Question 2: Will you get in touch with me so we can make things right again?
> Correct answer: Yes, I will.

The Devoted One had no doubt that they could get past this, that the two of them could get back together and move on, the last few weeks amounting to nothing more than a rough patch in what would otherwise be a long, happy life together. It was a shame the cops had to be involved, but if that's what it took to get some attention, to reopen the lines of communication, well, then that's what it took.

With a lighter heart, the Devoted One settled back under the covers.

FIVE
WAFFLING

Megan

Sure enough, the shoes that Brigit had alerted on featured the same waffle-style soles that had left the print on Adriana's patio. Sitting next to the shoes was a piece of newspaper covered in blue paint and weighted down with three orange bricks, all of which had the ACME imprint on the end just like the one that had been thrown through Adriana's window. *Sheesh. Some criminals don't even have the sense to hide the evidence, do they?*

I pulled out my phone and snapped photos of both the shoes and bricks. I'd bag the shoes and one of the bricks later, but first I wanted to see how Ryan reacted to my questions.

The guy had no criminal record. I'd checked before coming to his apartment. Given that fact, I might have hesitated to wake him at this late hour if not for the shoes and bricks out here on his porch. But with clear evidence of trespassing, vandalism, and assault right in front of me, I had no qualms waking the guy up. Besides, he might not even be asleep. Flickering light was evident through the window, telling me a television was on inside the apartment.

I put my knuckles to the door. *Rap-rap-rap-rap.* When there was no response, I tried again. *Rap-rap-rap-rap-rap.*

A moment later, a child's sleepy voice came from the other side of the door. "Daddy?"

Not quite, kiddo. "Hi, honey," I said with forced cheer. No sense scaring the kid. "My name is Megan. I'm a police officer. I'm looking for Ryan Downey. He lives here, right?"

A *click* sounded as the dead bolt released, followed by a *jink* as the safety chain drew taut. The face of a young, towheaded boy with ice-blue eyes peered through the crack. He looked to be about five or six. He made fists with his tiny hands, rubbed his tired eyes, and yawned a wide, gap-toothed yawn. Darned if I didn't find myself yawning, too.

When Brigit wagged her tail next to me, the movement caught the boy's eye and he looked down at her and squealed, half in surprise, half in delight. "Uncle Ryan!" he hollered as loud as his little lungs would allow. "Wake up! There's a dog!" The boy disappeared into the apartment, continuing to yell. "Uncle Ryan! Come quick! There's a big furry dog!"

A man's voice came back. Though it was gravelly with sleep, it also had an odd, kazoolike quality to it, as if he was speaking through his nose. "What the heck are you talking about, Toby?"

"Come and see!" Toby shouted, reappearing at the door a moment later.

"Is it something on TV?" came the man's voice again. "You better not have woken me up for nothing."

A few seconds later, a man appeared behind the kid. He was so thin you could see his ribs, but he had zero muscle tone, his thighs jiggling. How he managed to look both emaciated and flabby at the same time was beyond me. He wore nothing but an intrigued look and an ill-fitting pair of striped briefs his skinny hips had a hard time holding up. His chest bore just three visible hairs, but his bald chest seemed more likely due to insufficient testosterone than a wax job. His eyes were the same ice blue as the kid's and bore crusty goop in the inner corners. His dark blond hair hung to his shoulders, Viking style. If Thor had a thinner, less attractive younger brother, this guy would be him and his name would be Thonk.

Ryan's gaze drew a line from Brigit up to me. Unlike Adriana, who seemed to avoid direct eye contact, Ryan locked his gaze on mine with laser-like intensity. "Well, hello, there," he said, his voice full of innuendo.

A slow smile spread across his lips as his gaze left my face and raked my body up and down. The guy seemed to be mentally undressing me. As quickly as he mentally removed my clothing, I mentally replaced them with unappealing apparel. An argyle cardigan. A loose jumpsuit. A floral-print muumuu.

Reflexively, I crossed my arms over my chest, as if that could somehow block his imagination. "Are you Ryan Downey?"

"Yeah. That's me."

"I need to talk to you."

"Sure. Let me get the door open."

He closed the door, slid the chain aside, and opened the door fully. He raised one arm up over his head and grabbed the door frame, rocking back on his heels and thrusting his crotch forward a few inches. *As if I wanted a gander at his goods. Blurgh.* I was tempted to whip out my baton, poke it into his skinny gut, and use it to hold him at bay. This guy could really stand to learn something about boundaries.

He cocked his head to complete the pose. "What would you like to talk about?" He said it with the same tone a guy might use if asking the question of a woman he'd met in a bar.

"I can wait while you get dressed."

He glanced down at himself before looking back at me, a smirk playing about his lips. "It doesn't bother me if it doesn't bother you."

My first thought was that Ryan Downey was quite full of himself. My second thought was that he didn't seem a likely match for Adriana at all. But I realized I wasn't seeing him at his best. Heck, I'd look pretty scary to anyone who'd woken me in the middle of the night. And putting the eye crusties and sagging undies aside, he wasn't entirely repulsive, lookswise at least. But his buzzy nasal voice and suggestive manner were major turnoffs, making him a 4 to Adriana's 8. The arithmetic didn't seem to compute. Then again, other unknown factors could result in mathematical adjustments. For instance, a guy might be handsome enough to rank a 9.5 on looks alone, but a bad credit score could drag him down a couple of digits or more. Did this guy have some hidden secret that warranted an award of extra points?

He certainly seemed confident. What was the source of his self-assurance? Had he accomplished some big feat? Did he have some incredible skill or talent that wasn't immediately obvious to me? Or was he simply delusional and narcissistic?

I glanced past him, into the apartment. A crumpled blanket and pillow lay on the couch, the Thomas the Tank Engine pillowcase telling me Toby had been sleeping there. On the coffee table sat an empty bag of potato chips, fast food and candy wrappers, and three crushed soda cans. How this guy could eat so much and stay so skinny was beyond me. Looked like he'd retained that warp-speed metabolism many boys were blessed with during their teenage years.

Strewn around the floor and on shelves on the far wall were an assortment of electronic accessories, some loose, some in boxes, and none of which I knew the function. Heck, I still had no idea what the Ethernet was. Sounded like some type of mystical fantasyworld to me, a place where we'd all ride around on winged unicorns and live in castles made of mist. What was he doing with all of this technology?

Ryan's walls were adorned with framed posters of cartoon women in tight, low-cut clothing that showed off their disproportionately large cartoon breasts. I recognized the classic Wonder Woman in her red, white, and blue strapless leotard and knee-high red go-go boots. The thing I wondered most about Wonder Woman was how the hell she fought crime in an outfit like that. When she raised her hand over her head and twirled her golden lasso, how did she keep a boob from popping out? Next to the Wonder Woman poster was one of a female cheetah with generous human curves. Another featured a woman with platinum hair and icicles rising from her hands. I had no problem with people being into fantasy and superheroes, but did all of the female characters really have to be so busty? Then again, all of the males bore muscles on top of muscles, so maybe that evened the score a bit.

After I'd attempted to glean what I could about Ryan from the glimpse into his apartment, I returned my focus to him. "I'd like to discuss Adriana Valdez."

"Adriana? What about her?" the guy asked in his ka-zoo voice. Not exactly the sexy timbre a woman would want whispering sweet nothings into her ear. Not unless she were Betty Boop.

Before I could respond to Ryan, the kid chimed in from below with a question of his own. "Who's Adriana?"

Ryan glanced down at the boy. "Just some girl I used to see."

"You never met her?" I asked.

Toby shook his head. "Can I pet your dog?"

"Sure," I told him. "Brigit likes kids." So long as they weren't stepping on her toes or pulling her tail, that is.

Toby dropped to his knees in front of Brigit and began running his hand down the side of her neck. "She's so soft!" He buried his face in her neck. "And she smells like peaches!"

"It's her shampoo." Between you and me, I used the same flea shampoo on my own hair. No product designed for human use had ever given my locks such a nice shine and scent. I looked back up at Ryan. "Can you tell me where you were approximately half an hour ago?"

"Sure." A sly grin spread across his face as he leaned in closer to me as if to share a secret. When he spoke, his voice was low and sultry. "I was in my beachfront mansion making love to Eva Longoria while Gwen Stefani waited her turn."

Another smartass. What a surprise. I encountered two or three on every shift. I fought the urge to ask whether he'd even yet hit puberty.

"What's 'making love?' " the kid asked, still petting Brigit.

Ryan glanced down at his nephew. "It means kissing and stuff."

"Ew!" The boy made a face. "Yuck!"

Ryan chuckled and lifted his head, eyeing me intently. "You want to tell me why you're asking where I've been?"

I arched a brow. "You want to tell me the truth?"

His brow furrowed in puzzlement. "I did." He hiked a thumb over his shoulder. "Half an hour ago I was asleep. In my bed. Having a really nice dream."

Could it be true? He'd showed little alarm when I'd mentioned Adriana's name. Then again, some people were good at hiding their thoughts and emotions. I'd learned that the hard way when I'd inadvertently befriended a sociopath who'd planted bombs around the city.

"Uncle Ryan snores," Toby said. "Really loud. Sometimes it wakes me up."

I looked down at the boy. "Were you asleep when I knocked on the door?"

He continued to pet Brigit, not bothering to look up at me. "Mm-hm."

"When did you go to sleep?" I asked him.

"Uncle Ryan said I could stay up until ten," he said, "but I think I fell asleep before that."

A wary expression on his face, Ryan lowered his arm and stood up straighter. "I went to my room around nine-thirty so I could watch TV in there. I told Toby he could stay up and watch kids' shows out here as long as he was quiet and went to sleep by ten." His eyes narrowed. "What's with all the questions?"

Rather than answer his inquiry, I posed another of my own. "You're babysitting?"

"Yeah." His voice was impatient now. "For my older brother. I've got the day off tomorrow and offered to take the kid so he and his wife could have a night off."

Would Ryan have taken the kid with him when he threw the brick through Adriana's window? Or would he have left the kid home alone? If it were the latter, he might also be guilty of child neglect. A kid that young shouldn't be left home alone, especially at night. Having the kid here at his apartment sure would make a nice alibi, though.

I addressed Toby again. "Did you hear or see your uncle leave the apartment a little while ago?"

The kid shook his head. "Nope."

I wasn't sure how much stock to place in the kid's response. If Toby was anything like my three brothers had been when they were young, he'd sleep like the dead. Nothing short of a nuclear bomb would've woken them up. Ryan might have been able to slip out, throw the brick, and return without Toby even realizing his uncle had left the apartment.

"Told you I was here," Ryan snapped. "You want to get to the point?"

I'll get to the point when I'm good and ready. I returned my gaze to Ryan and angled my head to indicate the shoes on his porch. "I noticed you've got some muddy shoes out here."

"What are you talking about?" He stepped outside and glanced around.

"Behind the chair," I told him.

He walked over and exclaimed, "Hey! Never thought I'd see these again."

When he bent over to pick up the shoes, I reached out a hand to stop him. "Don't touch them."

He stood, his eyes narrowing. "Why not?"

Ignoring his question, I asked one of my own. "What did you mean when you said you never thought you'd see those shoes again?"

"I left them at Adriana's place before I broke up with her last month. I wasn't about to go back to get them. I'm not a man with a death wish."

Funny. Adriana said *she* had been the one to break up with *him*. Which one of them was telling me the truth? If Adriana had been the one to cut things off, could a cocky guy like Ryan take it? Or would his ego be too bruised to accept it without retaliating? "I take it things got ugly?"

He snorted. "Like you wouldn't believe."

"Try me."

He started to say something but stopped himself, looking over at the kid through the open doorway. "Toby, I'm going to close the door so I can talk to this police lady out here in private. I want you to lie down on the couch and go back to sleep, okay? If you do what I say I'll take you for doughnuts in the morning on the way to day camp."

"Doughnuts!" The boy leaped up from the floor, my fluffy partner forgotten in favor of sugar, sprinkles, and lard. "Yay!"

As the boy ran and dived back onto the couch, I motioned for Brigit to return to my side and Ryan closed the door behind her. Brigit plunked her hindquarters down on the concrete next to my right foot and issued a sigh. She'd been enjoying Toby's attention. She'd probably also understood the word "doughnuts" and was wondering why nobody had given her one.

After shutting the door, Ryan stepped closer to me. *Too close.* I reflexively took a step backward to put some distance between us. Not only had he invaded my personal space, but a law enforcement officer never wants a potential suspect within grabbing distance of her weapons.

He got right down to business. "You want the dirty details about my breakup with Adriana? I'll give them to you. She's the reason you're here, right? She's done something crazy again?"

Adriana? Crazy? What? My mind squirmed in confusion. But I knew that sometimes the best way to get the most information out of a person was to let them go ahead and spill the beans without any direction rather than for me to ask specific questions. Often, something a person offered voluntarily and spontaneously could lead to better tips than a purposeful interview. "Tell me what happened with you two."

"Okay." He inhaled a long breath as if taking time to organize his thoughts and scratched the crusty goop from his eyes before returning his focus to me. "Adriana and I dated for about three months. At first things were great. I mean, she's pretty and in good shape, and she likes to cook and I like to eat so we seemed like a good match. But it wasn't long before she started in on me. First it was about the junk food. She wanted me to give up red meat and fast food and only eat things she made for me. You know, skinless chicken and brown rice and steamed organic vegetables. Crap like that." He rolled his eyes. "She's a total health nut. She must've baked me a hundred loaves of zucchini bread. In the beginning I ate some of 'em 'cause I thought it was sweet, but then things got out of hand. She kept trying to get me to go to yoga or do Pilates with her. Do I look like the kind of guy who does Pilates?"

"No, you do not," I said, keeping my eyes off his thin yet jiggly thighs. *Hey, he can't fault me for agreeing with him, can he?*

He scowled. "She had a key made to my apartment one morning when I slept in. Didn't even ask my permission first! Just took my keys down to the hardware store and had them make a duplicate. I didn't know it until I came home from work and found all of the junk food missing from my fridge and pantry. She'd come over and thrown them out. She'd also cleaned and reorganized everything. My whole place smelled like bleach. Can you believe it?"

Yes, I could believe it. Adriana had struck me as a somewhat tightly wound person who liked things to be spotless, germfree, and orderly. Still, though Ryan had asked a question, I didn't think he was really looking for an answer and, even if he was, I wasn't inclined to give one. I was here to collect facts, not offer my own opinions. Luckily, after catching his breath, he launched right back into his tirade.

"She'd thrown out some of my clothes she didn't like, too. She got rid of my T-shirts and jeans and replaced them with khakis and polo shirts. She was always asking me to fix things at her house, too. I didn't mind taking care of her cable or Wi-Fi when it went out, but the plumbing and paint and stuff like that were her landlord's job, not mine. She treated me like I was her life-size Ken doll or her husband, like I was just supposed to do everything she wanted me to do whether I liked it or not."

Huh. Looked like Adriana had left out a few details about their relationship—assuming, of course, that what Ryan was telling me was true. After all, he could be the one lying. Something told me he wasn't, though. He wasn't pausing to come up with the story as he went along, and what he was saying wasn't so over-the-top as to be incredible. Then again, he might have realized law enforcement could become involved and had decided to have a story ready, just in case. For all I knew, he'd practiced this little speech in front of the mirror.

"She brought a bunch of her stuff over here, too," he continued. "Put some pillows on the couch and a bath mat by the tub and a bunch of her weird herbal teas and echinacea and gingko bilbo in the kitchen."

I fought the urge to tell him that Bilbo was the first name of the title character in *The Hobbit* and that the dietary supplement he was referring to was actually called ginkgo biloba. But no sense derailing his train of thought. It was rolling full speed down the track toward Information Station and I wanted to see what all it was loaded with.

He snorted again. "Needless to say, that shit got old fast. I warned her that I wasn't ready to get serious, and that I am who I am and I'm not going to change for anyone. I told her if she didn't like me the way I was, then she should go find someone else. I mean, it was insulting, you know? Like I wasn't good enough for her. Anyway, she started crying and said she was sorry and wouldn't do it again, so I gave her a second chance. We carried on for another week or two, but then she was right back at it, coming over when I was at work and going through my things. She swears she didn't do it, but my favorite pair of old shorts went missing and I know it was her. They might have had some holes in them, but they were really comfortable."

I could relate. I had a pair of old jeans like that. The denim had worn thin, but they were soft and fit like a second skin. I'd keep them around until they disintegrated.

"About a month ago," he said. "I decided I'd had enough. I changed my lock and went to her house to return her stuff and collect mine from her. I told her it was over. I tried to be as nice as I could about it. I gave her that old bullshit about it being me, not her. I said she deserved someone who would appreciate her and could make her happy and all that, but she just lost it." His face softened, and he gave a slight shake of his head before speaking more softly. "She said I'd made her feel worthless. She threatened to end it all."

"End it all?" I repeated.

"You know." He ran his index finger across his throat but, seeming to realize that implied murder, put the index finger to his temple, hooked his thumb, and acted out shooting himself in the head.

"Suicide, you mean."

"Yeah." He exhaled a long, loud breath. "Anyway, who'd want to be responsible for someone doing that, you know? I can't have something like that on my conscience. So I told her we could still be friends but that she should look for someone else if she wanted a romantic relationship. I left some flowers on her porch with notes suggesting places she might go to meet guys. You know, churches and those meet-up groups for singles, that kind of thing. She's a total homebody and hasn't dated much. Doesn't seem to have any real friends, either. She's awkward. You may have noticed."

I had indeed noticed. Adriana wasn't warm, and the lack of direct eye contact had been a little disconcerting. But I still wasn't sure whether she'd been intentionally avoiding my gaze. There were all kinds of reasons why one person might not meet another's eye. Besides a potential vision issue, the person might suffer from a social anxiety disorder or be on the autism spectrum and find direct eye contact to be stressful. She might have been fearful or distracted. Some people found authority figures intimidating. And the fact that she worked in a hospital environment could explain her seeming obsession with cleanliness.

"If she doesn't get out much," I said, "how did the two of you meet?"

"I went to her house to set up her cable and Internet

service. She was pretty, so I figured, why not? She seemed shy, so I tried to pull her out of her shell."

The picture he was painting of Adriana as an insecure, overly emotional social misfit didn't quite jibe with the relatively controlled woman I'd met earlier. My expression must have revealed my skepticism, because the next thing Ryan did was ask, "She told you I've got a protective order against her, right?"

No, she hadn't. My brows lifted of their own accord. "You do?"

He smirked, evidently buoyed by my surprise. "Hell, yeah, I do. She followed me to work one day last week and begged me again to take her back. I refused as nice as I could, but she starting screaming at me and slapped me. I told her not to touch me again but when I went to get back into my vehicle she grabbed my shirt and tried to pull me out. When that didn't work she clawed at me like a rabid cat. Drew blood on my neck." He angled his head and pointed to a spot below his ear. "You can probably still see the marks."

I could. Under his ear were three distinct pink lines of scarred flesh.

Huh.

Now I was more confused than ever. Here I'd thought Ryan might be lying to me, but now it was looking like Adriana could have been the one painting the misleading picture. Maybe she was like Picasso, distorting the image, putting things in unexpected places, mismatching facial features. Had her lack of eye contact been a sign of dishonesty rather than fear or discomfort?

"Did you call the police to report the attack?" I asked.

"Yes," he said. "But there weren't any witnesses

around and once she saw that she'd drawn blood she knew she was in trouble. She jumped back into her car and got the hell out of there before the cops arrived."

No witnesses. That seemed to be a theme with these two. "What day did this happen?"

"Wednesday."

I made a mental note to look up the police report. "You got the protective order handy?"

"It's in my place somewhere. Give me a minute. I'll find it."

He slipped back into the apartment, leaving me and Brigit on the porch to listen to the crickets chirp while we waited. When Ryan returned, he held the document out to me.

I took the paperwork from him and looked it over. Sure enough, it was a protective order signed by one of the judges at the Tarrant County Family Court. The order required Adriana to stay at least two hundred yards away from Ryan's residence and not to stalk or follow him. Ironically, it also required her to cease any direct communication with him, as well as any attempts to communicate threats or harassment through third parties. I was beginning to wonder if Adriana had used me to do that very thing—harass her ex. Then again, there would have been much easier ways to annoy Ryan if that was her aim. Ways that didn't involve the police and the potential for criminal charges for making false reports.

"Mind if I snap a pic of the order?" I asked him.

He shrugged. "Fine with me."

I snapped a quick shot of each page. "I'm also going to have to take your shoes in as evidence."

"Evidence of what?"

"Vandalism. There were footprints outside Miss Valdez's house that appear to match those shoes."

He rolled his eyes again. "You get what happened, don't you? She made those prints with my shoes and then brought them back here to try to frame me."

Could that be possible? There was no way I could know for sure. And he'd certainly come up with that theory quickly, almost as if he'd thought this scenario through in advance and had an explanation locked and loaded.

"Frame you?" I asked. "For what?" I hadn't mentioned the brick to him yet. How he answered might further implicate him.

He gave me a pointed look and grunted. "Hell if I know. Spying on her? Stealing her stupid zucchinis? You're the one with the information. You tell me."

When I said nothing, he went on. "If I were going to creep around her place," he said, "I'd have been smart enough to put paper booties over my shoes so they wouldn't leave prints. I've got a whole case of them in my apartment. I use them for work."

I fought the urge to tell him that while paper booties might corrupt a footprint, it wouldn't prevent one from being left entirely. After all, there were several factors involved. Weight. Ground surface. Moisture. Instead, I handed the paperwork back to him and asked about the bricks on the landing. "What are they for?"

"Toby and I were painting a model car out here earlier," he said. "Models are a hobby of mine. It was a little windy so I used the bricks to hold the newspaper down while we worked."

"Where'd you get the bricks?"

"Had 'em for years," he said. "They were leftover from when my parents built their house down in Crowley." He cast a glance at the newspaper and frowned. "Looks like one of them's missing now, though. There should be four, one on each edge of the paper."

"That fourth one ended up on the floor of Adriana's bedroom."

His head snapped back in my direction and the pitch of his kazoo voice rose in what seemed to be surprise. "Say what now?"

"Someone threw the brick through her window tonight. That's why I'm here."

His mouth gaped for a moment. "Well, it sure as hell wasn't me!" His eyes went wide and he shook his head. "I tell you, she's just trying to get me in trouble. She probably threw it through the window herself!"

At this point, my mind was reeling. Who was the bad guy—or bad girl—here, and who was the good one? I had no idea. Ryan was sort of a jerk, but what he'd told me about the demise of their relationship had seemed credible. Then again, Adriana had seemed believable, too, even if she was a little uptight. Until I figured things out, it was best to tell these two to stay away from each other. "I'll look further into this," I told Ryan, "but you need to refrain from contacting her, okay? Nothing good would come of it."

"Trust me," he said. "If I never see that woman again I'll die a happy man."

I dipped my head. "Looks like we're in agreement, then." I handed him my business card. "Here's my contact information in case you need it."

He glanced down at the card before looking back up at me. "Are you going to see Adriana again?"

"Probably."

"When you do, tell her I know she took my *Wonder Woman #1* and I want it back."

"Wonder Woman #1?"

"The comic book. I had one in good condition but I just discovered it's missing. I paid over two thousand dollars for it five years ago, and it's gone up in value since Wonder Woman was named girls' ambassador or whatever you call it."

I realized he was talking about the controversial decision to designate Wonder Woman as the United Nations Honorary Ambassador for the Empowerment of Women and Girls. Some thought the superheroine was more than worthy of the appointment. Others thought that naming a character who wore skimpy, overtly sexual clothing sent the wrong message, especially to girls in countries where modesty was valued. Personally, I was on the fence. I liked being a tough, smart cop, but I enjoyed being feminine and sexy on occasion, too. Why couldn't women be all of these things at the same time?

"How can you be sure she took the comic?" I asked.

"'Cause other than my nephew, Adriana's the only one who's been in my apartment since the last time I saw it. It had to be her. Besides, she got all pissed off when I showed it to her. I'd told her I wanted to show her something really cool that I'd dropped two grand on. I think she expected me to give her an engagement ring." He grunted. "Any guy who puts a ring on that woman's finger is nuts."

I wasn't sure what to make of this information. He'd certainly given me some food for thought.

"That'll be it for now," I told him. "If I have more questions I'll be back in touch."

Once Ryan went back into his apartment, I collected the shoes and one of the bricks. My work at the apartment done for the time being, I led Brigit down the stairs to the parking lot. On my way back to the cruiser, I stopped to listen for the telltale pings of an engine cooling. The only ones I heard were coming from my squad car. The painted numbers at the end of each parking spot told me that the shiny blue Camaro in the spot marked 206 must belong to Ryan. I led Brigit over to the car and put my hand on the hood. It was cool. The car hadn't been driven recently.

Looked like Adriana Valdez was mistaken about who had thrown the brick through her window. That, or she was the bold-faced liar Ryan claimed she was.

Either way, I was damn sure going to find out.

SIX
MIDNIGHT SNACK

Brigit

Megan had turned their car into the parking lot of the fire station, which meant two great things. One, Brigit would get to see Blast, the yellow Lab who'd become her favorite playmate. And two, she'd get some kind of yummy meat snack. There was always meat at the fire station. *Yippee!*

SEVEN
CRIMES OF PASSION

The Devoted One

Lying to the police might be illegal, but the cop seemed to have bought the story. *Good.*

So why was the Devoted One having such trouble sleeping? Because it's hard to fall asleep when your mind is going a mile a minute, thinking of that special someone, remembering how it felt when things were good.

Soon I'll have that feeling again.

And it would all be thanks to Officer Luz. She'd become their go-between.

Little did she know that her work had just begun . . .

EIGHT
SYRUP AND SUCKERS

Megan

It was nearly three in the morning when I pulled my cruiser to a stop in the parking lot of the fire station. Seth's seventies-era blue Nova sat in the adjacent spot. Orange flames adorned the sides and the license plates read KABOOM. Appropriate for a member of the city's bomb squad.

I let Brigit out of her enclosure, not bothering to attach her leash. Blast stood in the open, lighted bay of the firehouse, wagging his tail and barking in greeting. *Woof! Woof-woof!* His handler—*my boyfriend*—stepped to his side. Like the dog, Seth sported short blond hair and well-developed muscles. Unlike his dog, Seth wore more than just a nylon collar. *Shame . . .*

The two walked out to meet us as we approached the building. While Blast and Brigit greeted each other with a friendly sniff of each other's hindquarters, Seth greeted me with a warm kiss. For a guy whose job it was to defuse bombs and put out fires, he sure knew how to ignite a spark in me.

He nuzzled my neck. "Hey, you."

"Hey, yourself."

Along with the crisp smell of soap from the shower, Seth bore a faint scent of chlorine from his daily swims. Not that I was complaining. Those laps in the pool had given the guy shoulders as hard as the Texas granite used to build the Tarrant County Courthouse downtown. Between his muscles, gorgeous green eyes, and sexy chin dimple, he could easily land the cover of any firefighter fund-raising calendar. *Fifty copies, please!*

Of course there was much more to Seth than the hot guy that met the eye. Like the fires he fought and the water he swam in, he was a man of contrasts and con-tradictions. Underneath the strong, sexy exterior was a man who was more fragile than he'd ever admit. Not broken, but fractured. Whether those fractures would eventually heal or widen, only time would tell. Though his mother had recently come back into his life and was trying to forge a relationship with Seth, he still strug-gled with deep-seated abandonment and attachment is-sues arising from her leaving him as a child to be raised by his grandparents. Add in several harrowing years spent in Afghanistan working explosive ordnance detail for the U.S. Army, as well as the devastating things he'd seen on the job as a firefighter and member of the bomb squad, and Seth had some heavy things weighing on him. Not that he spoke of them often. But on rare occa-sions he let his tough façade slip, providing a glimpse of the hurt child and the battle-scarred soldier that lived within him.

But enough of that. I was here for one thing and one

thing only. "Any chance you've got a waffle maker in the kitchen?"

"Sure do," Seth said. "You got a craving?"

"Yeah." No sense telling him the hankering arose after I'd seen the waffle pattern on the bottom of Ryan's shoes. That was weird. Maybe even disgusting.

He motioned for me to follow him and turned to go into the building. "We've got real maple syrup, too."

Of course they did. If there was one thing firefighters knew how to do—besides fighting fires, of course—it was how to eat. I'd stopped by at mealtime before. They downed a day's worth of calories in one sitting. But given that they worked out routinely and burned a lot of energy carrying their heavy hoses and equipment, they managed to stay in great shape. I, on the other hand, spent most of my shifts sitting on my butt in my car. That's why I had to be careful about what I ate. Usually, anyway. Right now I wanted a darn waffle and nothing was going to keep me from getting one.

I patted my leg. "C'mon, Brig."

Our dogs trotting after us, Seth and I walked into the station, crossing through a lounge where two men and a woman were engaged in a penny-ante poker game. Judging from the pile of copper coins in front of the woman, she was thoroughly besting her male counterparts. The four of us exchanged nonverbal greetings. A lifted chin. A nod. A wave. A raised hand. Nothing more formal was needed. Seth and I had been dating several months and my presence was nothing new around here.

Seth pulled out a chair for me at one end of the long kitchen table. "Take a seat. I'll whip you up a waffle and fry Brigit some bacon."

On hearing her favorite word, Brigit issued a questioning *arf*?

Seth chuckled and reached down a hand to ruffle her head. "I'm moving as fast as I can, girl."

While he set the bacon to frying in a pan and whisked up the waffle batter, I told him about my night. "One of them has to be lying to me," I told him. "I'm just not sure who."

"Most stalkers are guys, aren't they?"

"That's true." While studying criminal justice at Sam Houston State University in Huntsville—*go Bearkats!*—I took courses in criminal psychology. I'd learned that the vast majority of victims knew their stalkers, and that while a small percentage of males would be the subject of a stalker at some point in their lives, females were far more likely to be the victims, with up to nearly a third of women being victimized. "I'm just not sure I can rely on statistics in this case."

"Sometimes stats don't hold up," he agreed. "Besides, hell has no fury like a woman scorned, right?"

"You've got a point. That crazy ex-girlfriend stereotype didn't come from nowhere. Unfortunately, these are just theories. They don't really tell me anything."

"Okay, then," he said. "What does your gut tell you?"

My gut was tied in a knot, telling me nothing other than that it was hungry. "My gut says it wants a waffle ASAP."

Seth cut me a grin. "Guess you'll have to use your brain, then." Seth plugged in the waffle iron to heat up. "You're smart. You'll figure it out."

"I hope so," I said, "and I hope I'll figure it out very soon. These types of things can escalate and get out of hand." Ryan had said he didn't want a suicide weighing on his conscience. I certainly didn't want a murder weighing on mine.

Would the situation between Adriana and Ryan come to that? I had no way of knowing. Those college courses I'd mentioned had also taught me that the reasons why people commit crimes weren't always as clear as they might seem, and could stem from any range of motives. Stalkers, specifically, could be broken down into five subtypes.

One type of stalker was the intimacy seeker, eroto-maniac, or "love obsessional" stalker. These types identified another person, often a complete stranger, as their one true love and behaved as though they had a relationship with the stranger. In these situations, the perpetrator was delusional, believing their target reciprocated their feelings. Country-western singer Shania Twain had been the target of such a stalker. He'd sent her love letters and attended her grandmother's funeral even though he had no connection to the family. *Creepy.*

Another stalker subtype was known as the incompetent stalker. Unlike intimacy seekers, incompetents realized their feelings were not reciprocated, yet they continued to pursue their love interest, hoping their affection would lead to a relationship. Having poor social skills, they did not engage in standard courting rituals and instead took actions counterproductive to their aims, frightening off their targets rather than enticing them. Britney Spears had been the victim of such a stalker, who'd sent her messages saying, "I'm chasing you." *Eeek.*

The resentful or "grudge" stalker subtype was motived

not by any desire to have a relationship with the victim, but rather by a sense of injustice and a desire for revenge. These stalkers saw themselves as the victims, and resented the humiliation and unfair treatment they believed their target inflicted on them. These types of stalkers commonly reported having highly controlling fathers, and the continual focus on their unhappy pasts contributed to mood disorders. John Lennon's killer, Mark Chapman, was a classic grudge stalker. He saw himself as a loyal rock fan and admired John Lennon until he read a Lennon biography. He murdered Lennon after becoming angry at what he felt was a major hypocrisy—that the former Beatle preached love and peace yet had amassed a vast fortune.

Predator stalkers weren't interested in having a relationship with their victims. Instead, they sought power and control, taking pleasure in gathering information and engaging in sexual fantasies about their victims. These types of stalkers generally had serious sexual disorders.

The most common type was the rejected or "exintimate" stalker. These stalkers were people who'd suffered the end of a close relationship and weren't happy about it. In most cases, the person who ended the relationship was someone the stalker had been romantically involved with, but rejected stalkers had also been known to target family members, coworkers, former friends, or other acquaintances. In most cases, the former relationship between the stalker and the victim had been abusive or controlling. Rejected stalkers often first attempted a reconciliation. When those attempts failed, they sought revenge. In fact, their behavior could fluctuate between conciliatory and vengeful. These types of stalking situations were the most likely to lead to violence, with fifty percent of such stalkers who made violent threats carrying them out.

While the motives for each stalker subtype differed, they shared some similarities. All tended to rationalize their behavior, making excuses and minimizing consequences, expressing little or no embarrassment or discomfort from their actions. Virtually all stalkers lacked good interpersonal and social skills, despite the fact that they tended to have above-average intelligence. They were often narcissists with a sense of entitlement, and loners with few personal relationships. They didn't take no for an answer and had obsessive personalities. They had mean streaks and leaned toward sociopathic ways of thinking.

Those with such deep fixations were psychologically unstable, and often suffered from undiagnosed personality disorders. Many had serious mental health issues. Treatment for offenders involved programs designed to teach empathy for their victims and social and relationship skills. Though they engaged in criminal behavior, at their core they were individuals in need of psychological help.

I wasn't sure whether the guilty party in this case was Adriana or Ryan, but I'd peg either as a rejected or ex-intimate stalker. Statistically, it was more likely Ryan was the perpetrator. But given what he'd said about Adriana's strict dietary regimen and her excessive cleanliness, she seemed to have the typical obsessive tendencies. And while there had been no witnesses to her alleged attack on Ryan, the judge who'd presided over the hearing regarding the protective order must have believed the story. On the other hand, Ryan sure was full of himself, a sign he could be a narcissist. He'd also been quick to say mean things about Adriana and to paint himself as a good guy, a virtual romantic hero who'd swooped in to rescue her from a life of loneliness and, later, thoughts of suicide.

The batter ready, Seth poured it into the waffle maker and closed the lid. The enticing scent of warm waffle filled the air. Seth rounded up a napkin and fork and set them on the table in front of me. My place set, he turned back to tend to the waffle iron. When the green light came on, he lifted the top of the iron and used a fork to pry the waffle free. He set it on a plate and slid it in front of me, along with a half-gallon jug of pure maple syrup. The way they ate around here, they bought food in industrial-sized quantities. "Here you go."

I grabbed the jug and made certain to fill every square with syrup. Evidently Adriana wasn't the only one with obsessive tendencies. I grabbed my fork and took a bite. *Mmm.* I cut my eyes to Seth, who was flipping the bacon in the pan. "You're the best."

A sly grin slid across his face. "You talking about my waffle-making abilities, or something else?"

"Both." It was true. While he made a mean waffle, he sure knew how to heat me up, too.

My demands met, he turned his attention back to the sizzling bacon, using the fork to lift the strips from the frying pan. The dogs sitting obediently at his feet wagged their tails and licked their chops. "You'll have to give it a minute," he told them. "Don't want you burning your mouths."

Much to Brigit's and Blast's disappointment, rather than giving them the fried strips of meat right then and there, Seth opened the freezer and placed the plate of bacon inside to speed up the cooling process. He turned back to me, angling his head to indicate the pot the station kept perpetually brewing. "Coffee?"

"Do you even have to ask?"

He poured me a cup, added a splash of the soy milk he kept on hand for me—*gotta love this guy, huh?*—and set the mug on the table. He went back to the freezer, removed the plate of bacon, and placed it on the table, taking his seat. Tearing a strip into pieces, he blew on each one to make sure it was cool enough before tossing the pieces to the dogs, alternating between them. The two snapped each piece out of the air with precise skill. "Did I tell you one of the guys is leaving the station?" he said. "His wife got a promotion at her job and they're moving out of state."

"So there's an opening here?"

"Yeah. If Frankie wants to apply I'll put in a good word for her."

Seth's station was only a couple of miles from the house I shared with Francesca "Frankie" Kerrigan. Frankie and I had become roommates on a whim after I'd pulled her over for reckless roller-skating. To make a long story short, her a-hole of a boyfriend had dumped her, leaving her with an empty room and rent she couldn't afford on her own. I'd used my badge to stop him from taking the television the two had bought together, and moved into the spare bedroom he'd been using as his man cave. The house provided a much better living arrangement for me and Brigit than the tiny studio apartment I'd been leasing, and Frankie had proven to be a thoughtful and considerate roommate. She'd recently given up her job as a nighttime stocker at a grocery store to attend the firefighter academy. Standing five feet eleven and with a strong physique honed from years of playing Roller Derby, she was a good candidate. Her training would wrap up at the end of the week, and she'd be seeking her first assignment. Seth's station would be a quick and easy commute for her.

"Thanks!" I told Seth. "I'll let her know to get her application in right away."

ERT! ERT! ERT! Before Seth could respond, the station's alarm went off, calling the firefighters into action. He stood and leaned over to give me a quick kiss. "Maple. Yum."

I kissed him back and put my index finger to his chin dimple, my special sign of affection for him. "Be careful!" I called after him as he rushed off to jump into his gear and secure Blast in his kennel while they were gone.

Brigit watched Blast run out after Seth, a look of doggie disappointment on her furry face. I supposed my face bore the equivalent human expression. But when Brigit realized Blast's departure meant the rest of the bacon was all hers, she changed her tune. Before I could stop her, she'd put her paws on the edge of the table, used her long tongue to swipe the remaining strips of bacon off the plate, and gobbled them down.

"Looks like our break is over, partner."

I picked up my mug and the plates, rinsed them in the sink, and put them in the dishwasher. Brigit and I returned to our cruiser and waited in the parking lot as the firefighters climbed onto the truck and turned on their lights and siren to head out to the fire. Seth raised an arm in good-bye as they careened out of the lot. *Dang, he looks hot in his firefighter duds.*

Turning my attention away from my sexy boyfriend and back to my work, I logged into the laptop mounted in my squad car and pulled up the police report detailing Adriana's alleged attack on Ryan. According to the officer's report, Ryan Downey worked as a subcontractor for Interstellar Communications, an Internet and cable company with an ambitious name. Adriana purportedly followed Ryan when he went to install equipment at a house in Ridglea Country Club Estates. At approximately one o'clock in the afternoon, he finished the job, came out of the home, and found her waiting by his truck. When he informed her that he had no intention of resuming their relationship, she physically attacked him. The report included photos of the injuries to Ryan's neck, the wounds raw. The report noted that the responding officer had spoken with the owner of the house where Ryan had been installing the equipment as well as a neighbor next door, but neither had seen anything. There were no witnesses. The report also noted that Ryan had expressed concern that Adriana had taken a valuable comic book from him. *Wonder Woman #1.*

One thing that caught my attention was the truck. Did Ryan drive one that was owned by the cable and Internet company, or did he own a truck himself?

I logged into the motor vehicle records and ran a search for those registered in Ryan's name. Sure enough, both the Camaro and a heavy-duty Silverado truck were registered in his name. Looked like Ryan was a Chevy man.

I chastised myself for not having read the report immediately after speaking with Ryan. Had I done so, I would have realized that Ryan owned a work truck in addition to the Camaro. But better late than never, right?

I started the engine, pulled out of the fire station, and returned to Ryan's apartment complex. My eyes scanned the parking lot, searching for his truck. *There it is.*

Brigit lifted her head from her cushion when I pulled to a stop behind the truck, and watched me as I exited our cruiser. I put my fingertips to the truck's hood, but felt no excessive heat. To be certain, I flattened my palm against the metal. It felt the same as the outdoor temperature. If Ryan had driven the truck to Adriana's earlier to throw the brick, would it have cooled off already? It was possible. After all, it had been well over an hour since I'd responded to the call, and the drive between the two locations was relatively short. And of course it was possible, maybe even likely, that he hadn't been to Adriana's house tonight at all. Adriana could have been trying to frame Ryan, as he'd suggested. Or someone else could have thrown the brick. The event might have had nothing at all to do with their relationship. ACME bricks were common, after all.

As I climbed back into my cruiser, my cell phone rang. I recognized the number as the one Adriana had given me earlier. I jabbed the button to accept the call. "Hello, Miss Valdez."

"Did you arrest Ryan?" she asked. "Is he in custody?"

"Not yet," I told her.

"Why not?"

"He had an alibi."

"I bet he had some woman lie for him, didn't he? Was there a woman at his apartment?"

If I didn't know better, I'd think she sounded jealous. Heck, maybe I didn't know better. She *did* sound jealous. I decided not to give her any more information. I wasn't sure who to trust here and felt it was better to hold my cards close to my vest. "Since you're still up I'm going to swing back by your place. I have some things I'd like to discuss with you."

"All right."

A few minutes later, I pulled back up to Adriana's house. She'd been watching for me out the window and met me on the porch. Her eyes were bright. But was it from eagerness, or worry? It was difficult to distinguish between the two.

"Did you find anything at his place?" she asked, again looking at my ear instead of my eyes. "Any evidence?"

Hmm. Is she fishing to see if I'd noticed the muddy shoes on his porch and the missing brick? I decided not to tell her about them. If she screwed up and mentioned them herself, I'd know she'd planted them and was truly trying to frame Ryan, as he'd claimed. "Nothing definitive," I said.

Her face clouded and her eyes sparked. "But you looked around, right?"

"As much as I could. I peeked in the windows of his car and checked the hood to see if it was warm. It wasn't. Without a search warrant I couldn't go into his apartment." I said no more for a moment, waiting to see if she might say something that would out her as the window breaker, maybe a reference to the shoes or the other bricks on his porch. When she said nothing, I gave her a subtle nudge. "Was there something in particular you think I might have missed?"

She stared at me for several seconds as if assessing me in return before lifting her shoulders. "I don't know. I guess I'd just hoped you'd find something incriminating and take him to jail so I wouldn't have to keep living in fear. I'm on edge all the time and can barely sleep at night. It's exhausting."

"I can imagine." I cocked my head. "Why didn't you tell me that Ryan had a protective order against you?"

She didn't hesitate before responding. "Because it means absolutely nothing, Officer Luz. I was served with a notice that he'd filed for an order based on an alleged attack that never happened. The notice said there was going to be a hearing, but I couldn't take off work the day it was scheduled. The other dietitian had already put in for vacation, and one of us had to be at the center."

"You could have asked the judge for a continuance," I said.

"Why would I bother? I don't want to go anywhere near Ryan, so what would I care if a court ordered me to stay away from him? Besides, I would've had to hire an attorney. Ryan was just trying to cost me money, and he was trying to force me to see him again by dragging me into court. The whole thing was nothing more than a ploy, and I wasn't about to play into his hands and give him what he wanted."

Could it be true? Had Ryan misused the court system to harass Adriana? If he had, did that mean he might have smashed her window tonight for the same reason? This situation seemed to get more complex by the second. "What about the injuries to his neck?" I asked. "If you didn't do them, who do you think did?"

"Probably a hooker," she spat. "I didn't get into this earlier because it didn't seem necessary, but Ryan has some weird sexual fetishes. It's disgusting. That's one of the reasons I dumped him."

An image popped into my mind of Ryan dressed in a horned Viking hat and a studded leather codpiece, wielding a whip in one hand and a microwave burrito in the other. *Ew!* I wasn't a prude, but I wasn't exactly comfortable with this topic, either. Still, it was my job to gather the facts. No avoiding it. "Are you talking about autoerotic asphyxiation?"

She pursed her lips primly. "That's exactly what I'm talking about. He was also into role-play. You know, dressing up in costumes. He's into comic books so at first I thought it was innocent fun. But when he bought me a crotchless tiger costume and wanted me to wear it during—"

I cut her off with a raised hand. "Say no more." *Please! Say no more!* I knew I was supposed to be gathering facts here, but in this case the general gist would have to do. I wanted no more details. "Do you know for a fact that he interacted with hookers?"

She frowned. "Well, no. It's only a guess on my part. But I don't think a woman would do the things he wanted unless she was being paid."

As long as the subject of comic books had come up, I figured I might as well ask her about the missing *Wonder Woman #1*. "Ryan told me one of his rare comic books is missing. The first *Wonder Woman* comic."

"He probably claimed I took it, right?"

I shrugged.

"You saw how messy his place is, didn't you?"

"It wasn't immaculate by any means, but I didn't go inside and I didn't see where he keeps his comics."

"I'll tell you where he keeps them. All over the place." She waved her arms around in demonstration. "He spends a small fortune on the dumb things and doesn't bother keeping them in a box or drawer or somewhere safe. His nephew Toby might have taken it to look at. Or Ryan could have tossed it in the trash by accident or something."

I had my doubts he'd be as careless as she was implying but, then again, I didn't know the guy. All I did know was that people did stupid, strange, and senseless things all the time. It was precisely those stupid, strange, and senseless things that kept the eighteen thousand U.S. police departments in business.

I admonished Adriana both to be careful and to refrain from any contact with Ryan. "I'm working the night shift all week," I told her. "I'll be sure to swing by here regularly to keep an eye on things, and I'll ask the other officers on duty to do the same." Of course I'd tell them to keep an eye on Ryan's place, too. With any luck, one of us would catch either Adriana or Ryan doing something they shouldn't to the other, and then I'd know which of them was the real culprit.

"Thanks, Officer Luz. I appreciate it." She offered a soft smile. "By the way, did you get a chance to tell Ryan that I've moved on? That I'm dating a doctor now? If he knows I'm dating someone else, maybe he'll move on, too."

"Sorry," I said. "It didn't come up." No sense antagonizing the guy. If he had thrown the brick through Adriana's window, why say something that might only encourage him to do worse? And if she was the guilty one here, why help her in her efforts to annoy him?

With a nod in good-bye, I returned to the cruiser, loaded Brigit into her enclosure, and slid into my seat.

I was at a loss as to where to go from here. Both Adriana and Ryan had made arguments that seemed reasonable and valid, yet one of them had to be a damn good actor. Unfortunately, I wasn't a casting agent and couldn't distinguish between who was telling me the truth and who should be nominated for an Emmy. Looked like it was time for *me* to escalate things.

I placed a call to Sergeant Spalding, the supervising officer on duty at the station. "I have an unusual situation," I told him.

"It's not another man with his pants down, is it?"

He was referring to my recent arrest of a Peeping Tom who had terrorized the Berkeley Place community in Fort Worth. When law enforcement hadn't been able to identify the perpetrator right away, the neighborhood watch group had nearly turned into a lynch mob. Luckily, Brigit and I had nabbed the guy before things got out of hand, though when we'd caught him he'd had something *in* his hand. But no need to disgust you with the details. Long story short, Brigit and I have a good "track" record of solving cases, pun intended.

"All the pants are up this time," I told Spalding. No need to get into Ryan's droopy undies, either. "But I've got an odd situation and I'm not sure whether to make an arrest." I ran through the events of the night for him, adding that Ryan had procured a protective order against Adriana after the alleged altercation last week.

"You made the right call not bringing anyone in," he said. "You were also smart not to tell Miss Valdez about the shoes on Downey's porch. Detective Bustamente will be in the office in the morning. Check with him and see if he thinks this warrants further investigation."

"Will do. Thanks."

Though I was loath to do so, I knew I should also talk to Derek Mackey, get his take on things. After all, he'd been to Adriana's place recently. Maybe he'd noticed something I hadn't. Then again, maybe not. Hard to notice much when your head is perpetually up your back end.

It was a few minutes past six A.M. and the sun was just beginning to light up the distant sky as I stood at the counter of a combination gas station and convenience store near the intersection of Rosedale and Hemphill, my notepad at the ready, my furry partner sniffing at the packaged pork rinds hanging from a peg below. I nudged her nose aside with my knee and returned my attention to the sixtyish clerk. "What was the shoplifter wearing?"

"Green scrubs," he said.

"Scrubs? Like nurses and doctors wear?"

"Yup. He was wearing a surgical mask and cap, too." He scratched at the horseshoe of gray hair encircling his balding head. My thoughts must have been written on my face because he followed up with, "I'm as surprised as you are. Most of the shoplifters I see are either kids or scuzzy types. Never would've pegged this guy for a thief if I hadn't seen him do it with my own eyes."

Like the clerk, I would've expected someone wearing scrubs to be above petty thievery. This culprit seemed dressed more for a big-time thriller-type crime, like illegal trade in prescription painkillers or human organs. But while there were profiles and stereotypes for those who committed certain varieties of crimes, I knew that books could not always be judged by their covers. Kleptomaniacs came in all shapes, sizes, colors, and attire.

While the clerk rang up a woman in a white lab coat who'd come in for coffee, I jotted some quick notes. *Suspect: male. Green scrubs. Surgical mask/cap.* Of course I'd need much more than these paltry details to go on. The store sat smack-dab in the center of Fort Worth's medical district. Both the Harris Methodist and Cook Children's Hospitals were located within a few blocks of where we now stood, as were the offices of dozens upon dozens of doctors with admitting privileges at the facilities. Add in the various clinics, laboratories, and the blood collection center, and there had to be hundreds if not thousands of health-care workers—most of whom wore scrubs—in the immediate vicinity.

When the woman left the counter, I addressed the clerk again. "What else can you tell me about the guy?"

"He's a white fella. Average sized." He shrugged again. "That's about all I can tell ya."

Caucasian. Medium build. I looked up from my pad. "What did he take?"

"Grape-flavored Tootsie Pops."

"Are you serious?"

"Serious as a heart attack," he replied. "Stuffed a whole handful of the suckers in his pocket." The man gestured to a purple lollipop lying on the floor of the candy aisle. "That's one he dropped. I's sitting here readin' the paper when I heard it hit the floor. I looked up, saw what he was doing"—he pointed emphatically down the aisle as if pointing at the now-gone thief— "and told him to 'hold it right there!'"

Obviously, the shoplifter hadn't obeyed, as evidenced by the fact that he was no longer *right there*.

"He didn't say one word to me," the clerk continued. "Just hightailed it out the door as fast as he could. By the time I got around the counter and out the door after him, he'd skedaddled."

"Did he get into a car?"

"I don't believe so. Don't think he'd've had time to get one started and pull outta the lot 'fore I got out there."

Good point. "Maybe someone was waiting for him with the engine running," I offered, though I thought someone waiting in a getaway car was a long shot. It was hard to comprehend that there could be a whole candy-stealing conspiracy going on.

"Suppose anything's possible," the man said with a shrug that said he didn't buy the idea any more than I did.

Still, the thief had to have gotten away somehow. Had he run off on foot? I glanced at the doors. While I could see no trail, my partner's special capabilities meant she could easily determine which way the thief and his stolen suckers had gone. I sometimes envied her super-powers. But if having her powers meant I'd have to crap in public and bathe myself with my tongue, I'd take a hard pass, thank you very much.

I gestured up at the security camera mounted high in the top corner of the wall behind the counter where it could take in most of the store. A monitor on the back counter showed the footage in real time, probably as a deterrent to would-be thieves. Of course it hadn't deterred the Lollipop Bandit. Right now the monitor showed the clerk's back, me gesturing to the camera, and Brigit again mouthing the bag of pork rinds below me. I nudged her face away from the bag a second time. "Can you show me the footage?" I asked the clerk.

"Sure can."

He fiddled with his keyboard for a moment before an image popped up on the screen. Sure enough, the monitor showed a man walking into the store. The surgical cap fully covered his head and the back of his neck, making it impossible to determine his hair color. Meanwhile, the mask covered his face from just below the bridge of his nose all the way to his chin. Though the clerk hadn't mentioned it earlier, the thief was also wearing latex gloves. No point in dusting for prints, then.

"Can you zoom in on him?" I asked.

The clerk maneuvered the mouse until the cursor was on the bandit's face and clicked several times to enlarge the image. Unfortunately, though the thief's eyes were visible in the narrow gap between the cap and mask, the resolution on the security camera footage was too poor to give me anything to go on.

"Any cameras outside?" I asked.

"Got 'em on the gas pumps," he said. "But since he didn't run past 'em they're not gonna help ya."

Looked like there was only one option left, and she was sitting at my feet, her eyes locked on the package of pork rinds as if she was willing them to fly off the peg and into her mouth.

I raised Brigit's leash. "I'll set my partner after him. See what we can find out." I looked down at my partner. "C'mon, girl." I led Brigit down the candy aisle to the fallen lollipop and gave her a chance to sniff the area. Once she'd taken it in, I ordered her to track.

She set off toward the door, her tail wagging. Despite being paid only in liver treats and chew toys, Brigit loved her job. To her, work was a game. I supposed it was to me, too. Each case was like a puzzle to be solved. In fact, the entire reason I'd gotten into police work was with the hope of making detective one day. Until I was eligible, I was biding my time as a beat cop and had befriended the detectives at the station, continuously picking their brains, trying to learn as much as I could from them.

I held the door open for Brigit and trailed along after her as she sniffled and snuffled her way down the front sidewalk and around the side of the building. She paused for a moment and lifted her head, scenting the cool and damp morning air before putting her nose back to the ground.

She continued through the dawn's early light, proudly hailing passersby as we made our way up Henderson, heading toward the hospitals. She went in one direction for a few feet, stopped to snuffle more intently, then headed off in another. As we drew closer to the hospital building, she repeated this behavior several more times. No wonder. There was a lot of foot traffic around the building, people coming and going. Surely it must be hard to stay on a track with so many scents and trails coming together and overlapping. But if any dog could do it, it was Brigit. She hadn't graduated first in her training class for nothing.

I issued words of encouragement. "Good job, girl. Good job."

We passed several people in scrubs and others in regular clothing as she led me past the multilevel parking garage. Next thing I knew, she was heading up to the automated sliding doors of Cook Children's Hospital and into the emergency room waiting area. People and children looked up as we came inside. A young girl who'd been mid-wail stopped for a moment to eye us before resuming her cry. *Waaaah!*

When Brigit trotted across the room and approached double doors marked AUTHORIZED PERSONNEL ONLY, I ordered her to stop. She turned and looked at me as if to say *but we're not done yet!* Maybe not, but taking a dog into a nonpublic area of a hospital seemed extreme, especially when the only thing at stake was a few grape lollipops valued at a mere two or three dollars. Besides, even though I had little doubt the thief had come this way—after all, Brigit's nose was virtually foolproof— there was no guarantee he was still in the building. Knowing the clerk had spotted him and likely called law enforcement, he might have cut through the ER as an evasive ploy. For all I knew, he'd exited the hospital elsewhere. He could be anywhere by now.

As I wound Brigit's leash tighter around my hand, the receptionist at the desk cast me a look mixed with interest and irritation. "Can I help you, Officer?"

"Maybe." I stepped over to her desk. "Did you see a man in green scrubs come through here a few minutes ago?"

"I've seen a dozen men in green scrubs come through here in the last few minutes."

"This one would have been average-sized. Maybe wearing a mask and cap and gloves." If he hadn't removed them.

The woman raised her palms. "You've just described the majority of the hospital staff. We're in the middle of the shift change, too. Everyone's coming and going."

In other words, she couldn't help me narrow things down. *Darn.*

She cocked her head. "Were you and your dog tracking someone? Do I need to alert security?"

"It's nothing serious," I said. No sense getting everyone worked up over a few lollipops when there were much more important things at stake here, like sick kids. "Have a good day."

As those waiting watched, I led Brigit back outside. The early morning seemed extra dark in contrast to the bright lights of the hospital, and I paused for a moment to give my eyes time to adjust. Once they did, we jogged back to the store. Other than the time we'd spent at Adriana's and Ryan's, Brigit and I had been sitting on our butts in the cruiser most of the night. We could both use the exercise.

The clerk looked up as we came back through the door. "Any luck?"

"She led me to the children's hospital, but we had to abandon the search there. Dogs aren't exactly welcome in sterile environments and I couldn't be sure he'd still be in the building."

"Thanks for trying," he said.

I nodded in acknowledgment. "I'll type up a report. If there are any developments, I'll let you know. And if you see this guy again, give us a call."

With that, I turned to go, but not before Brigit used her teeth to pluck the bag of pork rinds from the peg and trotted toward the door with them.

The man chuckled. "Looks like we've got another shoplifter."

"This dog has a mind of her own sometimes."

When I pulled out some cash to pay for the snack, he raised a hand to stop me. "On the house. She's earned it."

As if she understood, Brigit looked back at him, batted her eyes, and wagged her tail in appreciation. I offered a verbal thanks.

With that, we returned to the cruiser. I loaded Brigit into her enclosure, tore open the bag of pork rinds, and poured them into her bowl. While she happily began crunching away, I set back out on patrol.

Brigit was snoring loud enough to wake the dead when my cell phone rang a few minutes later. The readout indicated it was Detective Hector Bustamente. I'd left a voice mail on his office line after leaving Adriana's the second time, inquiring whether he might have some time to meet with me this morning.

I jabbed the button to accept the call. "Thanks for calling me back, Detective."

"I came to the station early to get a head start on the day. Come by whenever you can."

"I'm on my way."

NINE
DAYDREAMS

Brigit

As soon as she'd polished off the pork rinds, Brigit had lain down in her enclosure for a nap. Now, she was running through the woods, chasing a white-tailed bunny and gaining on the stupid, big-eared pest, when the cruiser rocked to a stop and woke her, putting an end to her dreams. *Rats.*

She opened her eyes and lifted her head. The world had a pale yellow glow. She knew that meant it would soon be morning. Usually that was the time she and Megan came to work. But sometimes, like last night, they worked while it was dark and went home when the sun came up. Brigit liked those days. Megan would sleep into the afternoon and Brigit could get away with doing things Megan didn't normally allow her to do. Helping herself to food from the pantry. Chewing on the legs of the kitchen table to clean and sharpen her teeth. Licking the sofa pillows just for the heck of it.

Megan opened the back of the cruiser and Brigit hopped down to the asphalt. It was cool now, thank goodness. Later in the day it would be uncomfortably hot on the pads of her paws. Megan had bought some type of booties to protect Brigit's feet, but they felt weird and Brigit didn't like to wear them. Besides, the booties had made better chew toys.

Megan clipped the leash onto Brigit's collar and led her into the station. As they walked down the hall, Officer Eklund and his Belgian Malinois, Brutus, approached from the other direction.

As their human partners exchanged greetings, Brutus turned his snout toward Brigit and sniffed her mouth. *You got bacon? And pork rinds, too? Lucky bitch.*

Brigit whipped out her tongue and swiped it across Brutus's lips. *Might as well give the poor dog a taste.*

He licked her back, sticking his tongue all the way into her mouth.

Officer Eklund laughed. "Get a room, you two."

TEN
BASKING IN THE GLOW

The Devoted One

Given that the Devoted One had slept little last night, it would be normal to feel tired this morning. But today, basking in the glow of the early-morning sun felt good. The rays seemed hopeful, promising.

Surely there'd be some contact after last night. An e-mail or text or phone call or, better yet, a personal visit. There had to be questions. *Why would you do this to me? What do you want from me? How can I stop this?*

The Devoted One sighed. *I did this because I love you. I want you back. I'll stop once you're mine again.*

Yes, it was a new day, and that meant the Devoted One was that much closer to reclaiming their lost love.

That love *would* be reclaimed.

Any alternative was unthinkable and unacceptable.

But, above all, it would be unforgivable.

ELEVEN
WHAT NOW?

Megan

After greeting Officer Eklund and his K-9 Brutus in the hallway, I led Brigit down the corridor to the detective's office and rapped on the door-frame. *Rap-rap.*

Detective Bustamente sat behind his desk. With his portly build, wrinkled clothing, and laid-back manner, it might be tempting to write the guy off as lazy and dim. Doing so would be a grave error. While he might not give his attire much attention, he didn't miss a detail when it came to his investigations. He reserved his energy for his work. And while he might appear relaxed, he was always exercising his mental muscle.

He looked up from the tower of files on his desk. "Good mornin', ladies. How was your shift?"

"It was . . ." *Confusing? Perplexing? Disturbing?* I went with, "Interesting."

Knowing Detective Bustamente was always good for a scratch, Brigit circled around the desk, plunked her hindquarters down at his feet, and looked up at him.

He reached out both hands to scratch behind her ears

and lowered his nose to hers. "How are you, Sergeant Brigit?"

My partner wagged her tail and licked his cheek to let him know she was doing just fine, thanks, and hoped he was doing the same.

I set the separately bagged bricks and shoes on the desk and slid into one of the chairs. When Bustamente turned his attention from my partner to me, I launched into a quick review of the night's events. "I took a call last night and I'm not sure what to make of it." I explained about the brick and the footprints at Adriana's place, then moved on to the shoes and bricks at Ryan's. "It looked obvious to me at first. Like he'd thrown the brick through the window and hadn't made any effort to hide the evidence of his guilt. But then he told me he'd left his shoes at Adriana's when they'd broken up, and that she'd attacked him last week. He had claw marks on his neck that he claimed were made by her. But when I went back to her house to ask about things, she said she'd never attacked him and that he was into some unusual sexual activities, and that's probably how he got the claw marks."

"Kinky sex, huh?" Bustamente didn't bat an eye. After all his years on the job, nothing surprised him anymore.

I went on. "Adriana said she didn't bother fighting the protective order because it would have cost money to hire an attorney and she didn't mind being ordered to stay away from someone she didn't want to see, anyway. Also, she couldn't take off from work on the day of the hearing."

"That sounds like a valid explanation." He seemed to

mull things over for a moment. "Either of them got a record?"

"No."

He leaned back in his chair. "Was last night the first time we've been called?"

I shook my head. "Ryan called the police after Adriana allegedly attacked him. Adriana said she called a few days ago when someone threw a tennis ball at her car during the night and set off the alarm. Officer Mackey handled the call."

"And?"

"Adriana says he told her there wasn't enough evidence to warrant any follow-up."

Bustamente reached for his keyboard, tapped a few keys, and leaned in to read Officer Mackey's report. Having perused the short post before leaving Adriana's house the first time, I knew it would be of little help. Mackey had put in a minimum amount of information, and had managed to misspell at least one word per sentence. *Victim reports car alarm going of. Beleives that her ex-boyfriend thru tennis bal at car. No wintesses.*

The detective snorted. "Mackey's no Hemingway, that's for sure." Bustamente was silent for a long moment, nodding slowly as the wheels of his mind seemed to be turning. He held out a hand. "Let me see the photo you took of the footprints."

I retrieved my phone from my pocket, pulled up the first photo on the screen, and handed it to him.

He stared down at the photo for a few seconds before tweaking the screen to enlarge the pic. "These prints seem exceptionally complete and clear." He looked up at me. "It hasn't rained recently. Where did the mud come from?"

"Adriana's garden," I said. "She raises her own vegetables. She works as a dietitian at a rehab center. Her ex claims she's an excessive health nut."

"Tomato, to*mah*to," Bustamente said. He turned his attention to the bagged shoes. "What's that squished on the sole?"

"A tomato," I said. "Or a to*mah*to. From her garden. I didn't tell her I'd found the shoes at Downey's apartment. He claimed he'd left them at her house when they broke up weeks ago and that she must have brought them back last night to frame him. I suppose it's possible he might have left them outside since they were muddy, but his apartment was a pigsty. He didn't seem like the kind of guy who would worry much about mud on his shoes. He also said he would have worn booties over his shoes if he were going to be creeping around her place. He uses them on his job as a cable installer."

Bustamente tilted his head to one side, then the other, as if mentally weighing the evidence and arguments. When his head went straight again, I supposed it meant he, too, wasn't yet leaning one way or the other. He eyed the smushed blob of tomato for a moment before gesturing to my partner. "Did you have Brigit track?"

"I did. She didn't seem to find a trail leading out of the backyard. Either the culprit climbed over the side fence or—"

"The culprit was Adriana herself so the trail led right back to her side door."

"Exactly."

He glanced down at Brigit. "Too bad you can't tell us if you smelled Downey at the house."

She cocked her head as if trying to understand him. It wasn't the first time I wished she spoke English so we could communicate better. She knew more than she could tell us. I knew it.

Bustamente patted her head before turning back to me. "I'll send a crime scene tech out to take a closer look at the footprints."

"Great. I'll let Adriana know someone's coming."

"When's your next shift?" he asked.

"Tonight. I told Adriana I'd keep a close eye on her place and ask the other officers to do the same. Of course I'll tell them to keep an eye on Ryan's apartment, too."

"All righty. I'll give this some thought." The detective twirled a finger in the air. "Let's circle back later."

When I left Bustamente's office, I made a quick detour into the administrative area shared by the street officers. Brigit lay at my feet while I ran both Adriana's and Ryan's names through the Internet. The night's events had left me befuddled. Might as well see what I could find out about them, see if it might help me make sense of things, get a better understanding about who they were.

The search gave me several links for Ryan Downey. The guy was an open book, though hardly a literary masterpiece. More like a picture pop-up book. His Facebook page included photos of him posing with big-breasted women dressed in tight-fitting comic-character costumes that showed lots of leg and cleavage. All wore heavy makeup and some wore colored wigs. Bright pink. Purple. One was blue, similar to my roommate's hair. There were a couple recent pictures of him with his arm draped around an unidentified woman with blond hair. He'd also shared dozens of photos of his Camaro, far more than others were interested in judging by the pitiful lack of likes and comments on the latter few.

According to his Facebook profile, he claimed to be in a relationship with a woman he'd identified only as "My Beautiful Blonde Boo." Was she the young woman in the posted pics? He hadn't tagged the photos on his page or provided names in his posts. *Hmm.* When I'd interviewed Ryan, he hadn't mentioned having a new girlfriend. But I hadn't specifically asked about his current romantic involvements, either. Was he really dating someone new? Or had he only made the entry to irritate Adriana if she happened to look at his page? Something else to ponder.

Ryan had also posted several photos of him with his nephew. *Toby, right?* The kid sure was a cutie. There they were blowing bubbles in a park. Another featured Toby feeding ducks by a pond. The Police and Firefighters Memorial wall in the background told me the photo had been taken at Trinity Park. Ryan had shared a photo originally posted by a Randy Downey—*Ryan's older brother?*—that showed Toby playing on a playground with a dozen other kids. A sign in the background identified the adjacent building as the Southside Recreation Center. The post read: *Toby having fun with friends at Camp Fort Worth!* When I was a kid, I'd attended one of the city's summer day camps myself, though my camp had been at the rec center closer to my parents' house in the Arlington Heights area.

I wasn't quite sure what to make of Ryan, but at least he appeared to be a fun and involved uncle. Similar photos of costumed women, his car, and his nephew showed up on Ryan's Instagram account. His name also popped up in regard to a local high school's robotics team. Evidently he'd been on the team himself years ago and still helped out as an adviser on design and electronics. Maybe his technical savvy was where his confidence came from, what made him feel self-assured and superior.

While I learned quite a bit about Ryan—his public persona, at least—Adriana was an entirely different story. When I ran her name through the browser, virtually nothing came up. It was almost as if she didn't exist. She had no Facebook page, no Twitter or Instagram accounts. She didn't Snapchat and had no Pinterest. I would've expected her to at least be sharing some kind of healthy hummus recipes, maybe one for that zucchini bread she'd made for Ryan. The only entry I found for her was a listing on the staff of the rehab center.

Given the lack of information online, it looked like Adriana had taken pains to protect her privacy. I supposed I shouldn't have been surprised. It's not like her home was all that inviting. She seemed to be the kind of person who kept to herself, an introvert. Of course there was nothing inherently wrong with that. I'd been a bit of a loner myself as a young girl, quietly reading my books under a tree rather than jumping rope on the playground. With my stutter, I couldn't trust my mouth to say the chants right. Different strokes for different folks. But Adriana's reserve did make it harder to get a feel for her, to know what she was thinking, what made her tick. What she might, or might not, be capable of where an ex was concerned.

So long as I was on the computer, I figured I might as well enter my reports on the incident at Adriana's place and the Lollipop Bandit. Once they were in the system, I became curious. Had the lollipop thief struck before, or was this morning's heist his first offense?

I pulled up the search page and typed in a selection of alternative key terms. *Tootsie Roll Pop. Lollipop. Sucker. Grape. Scrubs. Medical uniform. Nurse.* The machine whirred for a second or two after my finger tapped the enter key, then spat out a list of seven reports. A quick scan of the reports told me that five of them were irrelevant. The other two reports told me that the man in the scrubs was a repeat offender. Per the information contained in these reports, both of which had been filed within the last month, a man in scrubs had been spotted pocketing grape Tootsie Pops at not only a convenience store on Pennsylvania Avenue, but also a pharmacy on Henderson.

Like the gas station he'd hit this morning, both locations were within a few blocks of Cook Children's Hospital. The reports indicated that the man's head was covered with a cap, his face with a surgical mask. The first report indicated another customer had witnessed the theft and reported it to the store management, but the thief had left the building in the meantime. The second report stated that a store employee who'd been stocking sodas nearby had seen the man slip the lollipops into his pocket, but that the man had taken off running when confronted. Though the stocker had chased the thief out into the parking lot, he gave up when the thief turned a corner a block down. Given that nobody had been injured or threatened and the value of the property taken was nominal, the responding officers had filed the reports but performed no follow-up.

While I knew those of us in law enforcement had to set priorities, the type A personality in me wouldn't feel satisfied until we caught the guy, even if all he got was a slap on the wrists for his sucker stealing. I'd definitely be keeping an eye out for the masked bandit while I went about my patrols.

On the way out of the station, I stopped at the bulletin board to check the schedule. Looked like Derek would be working the night shift tonight, too. While I normally groaned when I discovered he was working my same schedule, it would be helpful tonight. I'd be able to catch him and discuss his earlier visit to Adriana's house.

Our current shift complete, Brigit and I drove home. The house we shared with Frankie and Zoe, Frankie's fluffy calico cat, was a modest-sized bungalow-style home with a broad, deep porch. The wood was mauve with ivory trim, the front door painted navy blue to provide a touch of contrast. A giant magnolia tree lorded over the front yard, shading the lawn too much for grass to grow. An ivy ground covering was doing its best to hide the bare spots. A prefab single-car detached garage had been added some time after the house had originally been built, though Frankie and I used it for storage only, parking our cars in the driveway. A six-foot wooden privacy fence enclosed the backyard, giving Brigit a safe placc to romp, dig, and do her dirty business, and me a nice, shady place to read in the hammock Seth had bought me as a gift.

I pulled my blue metallic Smart Car to the curb in front of the house. No sense blocking Frankie's red Juke in the driveway. She'd just have to wake me up to move my car later when she left the house.

Brigit and I went inside to find Frankie sitting at the kitchen table with a bowl of Fruity Pebbles on the table in front of her and Zoe on her lap. While Zoe was a fluffy ball of white, orange, and black fur, Frankie's blue hair matched her eyes and the azure flakes in her bowl, as well.

"Hey," she said in greeting around a mouthful of cereal. "How was your shift?"

"Weird." I gave her the Cliff's Notes version of what had transpired. "I'm totally befuddled. What do you think?"

"That you're the only person I know who uses words like 'befuddled.'"

I gave her my cut-the-crap look.

She lifted her shoulders. "Hard to say. On one hand, who in their right mind would throw a brick through their own window? It would be a pain to deal with and it probably wouldn't be cheap to get it fixed, either. But on the other hand, would the guy really risk making a false police report about being attacked? And I guess the judge must have believed he was in some kind of danger or they wouldn't have given him a protective order. Then again, if Adriana didn't show up to court to defend herself, the judge probably figured it couldn't hurt to issue the order, just in case."

In other words, she found the situation as confusing

as I did. It was impossible to tell which way was up. Enforcing the law was my job, but how could I enforce it when I wasn't sure who to enforce it against? Turning to more positive topics, I said, "I've got some good news for you."

Zoe hopped up onto the table as Frankie raised a hopeful brow. "Oh, yeah?"

"Seth's station has an opening. He said he'd put in a good word for you."

Her face brightened. "That would be great! I'll get my application in right away."

While Brigit took a drink from her water bowl—*slurp, slurp, slurp*—I reached over to give Zoe a scratch at the base of her tail, the same spot that was pure bliss for Brigit. Zoe lifted her hindquarters to press them into my hand and began to purr. When I pulled my hand back a moment later, she went from appreciative to angry in one second flat, standing up, swatting at my arm, and issuing an insistent *meow*.

"Sorry, girl," I told the cat. "I'm wiped out. I'm going to bed."

After brushing my teeth and washing my face, I headed to the bedroom, changed into my pajamas, and pulled my curtains tight. I'd had to buy the heavy, room-darkening kind. It wasn't easy to fall asleep in the daytime without fooling your biorhythms into thinking it was night. On occasion, I drank a glass of wine to relax myself, but a glass of chardonnay didn't sound enticing at all at the moment. I tossed and turned for a bit, but finally ventured into dreamland.

Around three in the afternoon, I began to stir. Something warm was pressed up against my back. At first I assumed it was Brigit, but when I realized there was a heavy human arm draped over me, too, I knew it had to be Seth. He must've come over after his twenty-four-hour shift was up. While I had yet to give him a key to the house, he knew we kept an emergency spare on a hook inside Brigit's doghouse out back. Still, him coming over like this was something new. In a way, it wasn't unlike Adriana having a key made to Ryan's apartment without his permission. But unlike that situation, I was happy Seth was here.

I raised my head to look around. Brigit and Blast were curled up together on her bed on the floor. Zoe had joined the dogs, stretched out along the edge of the cushion.

My stirring roused Seth and he lifted his head from the pillow. "Hey," he said, his voice gravelly from sleep.

I turned to face him. "Who do you think you are, sneaking into a woman's bed without her permission?" Just because I didn't mind didn't mean I wasn't going to give him a little hell about it. No sense letting the guy think he could take me for granted.

His kissable mouth spread in a sexy grin. "I'm the male version of Goldilocks," he said, "and this bed felt just right."

I felt myself warm at his words. Our relationship had been through some initial ups and downs. Given his rough childhood, Seth didn't trust or get attached easily. But somewhere along the way his defenses had broken down. I had no idea where our relationship might lead, but for the time being I was quite happy with the way things were. Besides, what woman in her right mind would complain about waking up to find a sexy firefighter in her bed? Still, it was fun to razz the guy a little. "I could have you arrested, you know."

"For what?"

"Breaking and entering."

"I didn't break in. I used a key. A key *you* told me about."

He had me there. "I only told you where I hid the key in case there was an emergency."

"There *was* an emergency." He slid me a grin. "I needed ten cc's of Megan Luz, stat."

"Okay, but you still entered."

"I've heard of people being charged with B and E," Seth said, "but never just E."

"When it's just E we call it trespassing."

He sat up and raised his palms. "All right. If you want me to go, I will."

When he went to slip out of the bed I pounced on him and pinned him to the mattress. "Not so fast, mister."

He nuzzled my ear. "How about we commit a crime of passion?"

"Misdemeanor or felony?"

"Felony. First degree."

We spent the next half hour committing crimes in which we took turns playing the role of perpetrator and willing victim. When we finished, we collapsed onto our respective sides of the bed.

"How bad was the fire last night?" I asked.

"The fire itself wasn't too bad," he said. "The problem was getting to it. It was in a warehouse and there were wooden pallets and rusty pipes and all kinds of junk around the building. I wrenched my back moving a barrel."

"Turn over," I told him. "I'll rub it for you."

He rolled over, exposing the army eagle tattoo that spanned his broad shoulders and the scars across his lower back that he'd earned when running from a grenade thrown by a young boy in Afghanistan. It was like a horrific diary entry eternally etched on Seth's skin.

Forcing that awful thought aside, I wriggled to my knees on the bed next to him and began massaging his shoulders, rubbing my thumbs over the eagle's feathers. "How's that feel?"

Seth moaned in delight. "Like heaven."

"Guess that makes me an angel, then." My mind flashed back to the fictional vixens on Ryan's wall. I supposed it made sense for me to be some type of angelic superhero. After all, my last name—Luz—meant "light" in Spanish. I only hope I wouldn't be like Lucifer, the other angel of light, and fall from grace, ending up in hell. Then again, hell couldn't be much hotter than the brutal Texas summers.

I reached over into the drawer of my nightstand and retrieved the peppermint pain-relief cream. I always kept a tube handy. Between chasing suspects who were trying to flee and the repetitive hand motions of traffic duty, cops constantly found themselves with a wrenched muscle or tight tendon.

I squeezed a dollop onto the small of Seth's back and worked it around his lower lumbar before moving up his spine. As I rubbed his sore back, I told him what Adriana had said when I returned to her house, about Ryan's penchant for role-play.

"A crotchless tiger costume?" he said. "Did you ask where I can get you one?"

I grabbed my pillow and put it over his head.

His muffled voice came from beneath. "What's your next move?"

Lest I suffocate the guy, I removed the pillow. "The supervisor on duty said I made the right call not to arrest anyone. We got Detective Bustamente involved. The detective had some suspicions about the footprints and sent a crime scene tech to the house to take a look."

My hands burning from the cream, I slid off the bed to go wash them.

When I returned to the bedroom, Seth had turned over onto his back. "Let me take you to dinner before your shift."

He'd get no argument from me. They say the way to a man's heart is through his stomach, but that theory worked just as well on a woman.

We cleaned ourselves up and left the dogs canoodling on the couch while we went out for an early dinner of Mexican food. As much as I would've loved a margarita, I wasn't sure the effects would wear off before I had to leave for my shift, so I settled for eating half my body weight in guacamole instead. I made a mental note to take Brigit for some long walks during tonight's shift to burn off the calories.

On the drive back to my place, I asked Seth to swing by the W1 station. Detective Bustamente's car was still in the lot. *Good.* "Mind if I run in for a minute? I want to see if he's heard anything from the crime scene techs yet."

"No problem." Seth slowed, turned down the next side street, and circled back, pulling to the curb just past the front doors to let me out.

I scurried inside and down the hall to the detective's office. I found him toying with a red rubber band, stretching it every which way between his fingers as he stared off into space, probably contemplating an investigation. When he spotted me in his door, he asked, "Who and why would someone steal two hundred bowling balls?"

I vaguely remembered dispatch announcing an alarm call late last night at the Cowtown Bowl 'n' Roll, a combination bowling alley and roller-skating rink. I'd been dealing with a speeder on Rosedale at the time. I'd assumed it was like most other such calls, a false alarm. Looked like my assumption was wrong.

"Fraternity prank?" I suggested. "Maybe a competitor trying to put them out of business?" I had no idea how much it would cost to replace two hundred bowling balls, but it wouldn't be cheap.

He pointed a finger at me. "You're thinking like a detective, Officer Luz."

"What did the crime scene tech think of the footprints at Miss Valdez's house?"

"He couldn't conclusively say the prints were real or faked," the detective said, "but he thought the ones in the garden soil might have been too deep to have been made naturally. It also looked like additional dirt had been spread in that particular part of the garden to ensure a good print."

"So it's likely Adriana made them?"

"Let's say it's 'possible.' It's also possible Ryan faked them to make Adriana appear vindictive, to throw suspicion off himself."

"What about the brick? Any fingerprints on it?"

"Two sets," he said. "One set matched prints that were found on the rubber toe of the shoe. Our best guess is that they're Mr. Downey's. The other set were small, like a child's."

"Ryan's nephew." It made sense that Toby might have touched the brick while they were painting the model.

"That's what I'm thinking, too."

If Adriana had been trying to frame Ryan, it looked like she'd been smart enough to keep her prints off the brick and shoes. "Did you contact Miss Valdez and tell her the results?" I asked.

"I figured I'd let you handle that task," Bustamente said with a wry smile. "After all, you're wanting to get into detective work someday. You might as well get a taste of it now. Consider it an opportunity to expand your skills."

I crossed my arms over my chest. "Who do you think you're fooling?"

He chuckled. "Certainly not a smart young woman such as yourself."

He'd pushed his dirty work off on me. I wasn't much looking forward to giving Adriana the news, but Bustamente was right. I better get used to uncomfortable conversations if I wanted to be a successful detective. And I knew he'd only asked me to handle the task because he was swamped and because he trusted me to do a good job. It was an implicit compliment, really.

I raised a hand in good-bye. "I'll let you know how it goes."

"Good luck, Officer Luz."

As I headed back down the hall, I passed Officer Hinojosa.

"Sucking up to the detectives again?" Hinojosa asked.

"Not sucking up," I snapped. "Doing my job."

He chortled. "Yeah. Keep telling yourself that."

Seth and I drove back to my house. I would have liked to plop myself down on the sofa with Seth and our dogs and watch television until it was time for me to get ready for my shift. But duty called and I, being the dedicated cop I was, had to answer.

I walked Seth and Blast to the door. While Seth gave me a kiss good-bye, Blast did the same to Brigit, licking at her mouth. I wondered if he could taste Brutus and realized Brigit had cheated on him and gone to first base with a coworker. If he could, he didn't seem to mind. I guess dogs don't get jealous. Humans, on the other hand, were prone to intense jealousy. Exhibit A was Adriana and Ryan. One of them didn't seem to be able to get over the other. But who was the one who couldn't let go?

I touched my index finger to Seth's chin dimple. "Thanks for dinner." I followed up with another warm kiss.

When we finally broke apart, Seth gave my long, dark locks a final twist, said, "See ya," and headed out to his car.

I dressed in my uniform and pulled my hair back into my usual tight, professional-looking bun. "Let's go, partner!" I called to Brigit. She bounded up and trotted after me as I exited the house.

After running by the station to get our cruiser, we headed to Adriana's house. I clipped a leash to Brigit's collar, gave her a moment or two to sniff around the mailbox and porch, and led her to the front door. *Knock-knock-knock.*

"Hello, Officer Luz."

I nearly jumped out of my tactical sneakers when a voice came from behind the oleander bushes to my left. Had one of those creepy gnomes from out back come to life? I reflexively whipped my baton from my belt and flicked it open. *SNAP!* Working as a cop had put me in some dangerous situations, and quick reflexes could mean the difference between life and death. They could also mean the difference between appearing in control or out of it. Right now, I was afraid I appeared to be totally out of it.

Adriana's face peeked out from between limbs she'd pushed aside. Her eyes went to my baton.

"Hello, Miss Valdez." Attempting to appear calm and nonchalant, I twirled the baton in my fingers, just as I'd done with my performance baton back when I'd been a twirler for my high school's marching band. *Swish-swish-swish. Yep, just playing with my baton. You didn't scare the bejesus out of me popping out of that bush. Nope.* I stepped down from the porch, leading Brigit with me, before collapsing my baton and returning it to my belt. "What are you doing back there?"

She held up an extension cord, looking at it rather than me. "Plugging in my new lights." She disappeared for a moment as she stuck the plug into an outdoor outlet, reappearing a moment later as she slipped out from between the bushes. She pointed up to a floodlight mounted on the corner of her house. "That's motion-activated," she said. "I put a couple of them out back, too. They'll light up the whole yard if anyone goes back there again."

She'd followed my instructions. I fought the urge to pat her on the head and toss her a liver treat and a "good girl!" But it also made me wonder. *Would she be going to all this trouble if she'd been the one to throw the brick?*

I gestured to the thick bushes. "You might want to cut these bushes back, too. They make a good place for someone to hide." *Obviously.*

"I'll get right on that," she said.

Brigit sniffed along the edge of the porch, dropping to her belly and shoving her nose through a spot where the wood had rotted, leaving a gap of several inches.

Adriana glanced at Brigit before turning back to me. As before, her focus was slightly askance. "What did the crime scene person say? Are you going to search Ryan's apartment?"

Brigit began to claw at the wood, trying to get at something under the porch. I ordered her back to my side and grasped the leash near her collar, holding her close. When I responded to Adriana, I chose my words carefully, watching her closely to see how she would react. "The footprint analysis was inconclusive," I said.

Her eyes flashed, but was it with fear or fury? "Inconclusive? What does that mean?"

"It means the tech couldn't be certain if the footprints had been made naturally by a person walking in your backyard."

Her face contorted in confusion. "How else would footprints be made?"

I raised one shoulder. "He said that given the parameters, it's possible they had been fabricated."

"Fabricated?" She spat out the word as if it was a bug she'd accidentally ingested. "He thinks the prints were faked?"

"Not necessarily," I said. "But the bottom line is a good defense attorney could make a sustainable argument to that effect, especially given that Ryan has an alibi and already successfully sought a protective order against you. We need to build a better case if we're going to search Ryan's place and bring him in on charges."

She sputtered, her eyes looking wild as she threw her hands in the air. "I don't believe this! I'm being treated like a criminal when I'm the victim here!"

I raised a conciliatory palm in an attempt to calm and appease her. "I'll be watching out for you, Miss Valdez. I promise."

Yep. I'll definitely be watching out for you.

TWELVE
MISSION IMPOSSUMABLE

Brigit

She smelled the possum. It was right there under the porch. She didn't scent fear, though. The stupid thing must be sleeping. If Megan would just give Brigit some slack on the leash she could claw through that rotten wood in a few seconds. She wouldn't kill the thing, just give it a nice chase, a fun scare, show it who was boss. *Dogs rule! Possums drool!*

But no. Megan was being a total party pooper. Looked like Megan needed to be shown who was boss, too.

"Come on, Brig," Megan said, turning to head back to their cruiser.

Not gonna happen. Brigit plunked her butt down on the grass and refused to budge.

Megan gave her the hand signal that meant "come." But Brigit refused to come. *Make me.*

Megan crouched down and looked her in the eye. "Only good girls get treats."

Treats? Well, now. That changes everything.

Brigit lifted her butt, wagged her tail, and followed Megan to the car, gladly accepting the liver treat Megan tossed into her enclosure before closing it. Megan put her face to the mesh screen and said, "Sometimes you're a real pain in the ass."

Brigit wasn't sure what Megan meant, but she knew the tone meant Megan wasn't happy with her. She didn't much care. Megan would get over it. She always did. Besides, Brigit had a treat to eat. That's all that mattered right now.

THIRTEEN

ABSENCE MAKES THE HEART GROW FONDER

The Devoted One

There's been no visit. No phone call. Not even a text or e-mail. Of course it had been less than twenty-four hours since the incident, but the longer things went on, the less likely it was that there would be any contact.

You do nice things for someone, try to show them how you feel and make them feel special, and what do you get in return? Taken for granted and dumped, that's what.

It wasn't fair. It wasn't right.

No one should have to put up with this kind of treatment, to be taken for granted like this.

But people appreciate things more when they no longer have them, don't they? Sure. That's where that old saying "you don't know what you've got till it's gone" came from. Maybe the only thing needed to bring the two of them back together was a little time apart.

It was worth a try.

FOURTEEN
EYES WIDE OPEN

Megan

After visiting with Adriana, I phoned Detective Bustamente to give him an update. "I swung by her house for
a quick chat. I told her that the footprints wouldn't hold
up under the scrutiny of a good defense attorney and that
fact, along with Ryan's alibi, meant there wasn't suffi-
cient evidence to make an arrest."

"How did she respond?"

"She was furious."

"Furious because she's scared? Or furious because
her plan to get Ryan in trouble isn't working?"

Hell if I know. "I don't know what to think."

"We'll figure it out sooner or later," Bustamente said.

"I hope it's sooner." Later might be *too late*.

After speaking with the detective, I made a pass by
Ryan's apartment complex. While his Camaro was in
his reserved parking spot, his work truck was nowhere
in the lot. Looked like the guy was putting in some overtime.

With a couple of hours to burn until our night shift

began, I drove to the Shoppes at Chisholm Trail, a mall located within the boundaries of our beat. To look at the place now, you'd never know a bomb had gone off there the previous summer. Thanks to Brigit alerting on the device, we'd been able to evacuate the food court before the explosive detonated. To this day, I couldn't figure out why she'd led me to the garbage can where the bomb had been placed. While she was trained to track and sniff for illicit drugs, she was not trained to scent for explosives. Best I could figure, either she heard the timer ticking and was curious about it or she smelled something else in the garbage that had caused her to alert. Either way, her actions saved untold numbers of lives. She and I had sustained minor injuries, but we'd lived to patrol another day.

Given that it was now August, the summer stock had been relegated to the clearance racks to make space for the incoming winter apparel. But given that we lived in Texas, summer weather would actually continue for a couple more months, the calendar be damned. Might as well see if the stores had any cute bathing suits or shorts on sale, right?

Luck was with me. I found a cute bikini in a mint-green color for half price, as well as a pair of shorts and a bohemian print top. I tried them on in the dressing room, turning this way and that to check myself out in the mirror. "What do you think, girl?" I asked Brigit. Ridiculous, since she wore the same outfit—her fur— every day and had little interest in fashion. Even if she did, she couldn't exactly express her opinion. Sometimes I forgot my partner wasn't human. Still, she wagged her tail when I spoke to her so I took that as a sign of approval. I decided to get them all. I worked hard. I'd earned them.

As we made our way through the food court with our purchases, Brigit lifted her nose in the air and sniffed her way along. We were passing through an aisle between sets of tables when a male voice called out. "Officer Luz! How are you?"

I turned to see Serhan Singh at the counter of his kebab restaurant, Stick People. Though Singh was from Turkey, he'd embraced American life, and the local sports teams, with fervor. He sported a full beard, jeans, and a Texas Rangers jersey.

"Let's go say hi," I told Brigit, changing course. As we headed to his booth, her tail wagged a mile a minute. She knew Serhan. Better yet, she knew he was always good for some warm beef or chicken.

We stepped up to the counter. "Good to see you, Serhan."

"You, too," he replied. "I have not seen much of you two at the mall this summer."

It had been a busy season for me. Between tracking the Berkeley Place Peeper and working an undercover drug sting at the university, I'd been tied up elsewhere the past several weeks. "We've had some investigations that kept us from our usual beat," I told him. "How are your wife and daughter?" I'd never forget their terrified faces the day the bomb had gone off and they'd been forced to flee the mall. The image was seared into my memory.

"Kara's excited about starting first grade," he said. "She can't wait to learn how to read better. She told me that she knows most of the three-letter words now and wants to learn the four-letter ones."

We shared a chuckle at her innocence.

He looked down at Brigit, who was smacking her chops and drooling so heavily her mouth was a virtual Niagara Falls, forming a small puddle at her front paws. "Would you like chicken or beef tonight, Brigit?"

She responded with a *woof!*

"Beef it is." He used tongs to pull three strips of beef from a warming tray and lay them in a cardboard basket. He handed me the basket, along with a napkin. Not that he thought Brigit would need it. She could wipe her mouth with her tongue. But he knew I'd tear the meat into smaller pieces to keep her from wolfing it down and would need to clean up afterward.

"Thanks so much."

He nodded. "My pleasure. Hope to see you again soon."

Lest someone slip in Brigit's drool, I wiped the floor with the napkin and led her outside. I parked my rear on a bench to feed Brigit. She snatched each piece of meat from my hands as soon as I tore it off. It was a miracle I didn't lose a finger in the process.

After visiting the mall, I drove to Forest Park and threw a Frisbee for Brigit, letting her get some exercise and have some fun. She ran after it, catching it every time as it began to come back down to earth. She even caught my bad throw, which ended up in the branches of an oak tree, falling down through the limbs like a pinball.

As we played, a smiling redhead came up the walk,

a black Lab at the end of her leash. Brigit trotted over to meet the dog. Both of their tails wagged as they greeted each other.

"Hi," I said to the woman as I bent over to pet her dog. "Who's your pretty girl?"

"That's Shae," the woman said. "She's sassy."

As if to prove the point, Shae bent down on her front legs, her rear in the air and her tail whipping back and forth as she attempted to engage Brigit in play. Brigit mirrored the gesture, adding a frisky *arf-arf!* as she jumped back and forth on her front legs. The two engaged in a playful dance for a few seconds before a squirrel scampering between two nearby trees drew their attention away.

"Enjoy the rest of the day!" I called to the woman as she and her dog continued on their way.

We spent another quarter hour at playtime before it was time to head to the station. "C'mon, girl!" I called to round up Brigit. "Time for work."

We arrived a few minutes early for our shift. Brigit and I waited in the parking lot for Derek to arrive. Our fellow officer Summer pulled into the lot not long after us. She drove an adorable white Miata with a colorful pink Hawaiian lei hanging from the rearview mirror. She had the top down, enjoying the night air. Not that it was cool, by any stretch of the imagination. But when the daytime highs had hit 104 degrees, the upper eighties felt virtually arctic.

Summer's name fit her perfectly. She was a bubbly blonde with bouncy curls. Like me, she'd joined the force right out of college, though she had three years' experience on me. Unlike some officers, who became jaded after dealing with lawbreakers day in and day out, Summer somehow managed to remain an optimist, retaining her faith in humanity.

How she managed to maintain her sunny disposition these days was beyond me. After Derek Mackey had lost critical drug evidence and a dealer had gone free as a result, the W1 captain no longer trusted the Big Dick to work alone. Nobody'd wanted to pair with the jerk and, unfortunately, Summer had drawn the short stick. Until such time as Derek proved himself again, she was stuck with him. *Talk about cruel and unusual punishment.*

When Summer spotted us, she waved and tapped her horn. *Beep-beep!* I raised a hand back at her. She pulled into a spot and activated the convertible top. It rose and arced over her head, slowly coming to a close.

"Hi, Megan!" she sang as she hopped out of her car. "Hi, Brigit!" She walked over, knelt down, and gave my furry partner a nice scratch and a kiss on the head.

"Hey, Summer," I replied. "Before you head out on patrol, I n-need to speak with Derek."

She looked up. "About what?"

I told her about my visits last night to Adriana's house and Ryan's apartment. "Derek handled an earlier call at Miss Valdez's place. I want to get his read on her. We're not sure she's on the up-and-up. She avoided eye contact with me and seemed a little squirrelly."

On hearing the word "squirrel," Brigit looked up and glanced around, seeking the rodent I'd mentioned. Seeing none, she cast me a dirty look for my poor word choice and let out a sigh.

Summer stood. "What about Ryan Downey? Did he seem trustworthy?"

"Not particularly. Other than the Big Dick, I've never seen a guy so full of himself for no apparent reason."

Summer offered a *hmph*. "So either one could be the bad guy, then."

"Exactly." I told Summer that the night crew needed to make extra passes by their residences tonight to keep an eye on things, and provided her with the addresses. "If you see anything suspicious, let me know. Okay?"

"Sure will."

We jumped back as Mackey's shiny black pickup careened into the lot, tires screeching. *What an ass.* I was tempted to write him a ticket for reckless driving.

He braked to a quick stop in the spot next to Summer's car, the rubber truck nuts hanging from his trailer hitch swinging wildly. He slid out, bleeped the door locks, and went into the station to clock in. When he came back outside, he sauntered over. "Let's go," he barked at Summer, swinging an arm to point to her squad car on the far side of the lot.

She was unfazed. "Not yet, buckaroo." She smiled sweetly. "Officer Luz needs to speak with you first."

He cut her a harsh look and turned to me, his lip twitching in a sneer. There was no love lost between the two of us. He'd never forgive me for Tasering him in the groin last year. But, hell, he'd asked for it by making one crude comment too many and pushing me over the edge.

While I'd like to say I regretted my momentary lapse of judgment and self-control, it would be a lie. How could I regret the incident that ended my partnership with a grade-A shithead and resulted in me being teamed with Brigit instead?

Derek and the chief of police were tight. The two were hunting buddies and spent time together regularly outside of work. As a result, the Taser incident had been kept quiet, the chief realizing I could bring his golden boy down with me if I repeated the filthy comments Derek had made. Still, Chief Garelik had given me an ultimatum. Pair with a K-9 or turn in my resignation. At first I'd been hesitant. I wasn't sure a dog would make a good partner. I couldn't have been more wrong. Brigit was loyal and dedicated, and she had special skills that enabled us to do things other partners could never accomplish. She was a good listener, too, always having a ready ear when I needed to talk things out. And she performed watchdog duty at home, too, which was an added benefit. Taking care of her 24/7 tied me down a little and I didn't enjoy having to pick up her poop, but these sacrifices were small compared to what she brought to my life.

"Well?" Mackey snapped. "What do you want, Luz?"

"You handled a call a while b-back," I said, "at the home of a woman named Adriana Valdez. Do you remember her?"

"I only remember the hot chicks," he said. "Even then I never remember their names."

Derek's charm knew no bounds. *Blurgh.* I figured a few details might jar his memory. "Her car alarm had gone off in the middle of the night and she suspected her ex-boyfriend had thrown a tennis ball at her car. Does that ring a bell?"

"Now I remember." A lecherous grin spread across his face. "She was the *chica* with the tight little—"

"Besides *that*," I snapped, "what were your thoughts?"

He grunted. "She was getting her panties in a wad over nothing. Even if her ex did throw a ball at her car, it was a harmless prank."

Summer and I exchanged glances. A lunk like Derek wouldn't understand how a woman might feel threatened to know her ex had been cruising by her house, keeping an unwelcome eye on her, showing that he harbored enough resentment to want to cause her some grief.

Though I doubted this conversation with Derek was going to yield any useful information, I might as well see it through, right? "Did anything make you believe she'd set off her car alarm herself?"

"That's a stupid question." He frowned. "Why the hell would she do that?"

Summer and I exchanged another glance. Derek was clearly not a deep thinker. Like me, he wanted to make detective someday. I doubted he had what it took. He was more physical than intellectual, with more bravado than brains. He was much better suited for SWAT than investigative work.

I didn't bother explaining to Derek that it was possible Adriana might be trying to frame her ex. All I said was, "There was another incident at her place last night. We need to keep a close eye on her house and her ex's apartment for a while. I've given Summer the addresses."

With a jut of his chin in acknowledgment, Derek turned to Summer. "Let's roll."

"Head on to the cruiser, cowboy," she said. "I'll be there in a minute."

"Whatever." He walked off, heading toward their squad car.

I eyed her. "Is there something else we need to talk about?"

"No," she whispered, a naughty gleam in her eye. "I just like pushing Mackey's buttons. He hates those pet names I keep calling him, and he hates to wait for anyone."

I held my palm out at my waist and she gave me a discreet low five. *Slap.* Seeing our exchange and not to be left out, Brigit raised her paw. Summer gave Brigit a low five, too.

Brigit and I set out on our shift. I wrote a speeding ticket, directed traffic around a fender bender, and raised a hand in greeting to a group of junior high kids gathered in the parking lot of a small neighborhood pizza place. "You kids be careful, now!" I called through the open window of my cruiser. Of course what I actually meant was, *Don't do something stupid or I'll be back here to bust your asses.*

I cruised by Adriana's and Ryan's places a dozen times that night, but the only suspicious thing I saw was a small gray possum sneaking out from under Adriana's porch. The nocturnal beast must have been what Brigit was trying to get at earlier. The possum's movement activated Adriana's new motion-sensing lights, turning a spotlight on him as if he was starring in his own Broadway musical. The little creature froze, his expression reading *What just happened here?*

The lights inside Adriana's place went off around eleven. Ryan's place went dark around midnight. *Good night, folks. Sleep tight.*

As I rolled through Ryan's apartment complex again

around two in the morning, Brigit whined to let me know she needed a potty break. "I hear ya, girl."

I parked in an unreserved spot in the center of the lot and let Brigit out of the cruiser, not bothering to attach her leash. At this late hour, no one was out and about. The only sounds were the rhythmic chirp of the crickets and the hum of the air-conditioning units as they battled the heat and humidity.

Brigit followed me to a small grassy area between Ryan's building and the one next door. After squatting to relieve herself, she sniffed around the bushes and trees, checking things out.

As long as we were out of the car, we might as well perform a more complete surveillance, right? I softly called for Brigit to follow me, and we tiptoed up the stairs to the landing outside Ryan's apartment. Tonight, his porch was clear. The newspaper had been removed, along with two bricks I'd left when I collected the other one for evidence.

Had he cleared his porch to prevent Adriana from taking something else she could use to implicate him? Who knew? Certainly not me.

Only the two of them knew the truth.

Too bad I wasn't a mind reader.

I worked the night shift the rest of the week and continued to cruise by Adriana's house and Ryan's apartment every hour or so. On one of my rounds, I crossed paths in the apartment parking lot with a patrol car from a private security company. The white sedan sported a single flashing orange light on top and the company's logo, which approximated a police shield, on the front doors. I rolled to a stop and stuck my hand out the window to get the driver's attention.

The car pulled up next to me and the window lowered to reveal a man who looked to be in his late sixties. Despite his age, he was nonetheless in trim shape, with a thick head of gray hair and alert eyes. "Everything okay, Officer?"

"Just wanted to see if you'd noticed anything unusual the past few days."

"As in . . . ?" He paused and raised his brows, inviting me to fill in the blank.

"Unusual activity late at night? Someone sneaking around, or coming and going at odd hours?"

"Haven't noticed anything out of the ordinary," he said.

I cocked my head and eyed the man intently. "Can you do me a favor?"

"Sure thing."

"Keep a close eye on unit 206," I told him. "The guy who lives there had a recent breakup and there's been some strife between him and his ex." I reached into my breast pocket and pulled out my business card. "If you happen to notice anything odd, let me know."

"I'll do that." He took the card and slid it under a strap on his visor.

With that, the two of us went about our business.

Other than another possum sighting at Adriana's house, nothing out of the ordinary caught my eye. No calls came in, either. Whichever one of them had thrown the brick had apparently decided to behave himself or herself. With any luck, their situation had resolved itself and whoever had been acting out had decided to stop being petty and get a life.

While I hoped Adriana and Ryan were moving on, I was beginning to think Seth was moving in. He'd showed up with fresh bagels Thursday morning as Brigit and I returned home from our shift. While I dozed with a box fan running to drown out the noise, he mowed and trimmed the lawn as Brigit and Blast played in the yard. When I woke in mid-afternoon, I found him in my bathroom shaving, getting ready to head to the station. He wore only a towel around his waist and a thick layer of shaving cream on his face.

I leaned against the door frame, admiring his muscular physique. No doubt about it, Seth was quite a catch. Unlike Ryan, Seth had obvious reasons to sport a big ego. Fortunately, he didn't.

His gaze met mine in the mirror. "Are you ogling me?"

"Maybe."

He held the razor aloft and arched a brow. "Want me to lose the towel?"

"I want you to *wash* the towels. And then do the dishes and sweep and mop the kitchen."

He scoffed in jest. "Fixing you waffles Monday and taking care of your yard today wasn't enough? I'm beginning to feel taken for granted." He sent me a wink and went back to shaving.

I continued to watch him. Although we'd become very comfortable with each other, there was still a lot about Seth I didn't know. He tended to be short on details, and didn't like to talk about anything too emotional. I'd learned to read his signals, though. The set of his jaw. The distance in his gaze. The vertical lines, or lack thereof, between his eyes as he thought. And damned if I didn't want to know more about him, to meet the grandfather who'd raised him, the man he'd continued to live with despite their obvious antagonism. Heck, Seth and I had been dating for months. It was due time, right? Still, I knew he had to get to the station and didn't have time for what might be a prolonged debate. I'd soon find a more opportune time to broach the subject.

"Careful with that chin dimple," I warned.

He cut me a sexy smile as he ran the razor down his cheek. "Always am."

FIFTEEN
PACK

Brigit

She and Blast tussled in the fresh-cut grass, rolling around and playfully chewing each other's necks. Blast was a beta male, which made him easy to get along with. When it came to food and toys and the best spots to sleep, he deferred to Brigit, just as he should. She was an alpha female, a doggie diva.

While Brigit knew she and Megan formed a two-member pack, she liked it when Seth and Blast came around. Maybe someday all four of them could be in a pack together.

A brown squirrel taunted the dogs from its place in the pecan tree. *Chit-chit-chit!*

How dare a mere rodent speak to her that way!

In an instant, Brigit was off her back, barking, and leaping as high as she could up the trunk of the tree. It wasn't high enough to catch the squirrel, but at least she'd scared it off. It scampered across the limbs into the adjacent yard.

Stay out of my yard! You're asking for it, you dumb nut-eater!

SIXTEEN
ANOTHER PLAN B

The Devoted One

The broken window hadn't worked, and neither had the silence. There'd been no communication, no card or e-mail or phone call saying, "I've missed you and come to my senses. Let's put this nonsense behind us and get back together."

Time to rethink things.

Absence might make the heart grow fonder, but only for so long. At some point, the heart no longer grows *fonder*, it begins to *wander*. No way would the Devoted One let that heart be stolen away by someone else.

It's time to get back in touch.

SEVENTEEN
AND A PINCH TO GROW AN INCH

Megan

On Saturday afternoon, the fire chief presided over the graduation ceremony for the fire academy graduates. It was held in a large meeting room in the Forth Worth City Hall on Throckmorton Street. Seth, Blast, Brigit, and I sat in the audience, along with Frankie's boyfriend Zach. Zach was a former paratrooper and a buddy of Seth's from their army circles. Zach was tall, like Frankie, standing six feet two inches. Like Seth, he continued to wear his hair in a short, military-style cut, but where Seth's hair was blond Zach's was dark brown. He worked as a supervisor in the shipping department of the Miller Brewing Company in south Fort Worth.

Frankie's parents were also in attendance, and sat in the third row with us. It was clear Frankie got her height from her father. Her mother, on the other hand, stood a mere five feet. But her mother didn't let her short stature hold her back. When the fire chief called out the name "Francesca Kerrigan," her mother leaped to her feet, pumped her fist, and let out a loud *whoop!* The rest of us applauded, and Zach added a whistle. Needless to say, we were happy for Frankie.

From the platform, Frankie turned and waved, beaming with pride at her accomplishment. She'd spent the last few years stocking groceries at night, not sure what she wanted to do with her life. It was Seth who'd first suggested the idea of firefighting to Frankie. I'd like to think that I was the magical kismet that had led her to discovering her life's purpose. But maybe I was just trying to flatter myself, to think my life served some cosmic objective. It seemed preferable to accepting that life was merely a series of random events with no inherent goal.

After the ceremony, we gathered around Frankie to congratulate her.

"Good job, Francesca!" her father bellowed, enveloping her in a warm hug.

Her mother gave her a playful jab in the arm. "That's my girl!"

Zach draped an arm over her shoulders and pulled her toward him to give her a kiss on the cheek. "Any word on the position at Seth's station?"

"About that," Seth said before Frankie could reply. "I was told I could give you the good news."

Frankie's blue eyes popped wide. "*Good news?* I got the job, then?"

Seth nodded. "You start Monday at seven A.M."

"Hot damn!"

"Don't get too excited." He flashed a mischievous grin. "Rookies always get put on cleaning detail. Come prepared to scrub the floors."

The six of us went out afterward for a celebratory dinner and drinks at a hibachi restaurant. In an ironic twist of fate, Frankie's mother unintentionally set her cocktail napkin too close to the hot grill. When the napkin burst into flame across the table, I gestured wildly with my hand and shrieked. "Fire!"

In a quick, smooth motion, Frankie snatched up the napkin and dunked it into her glass of water, dousing the flames. Yep, looked like firefighting was her destiny.

When dinner was over, we returned to our house. I'd ordered a cake decorated to look like a fire truck and hung police cordon tape as improvised streamers around the kitchen. *Thank you, taxpayers of Fort Worth.* Zoe jumped up onto the table and licked at the frosting, but we caught her before she got too far.

"No cake for you, kitty," I said, scooping her up and setting her back on the floor.

I gave Frankie a hug as I handed her the piece of cake I'd cut. "You're going to do great."

"I hope so."

"I *know* so." I also knew she was in for some very harrowing shifts and that she'd be faced with people and events, both good and bad, that would stay with her forever. Such is the life of a first responder. The job could take both a physical and emotional toll, but for those called to it, there was no other job that could bring the same sense of fulfillment.

On Sunday, I left Brigit at home while I went to mass with my family. My brothers Daniel and Connor had come home from college for the weekend, which meant they'd either run out of money and had come to beg for some funds, or they'd given in to my mother's incessant guilt trips. Regardless of their reasons, I didn't want to miss the chance to see them. It wasn't often these days that all seven members of my family were in the same place at the same time, and no way was I going to be the party pooper who kept the family from being complete.

My parents sat at either end of their five children in the pew, a habit formed when we kids were young and sometimes acted up in church. They'd strategically kept all of us within arm's reach, ready to smack us with the bulletin if we misbehaved. Though none of us had received a smack in years, traditions die hard.

After mass, we went to my parents' house in the Arlington Heights neighborhood for lunch. The three-bedroom, two-bath, one-story house bore faded yellow paint and peeling trim. While there had been a row of bushes along the front of the house when I was young, several had succumbed to either the hard freezes over various winters or the severe heat and droughts of any number of summers. Three struggling bushes remained, positioned randomly, two on one side of the centered front porch, one on the other. Obviously, the Luz home had never been considered for a yard-of-the-month award.

Mom, who was as much a cook as she was a gardener, threw together a platter of simple sandwiches, augmented by store-bought macaroni salad, a bag of corn chips, and a jar of dill pickles.

My sister Gabby lived up to her name, rambling on about the driver's ed course she was taking. Her sixteenth birthday was coming up and she couldn't wait to get her license, even if the only vehicle she'd have access to was the 1993 Buick Regal my father had bought when he first began working at the GM plant in nearby Arlington over two decades ago. Gabby would have to share the car with Joey, who was a year older. But still, wheels are wheels, and the ancient car would get her from point A to point B. Not in style, maybe, but at least in comfort.

"The instructor had us drive on I-30 Thursday," she told me as we took seats at the kitchen table. "We nearly got hit by a pickup. It was so scary! People drive crazy around here!"

I reached for the bowl of macaroni. "You don't know the half of it. I wrote a woman a ticket this week for backing down an entrance ramp she'd entered by accident. People had to swerve around her. It was a wonder she didn't kill someone." I spooned a helping onto my plate and passed the bowl to Daniel. "How's summer school going?"

"Good. I'm on target for As in both of my classes this semester."

"That's great." My eyes moved to Connor, whose college aims tended less toward maintaining a good GPA and more toward having a good time. "What about you?"

His eyes darted to our parents before returning to me. "Don't ask," he muttered under his breath.

His response caused my mother's Irish temper to flare and she cast Connor a pointed look. "You don't get your act together soon, Dad and I will cut you off."

My brother mumbled something under his breath, but she chose to ignore it. Irish tempers tend to flame out as easily and as quickly as they flare up.

One of my mother's indistinguishable orange tabby cats leaped up onto the table as Joey reached for a sandwich. He grabbed the cat and set him back on the floor. "Did Mom tell you I got a new job?" he asked me.

Despite the fact that he could have easily given me the information directly, it came as no surprise that my brother would run things through our mom. Like many mothers, she served as the family's central communications center.

When I turned to her for the details, she made a circling motion with her hand, letting me know the information would be forthcoming once she had a chance to finish chewing. A few seconds later she swallowed the bite of food in her mouth and said, "He's going to sack groceries at Central Market." The tabby who'd attempted to summit the table a moment before jumped into her lap, where she treated him to a piece of her tuna sandwich.

I turned back to Joey. "Sacking groceries, huh? You giving up your lawn-mowing business, then?"

"Heck, no," he replied. "You know how much people pay me so that they can stay inside in the air-conditioning?"

A pretty penny, apparently. No wonder the kid always seemed to be flush with cash.

"I could mow your lawn, too," he offered. "I'll give you a family discount. Twenty bucks."

I was tempted to remind him of all the things I'd done for him over the years without a single cent in payment. I'd changed his diapers, driven him to his friends' houses for sleepovers, helped him clean up untold numbers of spills and messes he'd created. He could mow my lawn gratis until the day I died and he'd still owe me. But no sense pointing this out. There's no arguing with teen-agers. They're irrational creatures.

"Thanks," I told him, "but no thanks. Seth takes care of my yard work."

"How much do you pay him?"

"He does it for free," I said. "Out of the goodness of his heart."

A smirk played around Joey's lips. "Yeah, right. That's why he does it." He elbowed Connor and the two of them shared a laugh.

I narrowed my eyes at them. "You know I'm trained to kill with my bare hands, right?" Actually, I wasn't. But these two punks didn't need to know that.

Joey raised his hands in surrender. "Okay! Okay!"

Luckily for me, Gabby changed the subject. "When are you going to take me to the Roller Derby, Megan?"

Gabby had enjoyed roller-skating as a girl, and I'd promised her I'd take her to see Frankie play derby sometime. It was always fun to watch the Fort Worth Whoop Ass clobber some lesser team.

I took a sip of my iced tea. "I'll check the schedule and get back with you. I'm sure there's a bout or two coming up soon."

We continued to make small talk until everyone had eaten their fill and began to leave the table. I offered to drop Connor at the bus station for his return trip to college in San Marcos. Given that Daniel attended the University of Texas branch only a half hour away in Arlington, he planned to stick around a while longer.

Hugs were exchanged as we headed to the door. The cats had come around to see us off, too, and I gave each of them a scratch under the chin. "Behave," I admonished them with a wagging finger. One of them swiped at my hand. *Brat.*

Out the door we went. It was nice not to have to wrestle with the darn thing anymore. After years of the door hanging askew, Seth had recently fixed it. Not only was he hunky and handsome, he was handy, too. Definitely a keeper.

The following week, I was back on the day shift. *Thank God.* Some cops dealt just fine with working in the dark. They must be part vampire or something. As for me, the night shift wreaked havoc on my biorhythms. Even in the brutally hot Texas summers, I much preferred working by daylight.

Monday was a typical day. Motor vehicle violations. Teens trying to sneak into the movie theater without paying for tickets. A hit-and-run on Colonial Parkway involving an S-class Mercedes sedan, a golf cart, and a motorized scooter. Okay, so maybe that last call wasn't typical. According to the driver of the Mercedes, who was the only one left on the scene when I arrived, a kid on a scooter pulled onto the road right in front of him. When the driver hit his brakes, he was broadsided by a trio of adolescent boys in a golf cart who'd been racing the scooter. Fortunately uninjured, the kids had backed up, made a quick U-turn, and zipped away before the driver of the Mercedes could gather his wits and follow them. No doubt the kids had hidden the cart in a garage and were in the process of making up a story for their parents to explain the damage. *The shelves fell over on it!*

"Did you get a good look at any of the boys?" I asked.

"Not really," the man said. "The only thing I can tell you is that the driver had blond hair and braces on his teeth. I saw them when he was screaming in surprise outside my car window. He had bright blue rubber bands. One of them broke when he was screaming and stuck on my window." He gestured to a small broken rubber band on the glass. "As far as what they were wearing or anything else?" He shrugged to complete the sentence. In other words, not a clue.

"I'll cruise the neighborhood," I told the man. "Maybe I'll spot the kids or the cart. In the meantime, see if your homeowner's association will put out an e-mail alert. Somebody's likely to know who the kids are. If you get a response, I'd be happy to go talk to them and their parents and see if we can't set things straight."

After snapping a photo of the rubber band on the window, I used tweezers to remove it and dropped it into an evidence bag. I took the man's information and typed up a report on my computer. The administrative duties done, I cruised slowly up and down the streets of the neighborhood. I saw nothing. No boys. No scooter. No golf cart with a damaged front end. The kids had probably scattered and were hunkered down in their bedrooms, fingers crossed their parents wouldn't find out they'd snuck out a golf cart without permission and proceeded to crash it into a car priced at over a hundred grand.

As I cruised by the fire station, I swung into the lot. Might as well see how things were going for Frankie on her first day.

Inside the station, I found Seth snoozing in one of the bunk beds, Blast in his bed on the floor. While Blast slipped out of the sleeping quarters to follow me and Brigit down the hall, I didn't wake Seth. The guy needed his sleep and, given that I was on duty, I didn't plan to stay long anyway.

The two dogs and I discovered Frankie pushing a bucket and mopping out the shower area. I leaned against the doorjamb. "Enjoying your first day, Cinderella?"

She cast a glance my way. "Not at all! Can you get me out of this? Isn't there a law against hazing?"

"There is." I stepped forward to shoo the dogs away from the mop bucket. "But it's intended for athletic teams and fraternities, not government employees."

"Darn."

"If it's any consolation," I told her, "it looks like you're doing a fine job. This tile is really gleaming."

She leaned on the mop handle and admired her handiwork with a smile. "It does, doesn't it?"

I left her with an encouraging pat on the back, returned Blast to his bed with a whispered order to "stay," and set back out on patrol.

Around four-thirty, I received a call from the owner of the Mercedes. My suggestion to contact the homeowner's association had proven to be a good one. Three people had contacted the man with the name of the kid they suspected had been driving the golf cart. He'd been identified not only by his blue rubber bands, but also a chronic lack of supervision. Looked like he was teenager non grata around his neighborhood.

"I went by his house earlier," the man said. "I could hear a television on inside, but nobody would come to the door."

"I'd like to say that surprises me." But it didn't. Avoidance was a common technique used by lawbreakers. They seemed to think that if they ignored their troubles long enough, they'd go away. *That's not how things work.*

"From what I hear," the man added, "the kid's an out-of-control brat."

Wouldn't be the first time I dealt with one of those. Kids could be a real pain in the butt sometimes, especially when their parents didn't hold them accountable. "Got his name and address?"

Once I had the information, I headed straight to the house. It was a grand home, a soaring two-story contemporary model with rows of narrow plate-glass windows, a tile roof, and a three-car garage with an additional smaller door designed for a golf cart. As I pulled up, I realized Brigit was panting heavily. *Time for a water break.*

I parked in the shade of a Bradford pear tree, retrieved a cold bottle of water from the small cooler on the passenger seat floorboard, and opened the door to my partner's enclosure to pour some into her bowl. She stood in the space and greedily lapped it up. *Slup-slup-slup.* I added a little more until she seemed satisfied. I poured the slimy dregs that remained in her bowl onto the grass and closed the door, leaving the windows down so she could get some air.

Feeling parched myself, I took a swig from the bottle and carried it to the door with me. On the porch was a large pot of purple petunias. Their dirt was dry, their leaves beginning to shrivel. Of course August was a month when people tended to neglect their outside plants and lawns. It was simply too dang hot to spend much time outside unless you were lounging in a swimming pool.

I poured a few ounces from the bottle onto the petunias. Given the godforsaken temperatures, I wasn't sure whether the water would save them from an untimely death or merely prolong their agony, but I'd like to think it was the former.

I rang the bell. The sound reverberated through the house. After waiting thirty seconds or so, I tried again. *DING-DONG-dong-dong-dong* . . .

Still nothing.

Were the residents away from home? It was impossible to tell given that the garage doors were closed. Might as well give them the benefit of the doubt. Innocent until proven guilty and all that. And I couldn't much blame the kid for bolting. Young people tended to panic when things went wrong. Still, this wrong needed to be righted. I scrawled *"Urgent—call me immediately"* on one of my business cards and crammed it into the space between the door and the jamb. It was the best I could do for the time being.

Tuesday was a hot and unusually windy day, warm bursts kicking up sand and grit and small bits of debris that pinged when they impacted the side of the cruiser. When Brigit and I took a break in Forest Park, she quickly tired of playing Frisbee. I'd send the disc sailing in one direction, and just as she was ready to snatch it out of the air the wind would pick it up and send it off another way. I could sense her frustration. It was much more fun to catch the toy in the air. Any old dog could pick a Frisbee up from the ground. She eventually flopped down in the grass, panting, leaving me to retrieve the toy.

Though I'd been waiting for a call from the parents of the boy who'd crashed the golf cart into the Mercedes, my phone had remained silent. Evidently they'd ignored the message on my card. *Blurgh.*

I was rolling south down Hemphill when dispatch came on the radio. "We've got a report of a shoplifter at the gas station on the corner of Hemphill and West Allen."

Had the Lollipop Bandit struck again? Only one way to find out. I grabbed my mic and squeezed the talk button. "Officer Luz and Brigit responding."

The store was a mere two blocks away. As I headed toward it, I passed both a medical office and a mental health clinic. I kept my eyes peeled for a medium-sized man in scrubs, but saw none outside the buildings.

The store's manager, a trim, fortyish Latino man, was standing outside waiting for us when we arrived. I climbed out of the car and retrieved Brigit from her enclosure, snapping her leash onto her collar. I led her over to the man. "I hear you had a shoplifter?"

He nodded, but then shook his head, incredulous. "A man wearing green scrubs ran out with a handful of candy!"

"Let me guess," I said. "Grape Tootsie Pops?"

His mouth gaped. "How did you know?"

"This wasn't his first offense. He's been hitting gas stations and convenience stores in the area for weeks."

The man scoffed. "He's obviously got a job. Why steal candy? It's cheap."

"Some people get a thrill out of taking things that

aren't theirs," I told him. "They like to see what they can get away with. Any chance you saw which way he went?"

The man pointed at a parking lot across the side street. "He ran into that lot. That's all I know."

I looked in the direction he'd pointed. The parking lot was full of cars, many of them pickups and SUVs and minivans with high profiles. It was no wonder he'd lost sight of the thief.

I raised my hand to indicate Brigit's leash. "I'll see if my partner can trail him."

I took Brigit inside to the candy aisle, stopped in front of the Tootsie Pop display, and issued the order for her to track. She put her nose to the floor. *Snuffle-snuffle. Snuffle-snuffle.* After snatching up an errant peanut someone had dropped on the floor, she set off toward the doors. We exited the store and I jogged along behind her as she headed toward the parking lot across the street.

With the trail relatively fresh, she moved quickly, darting up and down the rows and between cars. Clearly, the thief had done the same, making some evasive maneuvers to avoid detection. Eventually, we made our way out of the lot and across south Jennings, heading into another parking lot on the next block. The thief must have looked back and realized he wasn't being followed, because he took a much more direct tack through this lot.

We approached John Peter Smith Hospital. JPS was a public facility, the place where officers took potential psychiatric cases for diagnosis and treatment, and home to the only Level 1 trauma center in Tarrant County. Not long ago, ER doctors here had saved the life of fellow FWPD officer Matt Pearce, who'd gotten into a gun battle in a wooded area with a father and his adult son. Pearce had taken five bullets, including one in the face. Another had nicked his heart. Add in a collapsed lung, shattered femur, punctured diaphragm, broken jaw, and damage to his liver and spleen, and he'd been given a mere four percent chance of survival. Luckily, he'd beaten the odds. He'd spent two weeks in a medically induced coma, awakening on his oldest daughter's third birthday. He was still undergoing therapy nearly a year later, but the fact that he was alive and had fared as well as he had was nothing short of a miracle, as well as a testament to the great care provided at the hospital.

Three women in scrubs stood at the edge of the sidewalk, paper coffee cups in their hands as they chatted, apparently on break. A man in scrubs leaned back against the building, casually scrolling through screens on his cell phone. *Could he be the Lollipop Bandit?* He was average sized and thus fit what little description we had of the culprit. But the fact that he appeared relaxed, was paying little attention to what was going on around him, and wasn't trying to hide told me he wasn't the guy we were after.

Brigit continued to snuffle along, leading me around the perimeter of the building between the outpatient entrance and the parking garage. As we crossed south Main Street, I glanced up at the sky bridge that connected the main hospital and the patient care center that housed the ER. People dressed in scrubs and others in regular clothes made their way between the two buildings, moving to and fro behind the glass like fish in an aquarium. To the east, a freight train clickety-clacked its way down the tracks that separated the medical center from a narrow neighborhood that bordered Interstate 35. Colorful graffiti decorated many of the boxcars, carrying the names of taggers from far and wide.

I turned my attention back to my partner. Brigit trotted up to a pair of automatic doors and, once again, I found her leading me into an ER waiting room.

A man at the reception desk looked up as we came in. "Is there a problem, Officer?"

I ordered Brigit to stop trailing the scent and led her over to the desk. Speaking quietly, I said, "We're tracking a suspect. He's wearing green scrubs."

"That doesn't narrow things down much." He gestured to the green scrubs he, himself, was wearing. A young woman and older man behind him were similarly outfitted.

"He's average sized. Would've come in these doors just a few minutes ago."

The guy slowly shook his head. "I wish I could help you but to be perfectly honest I pay much more attention to the patients coming in than I do the staff. People wearing scrubs are in and out of here constantly. Doctors. Nurses. Orderlies. Techs. We're a big facility. I don't even know all the faces of the staff, let alone their names."

Given that this was the second time I'd tracked the Lollipop Bandit, I felt less inclined to let things slide. "Where's your security office?" I asked.

The man gave me an office number and directions. With Brigit trotting along, I exited the ER and circled around to the main entrance of the hospital. Unfortunately, the two of us came back out the main entrance fifteen minutes later, none the wiser. While security cameras mounted outside the ER picked up a man in scrubs, a cap, and a mask entering the building, he'd been smart enough to keep his head down. He also apparently knew where the security cameras were—and weren't—located in the building. While we'd managed to track him visually for a minute or two in the public areas, we'd eventually lost him. It was possible he'd removed the cap and mask, but we couldn't definitively identify anyone on the screens as the bandit. We had no idea what his face looked like or his hair color, and frankly, everyone looked similar in the loose-fitting scrubs. It was even difficult to distinguish the men from the women in some cases.

Brigit and I returned to the gas station and informed the owner that we hadn't been able to find the guy. "Sorry. He's a slippery sucker." I cringed at my unintentional pun.

"You gave it your best shot," he said. "Thanks for trying." Our business done, he turned back to the display of motor oil he was stacking.

Brigit and I set back out on patrol. Just after four o'clock, my cell phone buzzed with an incoming call. *Finally.*

It wasn't the parents of the boy with the braces and blue bands, though. It was Ryan. He sounded pissed off and then some. "Adriana tried to get into my apartment today while I was at work. That woman is crazy!"

"Are you at home now?" I asked.

"Yes."

"Stay put. I'm on my way." Looked like Brigit and I might be putting in some overtime.

I circled through the lot and headed back out, aiming for Ryan's place. When I arrived, he was standing at the bottom of the stairs, waiting for me.

I climbed out of the car, leaving the windows down for Brigit.

Before I even reached him, Ryan launched into a tirade. "Adriana showed up here today. She tried to get the maintenance guy to let her into my apartment. She had a bunch of balloons and told him she wanted to surprise me for my birthday."

"Happy birthday," I said.

He threw up his hands. "That's the point! It's not my birthday! She just said that to have a reason to try to get into my place."

Well, then. Consider my birthday wish retracted. "How do you know all this?"

"He told me." Ryan pointed across the lot to the mailbox area, where a burly man wielding a can of WD-40 was spraying hinges that had evidently become sticky. "That's him right there."

"I'll go have a chat with him." As I turned to go, Ryan began to come along with me. I held up a hand to stop him. "You wait here."

"Why?" Ryan asked.

Because I want to ask the guy some questions he might not answer honestly if you're standing there, that's why. But I couldn't say that to Ryan, so instead I went with, "Protocol." You can't argue with protocol, right?

Ryan stood at the curb behind me as I walked through

the lot. When I passed by the cruiser, Brigit pawed at the metal mesh of her enclosure, letting me know she didn't appreciate being left out of the action. "I'll be right back, girl," I promised her.

I continued across the lot and approached the man. He wore navy blue work pants, a light blue polo shirt, and a layer of sweat and grime that told me he'd had a busy day. "Good evening, sir."

He turned his face my way. "Hello there, Officer."

"Mr. Downey said someone approached you today about getting into his apartment?"

"That's right." A burst of wind blew past just as he went to spray another hinge. The greasy mist ended up all over the front of the mailboxes. "Cheese and grits! Would you look at that mess? This wind's giving me fits today." He used a dirty rag to wipe away the excess lubricant and knelt down to stuff both the rag and the can in a toolbox before standing again and turning fully to address me. "A woman came by with a bunch of red helium balloons and a big gift bag stuffed with tissue paper. She asked if I would let her into apartment 206. She said it was her brother's birthday and she wanted to surprise him by leaving the present and balloons."

"But you didn't let her in."

"No, ma'am," he said, "Could've gotten fired if I had. I told her to go the front office and talk to the people there, let them decide."

"Did she do that?"

"Far as I know." He shrugged. "She headed in that direction so I'm guessing she did. But I was busy replacing some broken sprinkler heads in the lawn so I didn't pay much attention."

"What did the woman look like?"

"She was wearing high heels and a tight black dress."

"How tall was she?"

The man shrugged. "About average, I guess."

Adriana was a little on the short side, but with heels on she'd appear taller, so his response didn't rule her out.

"What about her hair?" I asked.

"It was blond," he said. "Hung down to about here." He used his index finger to point to a spot along his bicep.

Blond hair, huh? *Hmm.* Was the woman who'd come by Ryan's *Beautiful Blond Boo*? Or had it been Adriana in a wig? Maybe Adriana had seen the recent pics of Ryan and the blonde on his Facebook page and tried to make herself look like the woman.

"What about her eyes?" I asked.

"Couldn't tell," he said. "She was wearing a pair of great big sunglasses." He formed circles with his index fingers and thumbs and held them up to his face.

The big glasses might have been her way of trying to hide her identity. Then again, the sun was out in full force today, hardly a cloud in the sky. Maybe the woman was simply protecting her eyes from glare.

"What about her skin tone?" I asked.

"From what I recall she seemed to have a nice tan."

"Was it a tan?" I asked for clarification. "Or was she naturally brown?

"How do you tell the difference?"

"Good question." Moving on, then. "How would you describe her build?"

He looked a little uncomfortable. "I know you want me to be honest, so I'll just come out and say it even if it's not polite in mixed company. She was stacked."

"Stacked" definitely did *not* describe Adriana. With her thin build, she was probably an A cup at most. But all it would take is two sizable wads of tissue paper or a couple of the helium balloons to make a woman's breasts appear much larger than reality.

"Anything else you remember?" I asked. "Did she have a distinctive voice, maybe, or any distinguishing characteristics?"

"She had a tattoo around her wrist," he said. "A circle of red hearts."

I'd noticed no such tattoo on Adriana. She didn't seem like the type to get a tattoo. She was too uptight. Of course I hardly knew the woman and might be making incorrect assumptions. Could it have been a henna tattoo? Something she'd drawn on with a marker? Maybe a tight bracelet the maintenance worker had mistaken for a tattoo? These alternatives seemed less likely. "Any chance she gave you a name?"

"Not that I recall. I only remember her saying she was the sister of the guy in 206."

I knew Ryan had a brother. He'd said so when he'd identified Toby as his brother's son the first time I'd met him. But did he have a sister, too? "What time did this take place?" I asked.

"Around twelve-thirty, I'd say," the man said. "I'd just come off my lunch break."

"Have you seen the woman around here before?"

"Not that I remember," he said. "If she'd come around here dressed like that, I think I'd remember."

The guy was a hound, but at least he seemed to be telling the truth. I had to give him that. "Did you see what kind of car she was driving?"

"No. Once we were done talking I got back to work and didn't see her again."

I lowered my voice. "Have there been any other issues with Mr. Downey?"

"Issues?" His eyes narrowed. "What do you mean?"

I raised a noncommittal shoulder. "Problems between him and another tenant. Coming and going at strange hours. Anything at all out of the ordinary."

"I don't know if this is what you're going for," he said, "but he has blown a fuse a time or two when he's been fooling around with some type of electronics or another. He seems to like his gadgets. 'Course I can't blame him. I enjoy tinkering with stuff, too. But other than that nothing's caught my attention."

I retrieved my notepad from my breast pocket, jotted down the information he'd given me, and took down his name and cell number in case I had further questions later. "Thanks for the information."

He nodded, picked up his toolbox, and set off.

I returned to Ryan.

"What did he tell you?" he asked.

"Same thing he told you earlier," I said. "Blond girl with red balloons and a gift bag." My mind went back to what Adriana had alleged about Ryan's sexual fetishes. I angled my head and eyed him. "Do you have a sister?"

"No," he replied. "Just one brother."

"Is there any chance the woman could've been someone other than Adriana? Maybe your sister-in-law, Toby's mother?"

"My sister-in-law isn't blond. Besides, she wouldn't

bring me balloons. She's been mad at me since I slept with her cousin."

Sheesh. "Could it have been the cousin?"

He shook his head. "She's not blond, either."

"Have you had any other bad breakups?" I asked. "Or maybe it was someone who wanted to surprise you in a good way and figured the birthday story would be the easiest way to get in." *Maybe one of those hookers Adriana had mentioned?* Of course she'd admitted she had no evidence he was a john. It was mere speculation on her part. But I had to admit I could see it. This guy gave off an overtly sexual vibe. "Are you seeing anyone else?"

"I've been seeing a girl since Adriana." He smirked. "She's a blonde, but the carpet doesn't match the drapes, if you know what I mean."

Oh, I know what you mean, all right. No pun intended, but why beat around the bush? I was tired of Ryan's innuendo. *Let's just get it out in the open, shall we?* "You mean that you have engaged in a sexual activity with this woman which enabled you to observe the hair growing in her pubic area and that it was not the same color as the hair on her head."

"Jeez!" His face contorted in disgust. "But yeah, that's what I meant."

If anyone should be disgusted here, it was *me*. I was the one being forced to deal with an oversexed man-child. "Do you think this woman with the mismatched drapes might have been the one who came by with the balloons?"

"I doubt it," he replied.

I knew I shouldn't, but I just couldn't help myself.

"So she didn't seem all that enthusiastic about you afterward?"

"It's not that!" he snapped. "It's just that we're keeping it casual. You know how it is."

No, I *didn't* know. I wasn't frigid, but sex for me had never been a casual thing. Frankly, I wasn't sure how someone could relax and enjoy themselves if they didn't know their partner reasonably well. I'd be too afraid of undisclosed diseases or hidden cameras, of finding naked pics of myself scattered all over the Internet.

"Can I get her name and cell number?"

He frowned. "You really need to call her?"

"I need to rule out all the possibilities."

"I could just ask her myself. Save you the trouble."

Gee. How nice of you to think of me. "If she wanted to surprise you, she might not tell you the truth," I said. Besides, unless I was party to that conversation, I wouldn't trust Ryan to tell me the truth about her response, either. I wanted to hear things straight from the horse's mouth, so to speak.

He seemed hesitant, but gave me the information I asked for. "I guess she wouldn't mind. Her name's Danielle Griffin." He pulled out his phone, accessed his contacts list, and rattled off a phone number. "I hope getting a call from the cops doesn't scare her off." His lips spread in a lecherous grin. "She's a lot of fun, if you know what I mean."

"Yes," I said. "You mean you enjoy engaging in sexual relations with her."

He muttered another "Jeez," as if I were the one being uncouth here. *Don't start something you don't want me to finish.*

"Do you happen to have any pics of Danielle?" I asked.

"Yeah. I've got a few."

He fiddled with his phone for a moment, then held up the screen, showing me a photo of him and a pretty blonde. It was a selfie taken from above. She had her glossy lips pursed and her elbows crooked inward to plump up her cleavage, which was nearly falling out of her tight, low-cut red blouse. Again, I was hit with the thought that this girl, like Adriana, appeared out of Ryan's league.

He scrolled through the pics, showing me some others clearly taken after they'd had their romp in the hay. In the latter photos, her makeup was smudgy and her hair was mussed. I figured she'd been more likely to look like she had in the selfie when she'd come by the complex, so I instructed him to text me the picture and gave him my phone number. A few seconds later my phone pinged as the picture arrived.

"Did you show this picture to the maintenance man?" I asked. "See if he could identify the woman with the balloons as Danielle?"

"No," he said. "It didn't occur to me to do that."

"Okay. I'll check with him. But before I do, we need to make sure we've covered all the bases. What about a neighbor or another acquaintance? Any other blondes you know of that might have come by?"

"I can't think of anyone else," he said. "I've talked to a few other girls at bars since I broke up with Adriana. Got their phone numbers. But none of them know where I live. Things haven't gotten that far, if you know what I—"

"Have you spoken to anyone in the management office yet?" I'd cut him off, but I simply couldn't take one more "if you know what I mean" or I'd whap the guy with my baton.

"No," he said. "I haven't been to the office. Why?"

"The maintenance man told me that after he refused to let the woman into your place, he suggested she try the office."

"You going to talk to them, too?" Ryan asked.

"As soon as I round up my partner." I let Brigit out of the car, leashed her, and instructed Ryan to wait for me there. Meanwhile, Brigit and I headed to the office at the front of the property, my partner's nails *click-click-click*ing as we went along.

We caught a young woman with heavy makeup and short, ginger-colored hair as she was locking up for the day. She looked up as we approached. "Uh-oh. Is there a problem?"

"I have a few questions about the woman with the gift bag and balloons who came by today."

The woman cocked her head, her brows forming a puzzled V. "A woman with balloons? I'm not sure who you're talking about."

I repeated what the maintenance man had told me. "He said she was here around twelve-thirty."

"That explains it, then," the woman said. "My lunch hour is from noon to one."

"Was anyone else in the office then?"

"We have a part-time leasing agent who covers for me, but she only works from ten to two, so she's already gone for the day."

Darn. I handed the woman my card. "Could you ask her to call me tomorrow?"

"Sure."

I took a quick look around at the eaves of the building but saw no security cameras. Of course it was possible they had hidden ones. "Any chance there are security cameras anywhere on the property?"

"No," the woman said. "We have a security company that drives by a few times at night, but that's it."

I'd already spoken with the security patrolman earlier in the week and given him my card. So far, he hadn't called. Like I'd done earlier with the maintenance worker, I lowered my voice. "Can you tell me if you've had any issues with the tenant in 206?"

"Two hundred six." She looked up in thought, as if mentally reading a roster. "That's Ryan Downey, right?"

"Yes."

"He's caused two or three late-night maintenance calls," she said. "Blown a few fuses with all of his electronics. He repairs devices on the side and sometimes overloads the system. I've warned him he needs to be more careful. But as for his rent, he always pays on time and we've had no noise complaints on him or anything like that. Seems like a nice enough guy. I see him with his nephew now and then. The kid's adorable."

I had to agree with her there. Toby was a cute little tyke. "All right," I said. "Thanks for your time."

I returned to where Ryan stood waiting and told him the news. "I won't know more until tomorrow. Until then, keep your doors and windows locked."

"Is this all you can do? Can't you go by Adriana's and tell her to leave me alone?"

"I've already told her to stay away from you."

He grunted. "Doesn't seem like she listened."

His words irritated me, mostly because they might be true. Why couldn't people just leave each other alone? Why couldn't they just do what they were told?

He stood taller. "Maybe I should go talk to her myself."

"That's a really bad idea," I told him.

"Why?"

Why? Shouldn't it be obvious? "Because she allegedly attacked you, remember? That was the basis for your protective order." If he really considered her a threat, why would he have even suggested speaking to her himself? Had the attack never really happened? I'd had some doubts before, and they were stronger now.

"I can take care of myself," he snapped.

Argh! Reflexively, my hand tightened around Brigit's leash. "Look, Ryan. It's possible the woman who came by today wasn't Adriana and simply had the wrong apartment number. She didn't fit Adriana's description at all."

"She could've put a wig on," he insisted, "and stuffed some socks in her bra. Figures she'd dress up to get me in trouble, but wouldn't do it when I asked her to."

So we're back to the crotchless tiger costume, huh? I'd hoped to never hear about that again. I tried to sound nonchalant when I asked, "Are you talking about the sexual role play?"

"Sexual role play?" He barked a laugh. "Ha! That would be the day. Adriana's strictly old-school when it comes to sex. I'm talking about dressing up for the comic convention. I tried to get her to wear a cheetah costume but she wouldn't do it."

"Cheetah?"

"You know, Minerva from the Injustice League?"

No, I didn't know. Comics weren't my thing, not that I faulted anyone for enjoying them. We all need some form of escape. Mine was mystery novels. "I'm not familiar with the character."

"DC Comics?"

I shook my head.

He pointed up to his apartment. "I have a poster of her on my wall. One of Killer Frost, too."

I remembered seeing the posters the first time I came to his place. "So you're saying you didn't try to get Adriana to dress up for sexual role play?"

"Heck, no," he said. "It's too hard to get in and out of those costumes to get it on. I mean, if you want to do it, just do it already."

Huh. Had Adriana been lying to me about Ryan's unusual sexual proclivities? Or had she merely misunderstood his intentions?

He repeated his request. "You'll go talk to her again? Tell her to leave me alone?"

I felt like he was goading me into making a stop at Adriana's, but I also felt like it couldn't hurt to give her another warning in case she'd failed to heed the first one. "I'll swing by her place," I told him. "But you continue to stay away from her, okay?"

He scowled. "Why are you treating me like the bad guy? She's the one causing problems."

Is she? I wasn't so certain. Nevertheless, I raised a

conciliatory palm. "I don't want to see either one of you get hurt." At least that much was true.

He seemed to accept my explanation, thanked me for coming out, and turned to go back to his apartment.

Once he'd gone, I went in search of the maintenance man. I found him in the pool area kneeling down on the hot cement, changing a filter. As I walked up to him, Brigit seized the opportunity to cool off in the pool, doing a belly flop off the side. *Splash!* Water splashed up onto my shoes and the legs of my pants. "Bad dog!" I scolded.

She ignored me as she began to dog-paddle. I had no choice but to release her leash and let her swim to the steps to climb out. Once she was back on dry land, she gave herself a solid shake, sending up a tsunami of water.

"Sorry about that," I told the maintenance man as I walked over to him.

"No worries," he said. "Can't say as I blame her. It's hotter 'n hell out here today. Got more questions for me?"

"Just one." I pulled out my phone and showed him the photo of Danielle. "Was this the girl who came by today?"

He stood to take a better look. His gaze went from her face to her cleavage and held there for a moment, as if he was trying to recollect the breasts he'd seen earlier today. When he looked back up at me, he wobbled his head. "Could be," he said, "but I can't say for sure. Like I said, she had sunglasses on and I only talked to her real quick."

Darn. "All right. Thanks again for your time."

I mulled things over as I rounded up Brigit and wrung the pool water from her leash. Was there any other evidence I could find here? *Hmm.* I decided it couldn't hurt to take a peek in the Dumpsters, see if anyone tossed a gift bag into the garbage when their plan was foiled.

I led Brigit around to the back of the complex. Despite her earlier shake, she left a trail of water droplets in our wake, though they quickly evaporated in the sun. We found three large metal Dumpsters situated behind an eight-foot brick wall. The place smelled beyond foul. While I was tempted to plug my nose, Brigit was having a field day, sniffing the stray trash that had fallen on the ground, enjoying the odors. I glanced down at my partner. "You're disgusting, you know that?"

She wagged her tail in response.

I pulled a pair of latex gloves from my pants pocket, slid them on, and lifted the lid of the first Dumpster. I had to stand on tiptoe to peek inside. A swarm of flies buzzed about, angry that I'd disturbed them. All I saw were black garbage bags and a few stray pieces of trash—ice cream wrappers and the like—that had been tossed into the bin separately. Ditto for the second Dumpster. The third Dumpster contained black garbage bags, but also a taupe couch cushion that had been soiled with what looked like red wine, spaghetti sauce, or blood. *Yuck.*

When I turned around, I found Brigit rolling on her back on some unidentifiable guck that had been spilled next to the garbage bin. *What the heck is that?* An empty white plastic container nearby told me it was rancid cottage cheese. "Brigit!" I shrieked. "No!"

While many people believed police dogs obey their

handlers perfectly, such was simply not the case. Like their human partners, they had minds of their own and could sometimes be stubborn and insubordinate. Like now, with Brigit. My partner ignored my pleas, continuing to squirm on her back among the sour cheese curds as if having the time of her life. *Dumb dog.* She'd be getting a bath tonight.

Having found no evidence, Brigit and I returned to the cruiser. I did my best to wipe her sticky, stinky back down with an antibacterial hand wipe, but it wasn't up to the task. The cheesy gunk was hopelessly stuck to her fur. *Blurgh.*

We climbed back into the car. The scent of sour milk filled the vehicle. "You're smelling up the cruiser!" I scolded her, rolling down the windows. Still, while my K-9 partner stunk to high heaven, she had nothing on Derek Mackey. That guy's body odor could be weaponized.

I placed a call to Danielle. When she answered, her voice was tentative. She probably didn't recognize my number and assumed I was a telemarketer.

"Hello, Miss Griffin," I said. "This is Officer Megan Luz with the Fort Worth Police Department. I need to speak with you about Ryan Downey. I understand the two of you have been dating?"

"We've been out a few times," she said hesitantly. "Why? Is something wrong?"

"We're not sure," I said. "One of the staff at Ryan's complex said a blond woman came by today with a gift and balloons and asked to be let into his apartment. We're just trying to figure out who that might have been. Ryan mentioned that the two of you have been going out. If it was you who came by today, you're not in trouble or anything. We're just trying to determine who it was."

She sounded peeved when she responded. "It wasn't me," she said. "I really don't appreciate him dragging me into this, either. I mean, he's an okay guy, but . . . "

When she paused, I prodded her to continue. "But what?"

She exhaled sharply. "He's been putting a lot of pressure on me. I'm not ready to get serious. I've told him that several times but he hasn't backed off."

Sounded to me like Ryan might not consider their relationship to be as casual as he'd claimed.

"Now this thing," Danielle continued. "The balloons and whatever? It's weird. I'm feeling very uncomfortable right now."

"I don't blame you," I said. "Is there any chance I could come talk to you in person?" Given what she'd told me, that Ryan was pressuring her, she might be able to shed some light on him, help me get closer to the truth. And given her discomfort, I figured I could get more from her in person than I might on the phone. I'd be willing to work late if I could get some answers.

"I'm double and triple-booked the rest of the day," she said. "But early tomorrow morning would work." She mentioned she worked as an aesthetician at a salon and gave me the address.

"Thanks," I said. "I'll see you then."

We ended the call, and Brigit and I pulled out of the lot. We were halfway down the block when my eyes spotted something atop a tree up ahead. *A bunch of red helium balloons.* They were tangled in a branch at the pinnacle of the tree and bounced in the brisk breeze, the string pulling the branch up and down.

Could these be the red balloons the woman— *Adriana?*—had taken to the apartment? Had they gotten away from her earlier, pulled out of her hands by a gust of wind? Maybe she'd let them go when she couldn't get into the apartment. Better than being caught with them if she was up to no good. What were the odds someone else in the area would have lost a bunch of red balloons today? Probably very small.

While obtaining fingerprints from the string would be impossible, the balloons themselves might have retained a print if the person who'd carried them had touched them, too. If the woman had come in a car, she would have had to push the balloons into the vehicle, right? Sure. Helium balloons tended to want to drift out and up. I remembered fighting a trio of them I'd bought for my brother's high school graduation. If our technicians could lift a print from the balloons, I could see about getting one from Adriana and determine whether they matched. If they did, we'd have a much stronger case against her for trying to get into Ryan's apartment.

But first, there was the matter of getting the balloons down from the top of the tree. Unfortunately, the tree wasn't some small, decorative variety, like a crepe myrtle. It was a tall, stately oak that appeared to have been standing since Texas had still been part of Mexico. *¡Ay caramba!* How could the balloons be retrieved?

The crime scene teams carried extension ladders in their vans, but I wasn't sure an extension ladder would be of much use trying to get to the middle of the top of a tree. There'd be too many limbs in the way. I sure as heck wasn't going to try to climb the thing, either. A gust of wind could blow me down and break my back, putting me out of commission. What would become of Brigit if that happened? I couldn't bear the thought of her being reassigned to another officer.

This is where it paid to have friends in high places. Or, rather, a friend who could get to high places. Why not call Frankie? After all, she had access to a ladder truck that was specifically designed for this type of thing.

I pulled into the parking lot of a bagel shop near the tree and placed a call to her. "Want to get something out of a tree for me?"

"Is it a kitten?"

"Nope. It's balloons."

"If you want balloons, I can buy some for you."

"You could also buy me a kitten."

"Yeah, but then the reporters wouldn't come out and put the rescue on the news. How cool would it be for me to be on the news my second day on the job?"

"Pretty cool," I agreed. "So can you come or not?"

"Hold on a second. Let me check." There was muffled discussion as she checked with one of the higher-ranking firefighters to see whether they could come by and help. She returned in a few seconds. "We're on our way."

I gave Frankie the address. In minutes, the ladder truck pulled into the lot with one of her coworkers at the wheel.

"I can't thank you two enough," I told them.

The guy at the wheel raised a shoulder. "Eh. It's a slow day."

After a minute or two of expert maneuvering, the ladder was angled so that the end was within reach of the balloons. Frankie ascended the ladder, reached out, and worked on untangling the balloons from the tree. *Respect.* I would've been chicken to go up that high without some type of harness as a safeguard.

She held the bunch up by the string. "Got 'em!" she called down to me.

"Great!"

She'd just started to descend the ladder when *WHOOSH!* Mother Nature sent forth a gust of wind so strong it rocked me back on my heels and parted Brigit's fur down to her skin. Unfortunately, the gust was also strong enough to yank the string from Frankie's hand.

"Oh, no!" She reached up, desperately trying to snatch the string out of the air.

"Don't fall!" I yelled in panic. I'd feel terrible if she got hurt trying to help me out.

The two of us watched with alternating hope and dismay as the balloons swirled around in the air. They'd swirl close, nearly close enough for her to grab them again, and then twirl out of reach as if they were teasing her. Maybe we'd get lucky and they'd catch on something else, something lower even, where I could reach them unassisted.

We didn't get lucky.

When another gust of wind came, the balloons spiraled upward, bumping and bouncing off each other, growing smaller and smaller as they headed toward the stratosphere. *Dang it.*

Frankie climbed down the ladder. "I'm so sorry. Were the balloons important?"

"Maybe," I said. "But maybe not." At this point they were halfway to Mars, rendering the issue of their importance moot.

I thanked the two again, saw them off, and drove to Adriana's place. She and I spoke briefly on the porch, while Brigit snuffled around the steps, probably looking for the possum.

"Were you at work today?" I asked her.

"Yes," she said. "Why?"

That's for me to know and you to find out. "What did you do for lunch?"

"I came home, like usual," she said. "It gives me a break from the center and that way I can do a chore or two."

"Were you alone?"

"Yes." Her eyes narrowed. "Why are you asking me all these questions? Something's happened, hasn't it?"

"Someone tried to get into Ryan's apartment today."

"Why would anyone want to get into that pigsty?" She rolled her eyes. "What did they do? Try to pick the lock or pry the door open?"

"No."

"No? Then how did they try to get in?"

I decided not to give her any detailed information. That way, if she slipped up, maybe I could catch her revealing something she'd only know if she'd been the one with the balloons. I merely said, "False pretenses. Do you know anything about that?"

She jerked her head back as if I'd slapped her. "Why would *I* know anything about it?"

I raised conciliatory palms. Seemed like I'd been

doing a lot of that lately. "I'm just asking, trying to figure out what's going on here."

"What's going on," she snapped, "probably has something to do with one of Ryan's girlfriends. I'll bet he's got two or three."

Two or three? Heck, I'd been surprised he'd had *one*. Even if he was handy at troubleshooting computer and Wi-Fi and other technology issues, that kazoo voice wasn't exactly a turn-on. "What makes you think that?" I asked.

"I saw pictures on his phone once," she said. "He claimed they were old photos from before he met me, but I didn't buy it."

"Why not?"

"He was late for our dates a lot," she said. "He canceled a few times, too. He'd say he had a headache or that he had to work overtime. I'm pretty sure he was seeing someone else while we were dating. That's another reason I broke up with him. I couldn't trust him."

She didn't trust him, but could *I* trust *her*? Was there any truth to what she was saying? I glanced at her wrists, but she was wearing a long-sleeved shirt. Odd, given the high August temperatures. Then again, some offices were cold, and hospitals were notorious for keeping temperatures low. Should I ask to see her wrists? On one hand, I didn't want to unnecessarily antagonize her, especially if she was innocent. On the other hand, I wanted to get to the bottom of things as soon as possible. After a quick mental debate, I decided to go for it. "May I see your wrists?"

"My wrists?" she repeated, her forehead furrowing in question.

"Yes."

"I guess so."

She pushed her sleeves back and showed me her wrists, turning them so I could see all sides. Not only were her wrists bare, they did not appear to have been recently scrubbed, either. There was no telltale pink tinge to her skin.

She pushed her sleeves back down. "I'm not sure what you're doing here, but if you think I'm behind anything at Ryan's place, you're mistaken. I'm done with that loser and I hope he's done with me."

"I hope so, too."

With that, I wished her a good evening and left, my mind swirling in confusion like that bunch of balloons.

EIGHTEEN
IN HOT WATER

Brigit

Uh-oh.

Megan was in the bathroom, calling in a pleasant voice for Brigit to come to her. But Brigit wasn't fooled. Megan had filled the tub with water but had not gotten undressed. That could mean only one thing. She planned to give Brigit a bath.

Well, good luck with that. Brigit had other plans.

The dog ran into the bedroom and wriggled until she was under the bed. With any luck, Megan wouldn't find her here. *If I just keep quiet . . .*

She saw Megan's feet appear in the bedroom doorway. A moment later, Megan's face appeared as she bent down to peek under the bed.

Busted.

Megan reached under the bed, grabbed Brigit's front paws, and dragged her out into the room. Brigit was tempted to snap at Megan, but as much as she didn't want a bath, she knew biting her partner would get her in big trouble. Besides, even though she didn't like that

Megan was trying to make her get in the tub, she loved her partner and didn't want to hurt her.

Her instincts kicked in, telling her what to do. If she couldn't fight, she must flee. *Run!*

Brigit's paws scrabbled on the floor, but before she could get any traction Megan grabbed her collar, dragged her to the bathroom, and slammed the door behind them so Brigit couldn't attempt an escape like she'd done before. Though Brigit flattened herself against the floor, Megan somehow managed to get her hands under Brigit and pick her up just high enough to wrestle her into the tub.

The jig was up.

There was nothing to do now but get it over with.

Brigit endured the bath, all the while wondering whether Megan realized Brigit could rip her throat out if she wanted to. Not that she ever would. Don't bite the hand that feeds you and all that. But it was kind of fun to think about sometimes.

Megan scrubbed her with that awful fruit-scented shampoo, rinsed her with the sprayer, and, after what seemed like forever, pronounced her "all done." Brigit knew what that meant, too. Time to leap out of the tub and shake before Megan could get that towel around her.

The dog shook like she'd never shook before, sending up a spray of water and fur that coated the walls, mirror, and cabinets. Megan made high-pitched noises that Brigit knew were protests, but she ignored them and shook herself again. This is what her handler got for dragging her out from under the bed.

Megan toweled her off and opened the bathroom door. Brigit darted out like she'd been shot from a cannon.

This fruity smell was disgraceful! She had to get this awful peach scent off her fur and make herself smell like a dog again!

She bolted into the living room, sprang over Zoe and onto the futon, and rubbed herself back and forth and back and forth against the cushion. Why not rub the bed, too? She leaped from the couch, ran to the bedroom, and flew onto the bed, rolling over and over and rubbing up and down on the bedding.

When she heard Megan call from the kitchen, she sprang off the bed and dashed into the room, her wet paws sliding across the flooring. She skidded toward the door and bolted outside when Megan opened it.

The grass! Sweet, wonderful grass!

Brigit ran three laps around the backyard at breakneck speed before diving onto the grass and rolling over and over and over until she ended up wriggling on her back under a pecan tree. That same stupid squirrel taunted her from above. *Chit-chit-chit!*

Wriggle-wriggle-wriggle! Wriggle-wriggle! Wriggle-wriggle-wriggle!

Finally, she'd rid herself of the peach scent and smelled like a self-respecting dog again. Only then did she stand and walk proudly back into the house to be served her dinner.

NINETEEN
BACK AND FORTH

The Devoted One

Love was such an odd emotion. It could make someone so happy when it was returned in kind. But it could make someone so sad when it was not.

The Devoted One was sad. Frustrated, too. Now and then even furious.

For weeks now, the Devoted One had wanted to get back together and tried to make it happen. Nothing seemed to be working. Now, the Devoted One had begun to wonder if revenge might be more satisfying than reconciliation. *Hmm . . .*

At any rate, one thing was clear.

We're not over until I say we're over.

TWENTY
LET'S PARTY

Megan

Brigit and I arrived at the salon where Danielle worked promptly at eight Wednesday morning. Every seat in the foyer was full, the clients patiently thumbing through fashion magazines as they waited to be called back for their appointments. We made our way past them and checked in with the receptionist. "I'm looking for Danielle. She's expecting me."

The woman pointed to the back of the room behind her. "Behind that curtain."

"Thanks."

I led Brigit through the salon, which was rife with the sounds of friendly chatter and the hum of hair dryers, along with the pleasant floral scents of shampoos, conditioners, and hairsprays. Brigit raised her nose in the air, her nostrils flaring as she took in the smells.

When we reached the back of the room, I gently slid the gauzy curtain aside. Behind it was a small, windowless room with three salon chairs situated in a semicircle. Only one was in use. A middle-aged woman lay in the chair while three other women worked on her as if she was a racecar and they were her pit crew. One of the salon's employees sat at the client's bare feet, buffing them with a pumice stone. Another sat near the woman's waist. She had the woman's right hand up on a rolling table and was trimming her cuticles. A third salon staff member, whom I recognized from the photo as Danielle, was applying a creamy, pink-hued goop to the woman's face. Slices of cucumber lay over the woman's eyes, a plastic shower cap over her hair, which seemed to be in some phase of processing. Highlights, perhaps?

On a small table near the woman's head sat the bowl of goop. An open container of yogurt sat beside it. The two substances were essentially the same color and consistency.

Danielle set down the spreader she'd been using to smear the mask on the woman's face and used a plastic spoon to scoop up a bite of yogurt before looking up at me. "Are you the cop I talked to on the phone yesterday?" she asked before sticking the spoon in her mouth. As busy as the salon seemed to be, it was no wonder she had to grab breakfast on the job.

"Yes, that's me," I said. "Is there somewhere we can speak privately?"

"There's really no need." She gestured to the other women with her spoon. "We all know everything about each other's business."

"Yeah," said the manicurist. "Even if you went off somewhere to talk, Dani would give us all the details after."

All righty, then. I sat sideways on one of the empty chairs so that I would be at the same level as Danielle, and instructed Brigit to sit at my feet. "We still haven't determined who went by Ryan's apartment yesterday with the balloons," I said, "or what the woman was after. You're sure it wasn't you? You know, just wanting to do something nice for him?"

She plunked the spoon back into the yogurt and picked up the spreader. "Nope. Like I said yesterday, it wasn't me."

Looked like she wasn't changing her story. Of course it was possible she was lying, that she was in cahoots with Ryan and was trying to implicate Adriana. But my gut told me she was being honest. She hadn't been the one with the balloons. And if my gut hadn't convinced me, the two other women did.

The pedicurist held the pumice stone aloft. "Dani was here at the shop all day yesterday."

"Yeah," agreed the other, who'd kicked off her shoe and stretched out her leg to pet Brigit with her bare foot. "We were crazy busy. We didn't even take a lunch break. We ordered sandwiches in."

I nodded at them in acknowledgment, and returned my attention to Danielle. "You said on the phone yesterday that Ryan was putting pressure on you. Can you be more specific?"

She shifted on her seat, as if the conversation was again making her uncomfortable. "It's not a big deal, really. It just that he's moving a little too fast. Every time we go on a date he shows up with something. Flowers. Candy. Jewelry."

"Oh, boo-hoo!" called the woman who'd been foot-petting Brigit. "You know what I wouldn't give to get some attention from a man?"

Danielle sent a frown at her coworker. "It's nice to get gifts if nothing's expected in return, but with Ryan it feels like he's trying to buy me. Like he thinks spending money on me means I owe him something." She turned back to me. "At first I found it really flattering. It was nice to date a guy who isn't cheap, you know? He's always been willing to take me to fancy places to eat and stuff like that. But now he's constantly calling me or texting or dropping by my apartment unexpectedly. I feel a little smothered."

When I first met Ryan I'd sensed he had a poor sense of boundaries. Danielle's words reaffirmed that conclusion.

"He tries to pin me down weeks in advance, too," she added. "He already asked me to go to a Queen concert with him. They've got Adam Lambert singing with them now. It sounds like fun and all, but the concert's a whole two months away. Who knows if we'll even still be dating then? He's a nice enough guy, but I'm only looking to have some fun. I don't want a serious relationship."

The manicurist giggled. "Yeah. Dani just wants a fuck buddy."

"Shut up!" Dani chastised her friend, her face reddening.

Ignoring that last exchange, I asked, "Has Ryan ever mentioned a woman named Adriana to you?"

She gingerly smoothed the mask onto the woman's forehead. "Adriana?" She looked up in thought. "No. Not that I remember. Who is she?"

"An ex."

"Some reason why he should have mentioned her?"

Once again, she set down the spreader and picked up her spoon, taking a bite of yogurt.

"From what I can tell, it was a bad breakup."

The woman with the buffer chimed in. "Is there ever a good one?"

The three women laughed, as did the client, who was unidentifiable under the mask and shower cap. Heck, for all I knew, it could be Adriana lying there.

Danielle scooped up another quick bite. I was fairly certain she'd inadvertently scooped from the mask bowl, but before I could say anything she'd put the spoon in her mouth and swallowed the pinkish substance. I hoped it wasn't toxic. She waved the spoon in the air. "He might have mentioned her, but if he did he didn't make a big deal about it. It must have been a long time ago."

"One month," I clarified.

That seemed to get her attention. She held her spoon aloft. "Well, then she must not have meant that much to him."

Was she right? Had Adriana been just another girl to Ryan? No one special? Had he meant far more to Adriana than she had meant to him? Did this mean Adriana was the one causing the problems? Or had he misled Danielle? Downplayed his previous relationships so she wouldn't get a strange vibe from him?

"Ryan had some scratches on his neck a few days ago," I said. "Did you notice them?"

"Yes, I did," she said.

"Did he tell you how he got them?"

"He had to go underneath an older house to wire it," she said. "There was a loose board with some nails in it that scratched him up."

That wasn't the story Ryan had told me, the officer who'd responded after Adriana allegedly attacked him, or the judge who'd issued the protective order. He might have lied to us. Then again, he might have told a white lie to Danielle in order to avoid the subject of his crazy ex, if indeed he had a crazy ex. No woman would want to have to worry about a dangerous ex-girlfriend coming around, especially if she wasn't all that into the guy. Ryan might have realized that telling Danielle about Adriana could put an end to things with the two of them.

Danielle must have sensed my skepticism because she said, "He didn't tell me the truth about the scratches, did he?"

I wasn't sure what to say here. If Ryan had fibbed to spare Danielle the anxiety and to avoid an awkward conversation, who could blame him? On the other hand, she had a right to know what she might be getting herself into. I decided to err on the side of caution. "He told the police and a judge that his ex had attacked him."

"Really?" Danielle's eyes clouded in concern. "If that's the truth, why wouldn't he just tell me?"

The manicurist waved her tool at Danielle. "He didn't tell you about the ex because he didn't want to scare you off."

Danielle grunted. "He's doing a good enough job scaring me off himself."

The mask had hardened on the client's face and she could barely move her lips when she spoke. "You better call him on it. Get some straight answers."

I'd come here hoping to get some straight answers, too, but again they'd eluded me. *Rats.*

"For what it's worth," I told her, "his ex denies that she attacked him."

She frowned and eyed me intently. "Who do *you* believe?"

"Between you and me?" I lifted my shoulders. "I'm on the fence."

"Well, poop," she said. "If a cop can't figure it out, how am I supposed to?"

Good question.

Given that Danielle seemed to have no concrete information, I stood to go. I handed her my card. "If Ryan happens to mention anything about her that could be important, please give me a call. This could be nothing, but I'm concerned that his ex might have been the one trying to get into his apartment yesterday."

Her face clouded in concern. "Do you think she's dangerous?"

Again, good question. "Honestly, Danielle? I don't know what to think. All I can say is that where Ryan is concerned, I'd suggest you be very careful."

Brigit and I spent the next hour and a half cruising W1. Driving through the medical district, I kept a sharp eye out for a man in green scrubs enjoying a grape Tootsie Pop. I saw none, though there were several people in green scrubs going to and from the hospital parking garages and medical offices.

As we passed the zoo, I slowed. The zoo was one of Brigit's favorite places to patrol, though there was little call for us to do so. Not much crime happened on the property. As always, my partner lifted her nose to the window to scent the air, to check out what the various animals were up to. From the distance came the trumpet of an elephant. Though they didn't speak the same language, Brigit nonetheless replied with a bark. *Woof-woof-woof!* I could only wonder what their exchange meant.

I supposed I could have waited for the leasing agent to call, but at ten that morning I found myself turning into Ryan's apartment complex. Patience might be a virtue, but so were hard work and dedication, right? I wanted to get this investigation over and done with, to enforce the law against whoever was breaking it. And I couldn't enforce the law until I figured out who that person was.

I led Brigit with me as I entered the management office. The ginger-haired woman I'd met the prior evening sat at a large desk at the back of the room. She was speaking to a tenant on the phone, advising the person it was a violation of the rules of the complex to hang towels from a balcony to dry. "I understand you were out of quarters for the dryers," she said, pinching the bridge of her nose. "But that doesn't change the rules."

A woman in her mid-thirties sat at a smaller desk perpendicular to the manager's. She sported dark hair in a loose style that said she was either carefree or didn't have much time to style it in the mornings. The photos of the two dark-haired schoolchildren on her desk told me it was likely the latter.

"Can I help you?" the woman asked.

"I hope so." I stepped over to her desk and explained that I was seeking information about the woman who'd come by the preceding day with a gift bag and a bunch of red balloons. "What can you tell me about her?"

"Not much," the woman said. "I was in a rush to get some paperwork done and the phone was ringing non-stop. I barely looked up when she came in. She said something about wanting to be let into her brother's apartment to leave him the birthday present. I told her we couldn't take her into the unit but that she was welcome to leave the gift and balloons with us and we could put a note on his door to come pick them up during business hours. She declined and left." She shrugged. "That's it."

"Do you remember what unit she wanted to get into?"

The woman cocked her head and sucked her lip in thought. "One of the two hundreds, I believe."

"Does 206 sound right?"

"Could be," she said. "But I really don't remember for sure."

Was it possible this entire thing was only a mix-up? Had the maintenance guy gotten the apartment number wrong? Maybe the girl had come to deliver the gift and balloons to someone other than Ryan. "Did she mention the tenant by name?"

"I don't think so," the woman said. "I'd be more likely to remember a name than an apartment number."

"Did she have any distinguishing characteristics that you remember?" I asked. "Maybe a mole or tattoo or scar?"

The woman slowly shook her head. "Wish I could tell you. Like I said, I was swamped and hardly gave her a second glance."

I hated to leave here empty-handed, even if it was only with metaphorical empty hands. I wanted some evidence, a clue. And I wanted it now. "Any chance I can impose on you to check your tenants' birth dates? I'm investigating the matter and I need to figure out whether the woman was trying to illegally gain access to the apartment or whether this was simply an innocent mistake."

The woman gave me an incredulous look. "You want me to look up every tenant's birth date?" She gestured out the window. "You can see how many units we've got. Two hundred and forty." As if I were dense, she repeated herself. *"Two hundred and forty."*

"I'd only need you to check the birth dates for the male tenants," I said, hoping that might appease her. After all, the maintenance man said the woman indicated it was her brother's birthday. "And I don't need a list of dates or anything like that. I only need to know if one of them had a birthday yesterday."

She looked over to the manager, who'd just hung up the phone, and told her about my request. The manager cast me an irritated glance and exhaled sharply, but acquiesced. "Go ahead. I'll order us a pizza for lunch and help you with those credit checks."

"Thanks," I told the two. "I really appreciate your help." I unbuttoned the breast pocket of my uniform where I kept some petty cash, and pulled out a twenty-dollar bill. "Lunch is on me, ladies."

At that, their expressions brightened. I handed the leasing agent the cash, as well as one of my business cards. "Call me when you have the information, okay?"

"Okay."

Brigit and I returned to our cruiser. I drove slowly through the lot until I spotted the maintenance man from yesterday working on a loose railing. I pulled up to the curb a few feet away and rolled my window down. "Sorry to interrupt your work," I called, "but I have a quick follow-up question."

He made three rotations with his screwdriver and looked over at me. "Shoot."

"Did the woman with the balloons who came here yesterday refer to Ryan Downey by name, or did she only give his apartment number?"

"Just the number," he said.

"All right. That's all I needed. You have a good day."

He raised the screwdriver in an improvised salute and set back to work.

As I pulled away from the curb, I eyed Brigit in the mirror. "Any ideas, partner?"

She met my eyes, wagged her tail, and woofed. Too bad I didn't speak dog. As smart as my K-9 partner was, she'd probably have some good suggestions.

I put in a quick call to Detective Bustamente and gave him an update on the investigation. "What now?" I asked.

"If you notice a party-supply store in the area, check in and see if they can tell you anything. The girl might have bought the balloons there."

"Good idea." Of course many grocery stores and dollar stores also sold balloons and gift bags, but it was worth a shot.

I pulled out my phone and searched for party-supply stores in Fort Worth. A map popped up showing a dozen or so spread throughout the city. Only one was close to where we now sat. The Par-T Corral. I vaguely remembered the place. My mother had taken all of us kids there to pick out Halloween costumes years ago. I'd chosen a black cat costume. Ironic for a girl who'd later become a K-9 officer, huh?

I aimed the squad car for the Par-T Corral, which, like many businesses in Fort Worth, was western-themed. The days of cattle drives might be long gone, but the city would forever retain its nickname of Cowtown and the cowboy culture that came along with it.

The store sat at the end of a strip center that contained several mom-and-pop type businesses. A bicycle shop. A florist. A small sushi bar. Bells hanging from the door tinkled as I led Brigit inside with me. She stopped to sniff the back end of a colorful donkey-shaped piñata standing near the door. *Maybe I'd spoken too soon about how smart my partner is.*

We made our way past a display of greeting cards to the front counter where a woman with spiky orange hair flitted about, snipping strands of curling ribbon. She looked up as we approached. "Why hello, puppy!" she called to Brigit. "Aren't you a furry girl?"

My partner wagged her tail as if to say, *Why yes, I am quite furry, thank you for noticing.*

As I said hello to the woman, I noticed both the large tank of helium situated behind the counter and the security camera mounted on the wall. "I'm trying to track down a blond woman who bought a bunch of red helium balloons yesterday. Any chance you might be able to help me?"

The woman set the scissors down. "I'll do my best. I didn't work yesterday but I can search the system and see what I can find out."

"I'd appreciate that."

The woman punched some buttons on her computerized cash register, opened a notebook on the counter, and used a handheld scanner to scan the bar code assigned to red balloons. When she was done with the notebook, she jabbed a final button on the machine. "Nothing's coming up," she said. "Is it possible they were purchased the day before?"

I supposed it was possible, though helium balloons tended to lose their buoyancy fairly quickly. I doubted they were purchased any earlier than two days ago.

The woman jabbed a few more buttons. "Nope. We've sold a solid blue bunch and several mixed, but none that were red only."

Dang.

She closed the notebook. "We sell helium canisters, too," she said. "Some people fill the balloons themselves to save a little money."

"Can you see if anyone bought a canister along with red balloons?" I asked. "They probably would have been purchased some time in the last week." I doubted Adriana would have planned any sooner. I assumed that if she was behind the attempt to access Ryan's apartment, she'd done so to retaliate against him for breaking her window. But who knows.

The woman jabbed some more buttons. "Looks like we sold a helium canister and some red balloons last Friday."

"How were they paid for?"

"Cash," she replied.

Cash. The preferred monetary medium of criminals. *Illegal* tender. "Did the person buy anything else?"

She glanced back at her screen. "Yep. Looks like they also purchased one of those bracelet tattoos. They're popular with the teen girls." She gestured to an aisle nearby. "They're right down there if you want to take a look."

"I do."

She circled around the counter and led me down an aisle of party favors. Plastic beads. Bouncy balls. Party blowers. "Here we go." She gestured to a display of temporary bracelet tattoos. The selections included skulls, shamrocks, a chain of daisies, and one with red hearts. *Bingo!* I plucked the package with the red heart tattoo from the display. "Is this the one that was purchased?"

"Mm-hm. The 'Circle of Hearts.'"

I was so close now. Whoever had been at Ryan's apartment had to be the same person who'd purchased these items. It was too much to write off as mere coincidence.

I looked back at the register, again noting the security camera mounted over the checkout area. If Adriana appeared in the video like I suspected she might, I'd finally have some solid evidence instead of what I had so far, which was diddly-squat. *This case could soon be resolved! Woo-hoo!*

Brigit looked up at me as if she could smell my excitement. Heck, she probably could. I briefly wondered what excitement might smell like. Cherries, I decided. Or maybe buttercream frosting.

I turned back to the woman and gestured to the security camera on the wall. "Can you show me the video footage from the time the purchase was made?"

The woman glanced back at the camera, then up and

down the aisle before leaning in to whisper to me. "Sorry, but I can't. The camera's a fake. We installed it as a preventive measure. The real ones cost too much."

Ugh! "Are there any cameras outside?"

She shook her head. "We've got an alarm system, though."

While an alarm might do them some good if anyone attempted to break into the store, it did absolutely nothing for my investigation, unfortunately.

The three of us returned to the register where I paid the woman for the bracelet tattoo and thanked her for her time.

"You want a copy of the receipt for the balloons and the helium?" she asked.

"That would be great."

She printed it out and handed it to me. "Have a nice day, Officer."

"You, too." With that, Brigit and I exited the store, the bells on the door tinkling behind us. I glanced around outside only to confirm that the woman was right. There were no cameras mounted on the exterior. The bicycle shop next door was closed, but when I cupped my hands around my eyes and peered through the glass I saw no cameras in the shop that might have been aimed at the window and picked up the license plate of the person who'd bought the helium, balloons, and bracelet. I sighed. *Oh, well.* It had been a long shot, anyway.

As I climbed back into the cruiser, the leasing agent called. "What did you find out?" I asked.

"We have two male tenants with birthdays this week,"

she said. "One is on Thursday and the other was this past Sunday. But nobody had a birthday yesterday."

This information confirmed that the woman who'd come to the complex yesterday had indeed had suspicious intentions. The only other question was whether that woman was Adriana or someone else Ryan knew. Had the guy left a string of broken hearts like Adriana claimed? Was the blond guise some type of sexual role play? Could the blonde have been someone from his comics convention circles? Or a hooker?

I dialed Ryan's cell phone. He answered on the fifth ring. "Give me a second," he said after I identified myself. "I'm doing an install and I'll need to go out to my truck so we can talk in private."

I held on for a minute or two, listening to the sounds of the phone being jostled about until finally I heard the slam of a vehicle's door being closed. Ryan returned to the line. "What did you find out?" he asked.

"The leasing agent didn't get a good look at the woman, either," I told him. "But she did tell me that none of the male tenants had a birthday yesterday. I was able to confirm where the balloons were sold, but they were paid for in cash and there's no security-camera footage to show who made the purchase."

"Dammit!" His words were followed by a muffled sound, as if he'd pounded a fist on his dash. "So you're not gonna arrest her, are you?"

It was more an accusation than a question. His kazoo voice had become high and he sounded a little fearful. I felt a twinge of guilt. After all, if this woman had already clawed at his throat and was now trying to get into his apartment, who knew what she might be capable of? Then again, maybe Ryan was trying to frame Adriana. Maybe she'd broken his heart and he'd set this whole thing up as a ploy to get her in trouble. Maybe Danielle wasn't the only girl he was involved with. Again, I wondered if maybe one of those women from the comic book conventions had agreed to do some non-sexual role play for him. *Maybe, maybe, maybe.* There were far too many maybes. What I wanted—*what I needed*—were some certainties.

"Without a positive identification or more evidence, I can't take Adriana into custody," I told Ryan. "But I've got all the officers in W1 keeping a close watch on both her house and your apartment. We'll do our best to keep you safe."

He snorted. "Famous last words."

I put two fingers to my forehead to keep my head from exploding. "For what it's worth, I'm really sorry we can't seem to get this resolved."

"You and me both."

We ended the call and I sat back in my seat. *What now?* I decided to call Bustamente with another update and seek his advice.

"Go see Miss Valdez," he suggested after I'd gotten him up to speed. "Show her the receipt and see if you can get a confession out of her. Be sure to show some empathy. She's more likely to spill the beans if she thinks you can understand where she's coming from."

"Will do. Thanks." As soon as I hung up on the detective, I called Adriana's cell phone. "There's been a development in the case. Can I swing by the rehab center and speak with you?"

She hesitated a moment. "Could we meet at my house during my lunch break? If you come to the center it'll only feed the gossip mill."

I agreed to meet her at her house at twelve-fifteen. That gave me an hour to serve and protect the other residents of W1. Also the opportunity to write one of them a ticket for driving fifty-eight miles per hour in a thirty-mph zone.

The guy tried to talk me out of it. "Can't you just give me a warning?" He smiled up at me as if he thought he was so charming I'd change my mind. "I promise I'll be good."

"Warnings are for minor offenses," I told him. "You were going nearly double the speed limit. Near the zoo no less. There's kids and families out here. You could've killed or seriously injured someone."

He snatched the ticket from my hand. "You don't have to be so melodramatic."

And you don't have to be such an ass.

After a quick lunch of kale salad and kibble—I had the salad, Brigit had the kibble—my partner and I drove to Adriana's house to wait for her. She pulled into her driveway at eight minutes after noon. *Can't beat that commute.*

I let Brigit out of our cruiser, not bothering to leash her. Adriana could deal with a police K-9 in her yard. While my partner trotted over to the porch to see if her possum friend was around, I met Adriana on the drive, whipped out the receipt, and held it out to her. "What can you tell me about this?"

She looked down at the receipt but didn't reach for it. "What is it?"

"A receipt from the Par-T Corral. For helium, red balloons, and a temporary tattoo."

"I'm totally confused." She lifted her head and looked at my left temple. "What does that receipt have to do with me? Does this have something to do with the 'false pretenses' you mentioned yesterday?"

For better or worse, officers are allowed to mislead witnesses during questioning if doing so could lead to evidence. I decided to go that route. "Come on, Adriana. The store has a video camera over the register that recorded the sale. The management is getting the footage ready to send me. If you're going to show up in the video, you're much better off coming clean with me right now. We might be able to work out a deal." I stared her down, willing her to confess.

Her mouth gaped. "You think I bought balloons? And helium? And that I did something with them? Something bad?"

"I think it's possible."

For the first time since I'd met her, I saw real, raw emotion. Tears began to well up in her eyes and her shoulders slumped inward. A fresh twinge of guilt puckered my gut. I hadn't done a good job of showing empathy, had I? And I might have just accused an innocent woman. *Ugh!*

"Look, Adriana," I said softly. "No one could blame you for being upset. Ryan hurt you, didn't he? It would only be natural to want to get back at him. Or maybe to try to force him into a conversation."

She slowly shook her head. "Whoever it was, whatever they did, it wasn't me. And knowing you think I could have . . . I feel so . . ." She continued to shake her head, as if waiting for the right word to shake out and fall into place. *"Wounded,"* she said finally.

On hearing the word, I felt as if I'd been sucker-punched in the belly. *It hadn't been her, had it?* I'd been wrong to think so.

She blinked back the tears.

"Look," I said softly. "I'm sorry this has upset you. I'm just trying to get to the bottom of things. I don't know you or Ryan personally so all I have to go on is the evidence. I'll continue to look into things, and we'll have the patrols keep a close eye on your house, okay?"

"Okay," she said on a hitched breath. She blinked again and wiped at her eyes with the back of her hand. "Can I go inside now? I need to get a tissue."

"Sure."

As she turned to go, my heart drooped inside me. I'd victimized a victim, made her feel worse, made her feel unsafe and unprotected. I felt like an absolute shit. That's why, when I received a text from my mother asking if I wanted to go to Wednesday-night mass with her tonight, I replied with a thumbs-up emoji. Some time with Mom might make me feel better.

"What did you do?" I asked my mother as she climbed into the passenger seat of my Smart Car at a quarter to seven that evening.

She cast me a glance as she buckled her belt. "Nothing. Why?"

"You normally only go to a midweek mass if you're feeling guilty about something."

She scoffed. "That's not true! Sometimes I go if your father and siblings are driving me nuts and I need to get out of the house."

Evidently this was one of those nights. "If it'll help, you can have my sip of the communion wine."

"You're on to something," she said. "Let's skip the mass and get a glass of wine somewhere instead."

"Mom!"

She waved a dismissive hand. "I'll go to confession later to ask forgiveness."

I shrugged. "It's your soul."

I drove to her favorite Italian restaurant, where we took seats at a high-top table in the small bar area. When the waitress arrived, my mother ordered a cabernet, while I opted for a Lambrusco. As I looked at my mother across the table, I realized it was one of the only times she and I had been alone together in months, if not years. Hard to get much one-on-one time with your parents when you came from such a big family, especially if you were one of the older children.

"How's Seth?" Mom asked.

"Good," I replied. "He's been helping Frankie get acclimated at the fire station."

At least my roommate hadn't had to get used to working nights. She'd worked the night shift in her former job as a stocker at the grocery store.

"He's a good guy." My mom cocked her auburn head and eyed me intently. "You think he's the one?"

"I don't know," I said. "Maybe." There was that word again. *Maybe.* "How'd you know Dad was the one?"

"Easy. The thought of settling down with him didn't make me want to run off and hide."

The thought of spending the rest of my life with Seth didn't make me want to run off, either, though I wasn't anywhere near ready to tie the knot. I enjoyed Seth's companionship, but I was enjoying my independence, too, thank you very much.

The waitress brought our wine and we each took a sip. I had to admit, it was nice talking with my mother like this, relating to her woman to woman. Heck, I realized then that I hardly knew who she was as a woman. She'd always just been *Mom*. Maybe it was time I got to know Maureen O'Keefe Luz, the real woman behind the frenzy and freckles.

"You ready for Gabby to get her license?" I asked.

"Yes and no." She toyed with her cocktail napkin. "Part of me is sad to see my youngest grow up. Another part of me will be glad that not having to shuttle her around anymore will free up some of my time."

"What are you going to do with that free time?"

While I'd expected her to say she might catch up on her favorite TV shows, binge-watch a sitcom or two, she surprised me by saying, "I'm thinking about going back to school."

"School? Really?"

Mom had been attending community college when she'd met my father. After they married, they'd begun to reproduce fairly quickly. When she got pregnant with me, she'd dropped out to become a full-time mother.

"I have no idea what I'll study. I keep trying to remember what I was interested in before all those years of diapers and dioramas and dentist appointments." She chuckled softly. "Forty-seven years old and I still don't know what I want to be when I grow up."

"Well, it's never too late to figure it out." I raised my wineglass for a toast. "Here's to you, Mom."

We clinked our glasses and sipped our wine.

"Speaking of careers," I said, "I've got a case I can't figure out." I told her about Ryan and Adriana and decided it couldn't hurt to get her perspective. "What do you think?" I asked. "Is it him or is it her?"

She shrugged. "I have no idea. The only thing I know is that you'll figure it out."

"Because I'm smart?"

"No. Because you're stubborn."

Ah, mothers. Gotta love 'em.

TWENTY-ONE
C'MON, GET HAPPY

Brigit

Megan hadn't talked much as they'd driven around that day. Brigit knew that meant her partner was upset. She could also tell that Megan wasn't happy by the fact that she didn't pull back her lips to show her teeth or sing along with the radio like she normally did.

Megan had left Brigit home after work and gone somewhere. Brigit didn't like being separated from Megan, but at least she had Zoe to keep her company. The two were curled up on the couch together, dozing, when Brigit's ears pricked as they detected the sound of a car engine approaching.

Is it Megan?

Brigit lifted her head off the sofa and looked out the window, spotting the car pulling into the driveway.

It is! It's Megan!

Brigit hopped down from the couch and ran to meet Megan at the door. When her partner and roommate came inside, Brigit could tell exactly what she'd been up to without Megan saying a word. Brigit's nose told her all she needed to know. Megan had been with her mother and she'd drunk wine. She'd petted those pesky tabby cats at her parents' house, too. Their scent was all over Megan's hand. *Yuck.* Well, Brigit could do something about that!

She pranced around, woofing her heart out, until Megan bent down and gave her the nice full-body rub-down she deserved, Brigit's much better dog scent overpowering the tabby stench.

"Did you miss me, girl?" Megan asked.

Brigit licked her cheek in reply. *Slup!*

As they climbed into bed a couple hours later, Brigit could tell that whatever had been bothering her partner earlier today was bothering her again. Megan's moves were rigid, her groans anxious. *I can do something about that, too.*

She plopped herself down at Megan's side and gave her a fresh lick. *Slup!* When Megan sat up and used her elbow to nudge Brigit back, the dog knew her partner was only trying to be brave. What she really needed was more loving.

Brigit pounced on Megan, forcing her onto her back, and licked her partner like she'd never licked before. *Slup-slup-slup-slup!*

Megan squealed and squirmed under the dog, but finally she made that *ha-ha-ha* sound that Brigit knew meant she was happy now.

She gave Megan one final lick. *Slup.*

My work here is done.

TWENTY-TWO
LOVE IS PATIENT

The Devoted One

Things were not moving along as quickly as the Devoted One had expected, not giving the results that had been hoped for.

All I want is to talk to you. If you just give me a chance, I know I can convince you to come back.

Patience would be required. Fitting. After all, love was patient. It had said so on the cross-stitched sampler hanging on the living room wall growing up. According to the verse spelled out in blue embroidery thread, love was also kind. It didn't envy or boast, either. Supposedly, love kept no record of wrongs, but the Devoted One thought, *1 Corinthians was being a little unrealistic with that one. We're only human, after all. It's natural to keep score.*

But the final verse was the one that hit home.

Love never fails.

Like love, the Devoted One wouldn't fail, either.

TWENTY-THREE

A FLUFF PIECE

Megan

The Lollipop Bandit had been lying low, no further reports coming in. Of course I'd been making extra circuits around the medical center. Maybe he'd spotted me and decided not to risk another Tootsie Pop heist. Or maybe all that sugar had caused his teeth to rot and he'd moved on to softer contraband, pudding cups, perhaps.

When I'd had no word from the spoiled rich boy or his parents by Thursday, I decided another in-person visit was in order. When I went to the door this time, I brought Brigit up to the porch with me. While she was of no help in formulating questions during an interrogation, her presence tended to encourage people to tell the truth, almost as if they thought she could smell bullshit when they spewed it. Or maybe they just didn't want me to sic her on them if I thought they were lying. Either way, here we were.

I rang the bell. Once again, the *ding-dong* echoed through the large house. I stood there a long moment, staring at the peephole, waiting. There were no cars in the driveway, but that didn't mean no one was home. They'd have multiple parking options inside the three-car garage. Heck, the house even had a narrow garage door for the golf cart.

I was about to push the bell again when Brigit's ears pricked up and angled toward the door. Still, nobody responded.

"I know you're looking out the peephole," I said loudly. "My dog just alerted to your presence. Open the door."

There was a short pause, followed by a metallic sound as the dead bolt was released. The door swung open only a few inches and a woman with perfectly coiffed copper hair poked her head out like an elegant jack-in-the-box. While her mouth offered a broad smile, her eyes attempted to cut me like lasers. "Hello, Officer. How are you today?"

"I'm doing fine, thanks. I left my business card at your door Monday afternoon with a message to call me." I'd recently dealt with people who thought they were above the law. I had no more patience for people who thought their position or bank account balance gave them the right to misbehave without penalty. The rules applied equally to everyone, and I was going to enforce those rules. "Care to explain why you ignored a direct request from a police officer?"

"I never saw the card," she said. "Are you sure you left it at our house?"

"I'm absolutely certain," I said. "I remember these purple petunias." I angled my head to indicate the flower pot. "They looked dry so I poured some bottled water on them."

The woman looked down at the petunias as if noticing them for the first time. Heck, that might be the case. She probably had a lawn service that replaced her plants, and many people entered and exited their homes through their garages, hardly ever crossing their front thresholds.

"I need to speak with your son," I said.

"I'm sorry." She pulled the door even closer to her neck. Much more and she'd choke herself. "He's not here. He's with his grandparents in Aspen this week."

In my peripheral vision, I saw Brigit's nose twitch. *Yep, girl. I smell the bullshit, too.*

"Aspen, huh?" I said, going up on tiptoe and peering through the narrow opening over her head. Not that I could see much. Just a wall. "When did he leave?"

"Last Sunday."

Yeah, right. "Well, then. I must be mistaken. I thought he might have been involved in an incident with your golf cart on Monday."

The woman thought she had me. *Oh, how wrong she is.*

"Yes, you're mistaken," she said. "Have a good day."

I put the steel toe of my tactical shoe on the threshold to prevent her from shutting the door. "Since I'm mistaken, I'm sure you'll have no problem letting me take a look at your golf cart then."

Her eyes flashed in anger and alarm, but she tried to play it coy. "I wish I could show it to you. But it's not here."

Uh-huh. "Did it go on vacation to Aspen, too?"

That snarky comment wiped the smile off her face. "No," she snapped. "My husband has it. He's got a hitch on his SUV he can attach it to. He's playing another course today."

"Where?"

"He didn't tell me."

From inside the house a boy's voice bellowed. "Mo-om! We need more pizza rolls up here!"

"Aspen, huh?" I arched my brows.

She pursed her lips. "Well. It looks like *I* was the one who was mistaken."

I stepped closer to the door. "Hey, kid!" I hollered. "Get down here!"

A second later the voice called, "Who's at the door?"

Realizing the jig was up, the woman swung the door fully open now. "Just get your butt down here, Brock."

Footsteps thundered down the stairs, and a boy with gelled hair and a golf shirt with the collar pulled up stepped up beside the woman. When he saw me, his mouth went agape. Sure enough, he had braces on his teeth and the rubber bands were blue. His lip quirked as if he were disgusted by the presence of police officers who dealt with scumbags on a regular basis. *Yep, you little twerp. You're only one degree of separation from killers, drug dealers, and rapists.*

"I've got something that belongs to you, Brock," I said. I reached into my pocket and pulled out the baggie with the broken blue band in it.

"That's not mine!" he snapped. Unfortunately for him, one of the bands he was now wearing snapped, too, shooting out of his mouth and landing on top of Brigit's head. She looked up, her eyes nearly crossing.

I plucked the band off her head. "Cut the crap, kid.

You want to be charged with property damage, hit-and-run, and lying to a cop? End up in juvie with a bunch of gang members?"

He shrugged, as if the thought didn't scare him. *Idiot.* The kids in juvie would eat this pampered little prick alive.

Before he could speak, his mother answered for him. "No, he doesn't want to be taken to juvenile detention. We're not going to admit anything, but we'll pay any damages. Out-of-pocket. We don't want this going on our insurance."

Finally, one of them was using their sense. I told her the owner of the Mercedes would be in touch. "If you give him any grief, I'm coming back here. Understand me?"

"We understand," the woman hissed.

I pointed to the kid. "You could've killed yourself or your friends driving the way you did. You're grounded for two weeks. No TV or Internet."

"You can't do that!" he cried.

"No," I said, "but your mother can. And unless she wants me to come back and arrest you on those charges I just mentioned, she'll enforce it."

I looked from Brock to his mother. She scowled, but gave a small nod of agreement.

Ah, justice. It comes in so many forms.

The boy now hopefully saved from a life of crime, Brigit and I returned to the cruiser, but not until after I let her take a dump in the ivy growing about their mailbox. I didn't pick it up, either, but rather left it there as a memento, a reminder of who was boss. I phoned the owner of the Mercedes and told him his losses should be covered.

"Thanks, Officer Luz."

"They give you any guff," I told him, "call me right away."

"Will do."

It sure was nice when cases essentially solved themselves. Was it too much to wish the stalking investigation would solve itself, too?

After my shift, Seth picked up some takeout Chinese food and brought it to the house. He'd bought enough for Frankie, too, so the three of us fixed our plates and took them out onto the patio to eat. Between chasing bugs and romps around the yard, Brigit and Blast begged for bites of our egg rolls and lo mein noodles.

I handed a packet of soy sauce to Frankie. "How're things at the station? Are you still on latrine duty?"

"Yeah," she grumbled. "I've been out to two fires but all I've gotten to do so far is hold the hose."

Seth cut a glance her way. "Entering a burning building is dangerous stuff. You've got to work your way up to it."

"I know, I know," she muttered. "But I want to show off my mojo."

"Don't you get enough of that on the derby track?" I asked, referring to her Roller Derby bouts with the Fort Worth Whoop Ass.

A grin played about her lips. "You can never get enough of it."

I had just cracked open my fortune cookie when my

cell phone came to life. The readout indicated it was Detective Bustamente calling. I grabbed the phone. "Hi, Detective."

Brigit nuzzled my hand, snagging the fortune cookie and wolfing it down, paper fortune strip and all. Now I'd never know my destiny. It was making its way through my K-9's digestive system.

"Come on over to Adriana's," Bustamente said. "We've got ourselves a sticky situation." He ended the call without further explanation.

"Duty calls," I told Frankie and Seth.

"When will you be back?" Seth asked.

"I don't know. I'll check in with you once I know something." I scurried to my bedroom. Rather than put my full uniform back on, I opted for a FWPD tee along with my pants, tactical shoes, and belt. I rounded up Brigit and out the door we went.

We transferred to our squad car at the station and made our way to Adriana's place. I found Detective Bustamente standing on her curb, shooing at cars that were cruising slowly by. *What the hell is going on?*

I pulled to a stop behind his plain sedan, retrieved Brigit from the back, and met him on the walkway. "What are you doing out here?"

He responded by holding out his phone. I took it from him and looked down at the screen. He was logged into an app called Kinky Cowtown. The screen showed a pic of a smiling Adriana in a tank top. Below her photo was a bio. *I'm Adriana. I live alone and would love your company. Bring a leather whip and marshmallow whip and let's get nasty.* The short bio was followed by her address.

"Holy crap!" I looked up from the phone. "What is this?"

"Sexual hookup app. Someone put Miss Valdez's profile and address on it."

"Ryan Downey?" It had to be him, right?

The detective shrugged. "Don't know yet."

As the detective and I spoke, a dented orange Ford Fiesta pulled to the curb and parked. A man in his forties with a beer belly and three days' growth on his face climbed out. He had a jar of marshmallow fluff in one hand and a horse whip in the other. With hardly a glance in our direction, he headed past us up the walk. Instinctively, my hand went to the baton on my belt and yanked it out. I flicked my wrist and it opened with a *snap!*

"Hey!" Bustamente yelled after the man. "Where do you think you're going?"

The man stopped and pointed at Adriana's door with the whip. "Right here."

The detective gestured to me and Brigit. "You see these police officers standing here, don't you?"

"Yeah, but it's not illegal to meet for sex so long as I don't pay for it." The guy gave a grunt. "Learned that the hard way."

To borrow a phrase from the maintenance worker, *cheese and grits.*

"Hit the road!" Bustamente barked. "Now!"

The guy threw up his hands, inadvertently causing the whip to snap. *Snap!* "Chill out, man!" He tossed the marshmallow fluff aside and returned to his car, muttering and slamming the door. *Bam!*

I was tempted to write the creep a citation for littering,

but the thought of getting any closer to him made my skin crawl. *Poor Adriana.* I wondered how many strange men had come to her door before she figured out what was going on. She must be disgusted and terrified.

Bustamente turned from the man back to me. "I've spoken briefly with Miss Valdez, but she specifically requested that you come."

"She did?" That was surprising. The last time I'd seen her she had been less than happy with me.

"Yep," Bustamente said. "I guess she trusts you." He angled his head to indicate the door. "Let's talk to her. Then I'd like the two of us to go have a little chat with Ryan Downey. I've put in a call to get an officer out here to stand guard."

The detective held out a hand to indicate I should lead the way. With Bustamente following, I led Brigit up to the porch and knocked on the door. "Miss Valdez?" I called. "It's Officer Luz and Detective Bustamente."

A moment later the door swung open. Adriana stood there, a blanket wrapped around herself despite the warm temperature. Her eyes were pink and puffy from crying, but that didn't prevent her from giving my cheekbone a pointed look. "Now do you believe me?" she asked, an involuntary whimper following her words.

I swallowed the lump of emotion in my throat. "I'm really sorry you're having to go through this."

"Me, too," Bustamente added. After a short pause, he asked, "Why marshmallow whip? Any idea?"

"I know *exactly* why." She rolled her puffy eyes. "Because Ryan loves it and he got angry with me when I threw out a jar of it that was in his pantry. It's full of corn syrup and sugar and artificial flavors. It's basically poison. I was only trying to look out for him, but he never seemed to appreciate it."

Bustamente cut me a look that said, *Yeah, funny how men don't appreciate their women throwing out their beer and potato chips and porn collections.*

The mystery of the marshmallow fluff solved, I moved on to other matters. "I'll cordon off your yard with police tape. We've got an officer on the way who will keep an eye on your house. After the detective and I speak with Ryan I'll come back and stay the night out here, too, make sure you're safe."

She expelled a shuddering breath. "I'd appreciate that. This is a nightmare."

I could only imagine. "I'm worried about your safety," I told her. "Even after your profile is taken down, there will be men who know you live here alone. It might be time to think about moving."

"I can't. I've got over seven months left on my lease."

Bustamente chimed in now. "Texas law allows a tenant who's been the victim of domestic violence to break a lease without penalty. What's happened here, the brick through your window and these men tonight, would qualify you for relief."

She looked down at the floor before looking up again, her gaze going between me and the detective. "But I like this house. It's close to work and I've got my garden. I just moved in a few months ago. It costs a lot to hire movers and pay deposits. I can't afford to move again. Besides, it doesn't seem fair that I'm the one who has to move when Ryan is the one causing problems."

She looked so scared and small and alone. While we police officers could see to her physical safety, she looked like she could use some emotional support. Having some company inside the house couldn't hurt, either. "What about your new boyfriend?" I asked. "The doctor? Could he come stay with you?"

"He . . ." She hesitated a moment before finishing her sentence. "Didn't work out."

"Oh." *Too bad.*

She looked past us, where a young man with a pizza delivery sign atop his car had slowed to a crawl. The sign promised delivery in thirty minutes or the pizza was free. If the driver stopped for some nookie, he wouldn't make it in time. Then again, he looked all of seventeen. He'd probably finish in two minutes flat and have his pizzas delivered with time to spare.

I waved my baton while the detective yelled, "Beat it, kid!" *Ironic words, huh?*

The boy hit the gas and pulled away with a screech.

We turned back to Adriana.

She chewed her lip. "I know it will be impossible to prove Ryan entered the profile, but it's obvious he did this. You'll arrest him, won't you?"

"It depends," Bustamente replied. "We'll have to see what he says to me and Officer Luz tonight. No guarantees, but we may also be able to get a search warrant that would enable our tech specialists to trace the profile."

"You mean they can figure out who input the information on the app? I didn't think that was possible."

"Not exactly," he said, "and I can't even pretend to know how all that tech stuff works."

Neither could I. While I could use technology as well

as the next person, its inner workings were beyond my pay grade.

The detective continued. "Our tech people can sometimes get the code that identifies the computer that was used in a crime. It's called an IP address. IP stands for Internet Protocol. If they find an IP address for a computer that belongs to Ryan, we should be able to bring him in. Of course the process will take a few days."

"A few days?" She expelled a long exhale that said just how frustrated and disappointed she was. She looked past us again, though this time there was no sex fiend at the curb, only one of the swing-shift officers pulling up to keep watch. "I'm going to go back inside now, okay? I don't want any of the men driving by to see me."

"I understand," I said. "If you need anything tonight, just call my cell and I'll be at your door in seconds."

"Thank you, Officer Luz." With a final nod, she closed the door and it latched with a soft click.

I returned my baton to my belt and stepped down from the porch, leading my partner with me. Bustamente stepped over to the curb to speak with the officer who'd just arrived and give him an update on the situation.

Back at my cruiser, I retrieved a roll of bright yellow cordon tape from my trunk and tied an end to Adriana's mailbox as a starting point. I dropped Brigit's leash to give her the freedom to sniff around while I worked. I navigated the perimeter of the yard, affixing the tape to a bush, a fence post, and a scraggly Bradford pear tree on the property line, keeping the tape at waist level where it would act as an impediment to anyone attempting to enter the property. When I had the entire front yard roped off, I used my teeth to chew through the tape and returned the rest of the roll to my trunk. Brigit trotted up to the car, the jar of marshmallow fluff in her teeth.

I wrestled it from her. "Sorry, girl. This stuff will give you cavities."

Bustamente came over and reached for the jar. "I'll take that. My wife uses it in her pecan fudge."

Yum! I held the jar back, out of his reach. "Promise you'll bring some to the station?"

He chuckled. "I will. Can't promise how long it will last, though."

A van from a Dallas TV news team pulled to the curb. I issued an involuntary groan as Trish LeGrande hopped down from the passenger seat dressed in her trademark pink, tonight's outfit being a formfitting knit dress and strappy wedges. Her circus-peanut hair was pulled up in a French twist on the back of her head. Before graduating to more hard-hitting news stories, Trish had handled the feel-good fluff pieces for the channel. I supposed tonight's story was the first *literal* fluff piece she'd be covering.

Though she'd been on the scene and spoken with me at the mall bombing, when a pickpocket and purse snatcher was targeting people at the rodeo, and on various other cases, the woman never seemed to remember me. It could be due to the fact that she interacted with a lot of people and simply couldn't recall everyone she'd met. Or it could be that she didn't truly care about the stories she was reporting, she simply liked to be where the action was and be the center of attention. My money was on the latter.

She stepped over to me and the detective. "We heard something about an unusual stalking incident here?"

They must've been listening on a police scanner.

The detective and I exchanged glances before he addressed her. "This is an ongoing investigation. We have no comment at this time." When the cameraman stepped up with his camera on his shoulder, Bustamente turned to him. "We'd appreciate it if you don't put the residence on the news. This is an extremely sensitive situation."

All Trish said was, "We'll see."

Grrr. The media and law enforcement had a tenuous relationship. While news outlets could be of great help in tracking fugitives and helping us solve cases with their crime-stopper programs, other times the journalists could hinder our investigations, getting in the way or revealing facts we had hoped to keep under wraps.

A car slowly rolled up and Trish raised an arm and trotted toward it on her heels. "Sir?" she called to the driver. "Would you be willing to speak to me on camera?"

When the driver spotted the TV van and cameraman, he couldn't get out of there fast enough. He floored the gas and burned rubber, sending up a cloud of dust. *Screeeeech!*

"Dammit!" Trish sputtered, waving dust out of her face.

While Trish attempted to stop another car cruising by, I loaded Brigit into her enclosure. Bustamente climbed into his car and pulled out. Just as he vacated the spot at the curb, a motorcycle pulled into it. The rider held a whip in one hand and a jar of marshmallow fluff cradled between his legs.

Once again, I yanked my baton from my belt and extended it with a *snap!* I used the baton to point at the jar of marshmallow whip and wiggled my fingers in a give-it-here motion. Technically, I had no legal right to confiscate the sugary stuff, but if he voluntarily turned it over without question, that was on him. After he handed me the jar, I swung my baton in the direction the man was facing and gave him a look that said *keep moving or I'll take this baton to your boys.* He scowled, revved his engine, and was gone.

I followed the detective to Ryan's apartment complex. Luckily, both his blue Camaro and his work truck were in the lot, which meant he was likely to be home.

We parked in a couple of adjacent, unreserved spots. After I handed the second jar of marshmallow whip over to Bustamente, we made our way up the steps to apartment 206. While Bustamente knocked on the door, Brigit snuffled around the bottom of it, probably scenting the fast food wrappers that comprised a significant part of the apartment's décor.

Ryan opened the door. Fortunately for me, he was fully dressed this time. He wore a pair of gray pants and a white short-sleeved button-down with the name Interstellar Communications embroidered on the breast pocket. The lowercase *i*s were dotted with silver stars.

Before either the detective or I could say anything, Ryan kazooed at me. "You got Danielle all pissed off at me. Thanks a lot!"

I took a breath to keep myself from kicking him in

the kneecap. "You realize I was only doing my job, trying to keep you safe. Right?"

"I guess." He exhaled a loud breath. "It just sucks, that's all. I still don't see why you had to drag her into it."

The detective extended his hand. "Hello, Mr. Downey. I'm Detective Hector Bustamente."

Ryan tentatively shook Bustamente's hand before looking from one of us to the other. "Did you prove Adriana was the one who came by with the balloons? Did you arrest her?"

Bustamente and I exchanged glances.

"That's not what we're here about," I told Ryan.

He cocked his head, his eyes narrowing. "It's not?"

The detective didn't hold back. "I hear you've got quite a hankering for marshmallow whip."

Ryan snorted out a laugh. "Love the stuff. How'd you know?"

"How?" Bustamente repeated. "Because half a dozen men have brought jars of it to Miss Valdez this evening."

Ryan's smile faltered and his expression froze for a few seconds as he purportedly tried to make sense of what the detective had told him. Seemingly unable to do so, he said, "Say what now?"

Bustamente responded by holding out his phone to show Ryan the profile of Adriana on the Kinky Cowtown app.

After reading the bio, Ryan belted out a belly laugh and slapped his leg. "Holy shit! That's priceless!"

It wasn't priceless. It was *criminal*.

"Sure was original," Bustamente agreed, taking the phone from Ryan's hand. "Can't fault you for putting up the profile given what Officer Luz has told me about Adriana trying to get you in trouble. I'd have been upset about that, too."

There was that empathy the detective had mentioned.

"Wait." Ryan's eyes narrowed, his expression becoming wary. "Are you saying you think I put that profile up?"

The detective offered a casual shrug that I knew was anything but. He was trying to throw Ryan off his guard, procure an accidental confession. "Certainly couldn't blame you if you did. I'd be madder'n hell if some woman attempted to frame me for breaking her window and then tried to sneak into my place to do God knows what."

Ryan's eyes popped wide. "I had nothing to do with this! Interstellar is running a free-tablet-with-new-service promotion. We're busy as hell. I had back-to-back installations today, barely had time to stop and take a piss. Another guy was working with me to speed things up. He'll vouch for me."

In other words, Ryan had a potential alibi. Still, it was far from ironclad. After all, he could've used his phone or computer during a coffee break or when, as he'd so eloquently put it, stopped to *take a piss*.

"C'mon, Ryan," Bustamente said, offering a placating smile. "We know Adriana's been harassing you. It's only natural to want to even the score."

Ryan's mouth gaped and he looked from the detective to me, his expression incredulous. "I can't believe this is happening! This is bullshit! Adriana's behind this, not me!"

Bustamente switched tactics, going from friend to foe in five seconds flat. "You expect me to believe that a young woman would go so far as to invite total strangers to her house with the promise of kinky sex just to get back at an ex? That sounds pretty far-fetched to me. I think it's far more likely you posted that profile. Stalking is a third-degree felony, Ryan."

Ironically, though stalking convictions came with some stiff penalties, stalking statutes were relatively new. In fact, the first stalking law wasn't enacted until 1990, after a young, promising actress named Rebecca Schaeffer was shot to death by a crazed fan in California. Other states soon followed suit, enacting laws to punish stalkers and protect their victims.

"If you confess," Bustamente continued, "I might be able to swing you a deal, have the charges reduced to a misdemeanor or maybe even get you deferred adjudication so you'll remain free and it'll stay off your record. If not, you're likely looking at some jail time."

"What the hell?!?" Ryan sputtered and threw up his hands. "I'm not going to confess to something I didn't do! That's crazy!"

"If you didn't do it," Bustamente said, "then I suppose you wouldn't mind if I get one of our tech specialists out here to take a look at your computer and phone, check your browser history and whatnot."

Ryan's facial features hardened. He looked the detective directly in the eye as he ground out his words through gritted teeth. "Bring it on."

Wow. I had to give Bustamente credit. He might not have been able to get a confession out of Ryan, but he'd successfully goaded the guy into agreeing to a voluntary search. We wouldn't need a court order now. *Yippee!*

Ryan turned to me and damned if there wasn't hurt in his eyes. His voice sounded hurt, too. "I thought you were on my side, Officer Luz."

"If you're innocent," I told him, my guts squirming inside me, "I am." My Lord, this case had pulled my mind and emotions in so many directions it was a wonder my brain and heart hadn't snapped like taffy.

Who was the victim here?

Who was the guilty person?

What was it going to take to find out?

TWENTY-FOUR
WATCHDOGS

Brigit

It was getting dark when Megan drove back to the house with the possum under the porch. Brigit lifted her nose to the metal mesh of her enclosure and sniffed. She could smell the beady-eyed little beast. She'd love to give it a nice chase. Of course the dumb things didn't know how to play chase very well. She'd run after one before and instead of bolting for its life it had gone still, playing dead. A useless defense against a dog in most instances, but Brigit decided that even though the thing was too stupid to live she wouldn't kill it. It wasn't a fair fight.

She and Megan stayed in the car with the windows down. Looked like they were on watchdog duty tonight. That was okay with Brigit. That gave her a chance to gnaw on the new bone Megan had bought her at the store. If she couldn't be playing chase or wrestling with another dog, gnawing wasn't a bad substitute.

She picked the chew toy up with her mouth, used her paws to hold it in place, and set to work on it.

TWENTY-FIVE
SWEET REVENGE

The Devoted One

The idea had been brilliant. It created a sticky situation, made for some sweet revenge. And all it had taken was a few keyboard clicks.

The Devoted One could be furious about it, but instead the prank provided hope. It proved that the tactics were working, that the two still shared a connection, even if it was indirect and weak at the moment. But that connection could grow stronger. It *would* grow stronger.

The Devoted One was more determined now than ever.

TWENTY-SIX
DREAM GIRLS

Megan

After settling back in the cruiser at Adriana's, I placed a quick call to Seth.

"So you're not coming home tonight?" His disappointment was clear in his voice. As much as I hated to let him down, it was nice to know he cared.

"Sorry," I said. "I promised Adriana I'd keep watch in front of her house."

"You're not even supposed to be on duty tonight. Can't another officer handle that?"

"There's another one here," I told him, "but she specifically asked for me. I think she feels more comfortable with a female officer." I had to admit I was flattered she'd asked for me to be involved tonight. I hadn't been able to solve this stalking case or make an arrest yet, but I must be doing something right if I'd gained her trust.

"All right," he acquiesced. "But we're still on for the Kimbell this weekend?"

"Yep." I knew Seth had little interest in seeing the

Kimbell Art Museum's exhibit featuring Monet's early works, but the guy was willing to go along for my sake. Gotta love a guy who's willing to make sacrifices. Besides, I'd attended more than one classic car rally with him. Healthy relationships were about give-and-take. Too bad Adriana and Ryan didn't have a healthy relationship.

I signed off with a smooching sound to let Seth know he, too, was appreciated, and went back to watch duty. When my butt went to sleep in the seat, I retrieved Brigit from her enclosure and let her roam the yard while I strolled up and down the walkway to get my blood flowing.

My fellow officer, Brigit, and I spent the next hour and a half dealing with horny losers.

Some spotted the cruisers or saw me and Brigit in the yard and moved along on their own. Others needed some encouragement from my baton. Another slowed down and rolled down his window. "Something happen to Adriana?" he called.

"That profile was a prank," I told him. "Three male cops live here. With their Rottweiler."

That ought to keep the guy from coming back.

While I walked and watched, I worked my baton, twirling it through my fingers and performing a flat spin like I'd done back in high school when I'd been a twirler with the marching band. The sound of the spinning baton soothed me. *Swish-swish-swish.* I could only hope Adriana had something to soothe her. She'd need it tonight. I had little doubt Ryan was behind this prank. I mean, how nuts would a woman have to be to purposely draw sexual deviants to her home? But I knew Detective Bustamente believed we needed to tread lightly here, given Ryan's protective order and all. We wanted to make sure we were doing the right thing, nabbing the guilty party. Besides, a wrongful arrest could make a mockery of the FWPD. Yep, we had to get all of our ducks in a row before we nabbed our goose.

Eventually, I tired of pacing and took a seat on the porch, Brigit lying beside me and panting softly along with the electric buzz of cicada song. As I sat, I wondered what the technicians would find. Would they track the Kinky Cowtown profile back to Ryan's computer or cell phone? I had my doubts. After all, if he'd posted it through either device he wouldn't have offered them up for analysis. Of course that didn't mean he hadn't posted the profile. He just might have used someone else's computer or phone. Only time would tell. And it was still entirely possible that someone other than Ryan was behind the events at Adriana's place. Just because she couldn't name another potential culprit didn't mean there wasn't one. Maybe one of her coworkers had set her sights on the doctor Adriana had been dating and was taking it out on her. Maybe she'd angered a patient at the rehab center by denying him salt or sugar or Jell-O and he'd decided to take revenge. Maybe a neighbor was jealous of the size of Adriana's prized zucchinis. Or maybe I was just trying to entertain myself by coming up with outlandish ideas.

As the night grew darker and the stream of perverts dwindled, Brigit and I returned to the car to wait. It was more comfortable than sitting on a porch with no back support, and at least in the cruiser we could listen to NPR.

I must've inadvertently dozed off, because the next thing I knew I woke with a start as someone rapped at the window of my cruiser. *Rap-rap-rap.*

I looked up to see the officer from the other car outside. I rolled down the glass.

"I've had enough fun out here," he said. "I'm going back out on patrol. Hinojosa's on his way to help you out."

"Great. Thanks."

A few minutes later, Officer Hinojosa pulled his cruiser to the curb facing mine. With fresh eyes on Adriana's house and my eyelids so heavy I could no longer keep them open, I took the opportunity to climb into Brigit's enclosure and curl up on her big comfy cushion. She cocked her head in confusion. I'd never climbed into her space before. But there's a first time for everything, right?

I woke at first light. My eyes still felt heavy and my teeth felt like they were coated in felt. *Ick.* I couldn't wait to get home and freshen up. I might even be able to get in an hour's sleep before reporting for my day shift. As I sat up, a sharp pain zinged through my neck. *Great. A crick. Just what I need right now.*

I climbed out of my car and went to the front door to speak with Adriana. Fortunately, she was already up and dressed.

"We're going to be heading out," I told her. "No one has come by in a while. If you'd like I can see about g-getting one of the spare cruisers parked out here as a deterrent." If any other creeps came by, maybe they'd assume a cop was inside the house.

"That would be great," she said. "Thanks again for all you've done."

"My pleasure," I lied. It hadn't been pleasurable at all. I had the crick in my neck and my back was sore, too. I hadn't been able to stretch out in the confined space, especially with Brigit in there with me. Given the way my back felt at the moment, it would be a wonder if I could ever fully straighten my spine again. I'd walk around like a female Quasimodo.

When I returned to the station, Captain Leone caught me in the lot. "Detective Bustamente told me what you did last night," he said. "Going above and beyond."

I shrugged, not so much out of humility but because I was too tired to congratulate myself on my dedication. Of course the shrug only exacerbated the shooting pain in my neck.

"We can survive without you this morning," the captain said. "Get some rest and come in at noon."

Thank goodness. I'd been afraid I'd nod off while writing a ticket, fall into traffic, and end up under the wheels of a city bus. That would be no fun for anyone, especially whoever would be charged with scraping my squashed remains off the asphalt.

When I went home, I discovered that Seth had left the razor and shaving cream he'd been using the other day in my medicine cabinet. He'd left a toothbrush, too. *Hmm.* Looked like he and I would need to have a talk about our relationship status.

I peeled off my uniform, brushed the felt from my teeth, rubbed some mint-scented pain relief cream on my neck and back, and fell into bed.

I slept like the dead. When I woke four hours later, I felt only mildly refreshed but at least the soreness in my back and the crick in my neck were gone.

When I arrived at the station at noon, I checked in with Detective Bustamente for both an update on the case and a piece of his wife's fudge. Though I tended to be health conscious, I'd been falling off the wagon more and more frequently lately. I made a mental note to try to do more walking on my shift to burn off the extra calories.

I bit into a square of fudge. The delicious stuff melted on my tongue. "This is so good!" I gushed, quickly grabbing another chunk to take with me. "Any word from the techs on the Kinky Cowtown profile?"

"Yep. There was nothing on Ryan's phone or computer to indicate he was the one who'd posted the picture and bio."

"Really? Nothing at all?" I supposed I shouldn't have been surprised. After all, if Ryan had used either of the devices to upload Adriana's profile, he would not have so willingly given the techs access to them.

"*Nada,*" Bustamente replied.

"What about the IP address?" I asked. "How's that going?"

"It'll be Monday at the earliest before the techs can track that down."

Ugh. The wheels of justice moved too damn slow sometimes. Until this investigation was resolved and the stalker was behind bars, my mind would continue to work on it nonstop, examining the evidence over and over, taking in all the angles, playing back everything Adriana and Ryan had said, their gestures, expressions, and tics. I wished I could turn that part of my brain off and just enjoy the weekend, but I knew it would be difficult.

It was indeed difficult to turn off my brain, but the two glasses of sangria I downed Friday night at a Mexican restaurant with Seth helped me take my mind off things for a while. So did the things he did to me later, back in my bedroom.

The next morning, movement in the bed woke me. I opened my eyes to see Seth sliding out from under the covers. He went over to my dresser, opened the bottom drawer, and pulled out a pair of fresh underwear and socks.

I propped myself up on my elbow. "You've got underwear and socks in my drawers now?"

He cast a glance back at me. "I figured I'd leave a pair or two here," he said. "For convenience."

"Convenience, schmonvenience." Okay, that old verbal ploy didn't work so well with such a long word. But still, I maintained the sentiment. Seth was full of crap here. "You've got a locker at the station. Can't you leave clothes there?"

"I do." He raised a shoulder. "I just figured it made sense to have some here, too."

I sat up in bed, putting a pillow behind me. "You're a squatter."

"Am not."

"Are too. I saw your shaving cream and razor and toothbrush in my bathroom."

He cut a sideways glance at me. "Does it bother you?"

"No," I said. "I just want to know what's going on."

He scrubbed a hand down his face and let loose a loud groan. "Let's just say I'm tired of living in an igloo." In other words, things between his grandfather and his mother were as cold and frosty as ever.

"Well, at least it won't last forever," I said with a chuckle. "With global warming, you'll be knee-deep in water in no time."

He didn't laugh. In fact, he cut me an irritated look.

"Sorry," I said. "That must really stink."

He stared quietly at the wall for a moment before turning back and giving me his best sexy eyes. "You really can't fault me, you know. You make being here a lot of fun."

"I do, do I?"

"Yeah. Maybe we should have some more fun before breakfast." With that, he began crawling toward me across the bed.

That's when I realized the opportune moment I'd been waiting for had arrived. After all, a guy will agree to just about anything if he thinks sex will be part of the bargain. I put a hand against his shoulder to halt his approach. "I want to meet your grandfather."

He closed his eyes and groaned again. "You sure know how to spoil the mood."

"It wouldn't take much to get you back in the mood and you know it."

He sat back on the bed and stared at me for a long moment, his eyes narrowed at first, but eventually relaxing as he gave in. "Okay. You want to meet the jerk? You can meet the jerk."

"Good. When?"

He let out a long, loud breath. "I suppose next weekend is as good a time as any. I've got reserve duty, but I'll be back this way by six o'clock Sunday. I could pick you up on my drive home and we can get stuff to cook out in the backyard."

"That sounds great, Seth."

He cast me a pointed look. "If he acts like an ass, just remember this was your idea. Don't hold it against me."

I reached out and gave his arm an affectionate squeeze. "I won't."

Later, we left the dogs at home in each other's company and drove to the Kimbell Art Museum. We meandered around the space, taking a moment or two to stare at each of Monet's paintings. While I'd never had any talent for art, I could appreciate the time and skill involved in creating these masterpieces. The artist proceeded brushstroke by brushstroke, sometimes leaning in with a small brush to take care of an intricate detail, other times taking a step back to get the bigger picture. In some ways, the process was similar to a criminal investigation. The problem in the stalking case, though, was that I could only see a few of the colors around the edges and had no idea what the big picture was. But come Monday, when the tech team finished their analysis, we should be able to see things much more clearly.

I was sitting on pins and needles during my Monday shift, waiting to hear from the detective. Would the techs discover something that would prove Ryan had uploaded Adriana's profile to Kinky Cowtown?

I repeatedly checked my cell phone to make sure I hadn't missed a call or text. *Nope. Still nothing.*

After cruising through the medical district, eyes

peeled for a man in scrubs enjoying a grape Tootsie Pop, I drove over to the Colonial Country Club neighborhood. I pulled up to Brock's house, taking Brigit to the door with me. I rang the echoing bell. Brock's mother quickly answered the door. *Good.* She realized I wasn't fooling around.

"Hello," I said. "Just checking in."

A voice came from above us and I looked up to see Brock with his arms draped over the railing of a catwalk that connected one part of the upstairs to another. "I'm here." Both his face and voice were sullen. "My life sucks. You got what you wanted."

What I'd wanted was for the kid to take responsibility for his actions. But at least he'd likely think twice next time he screwed up.

"He's been working on his summer reading assignment," his mother said. *"A Tale of Two Cities."*

"Well, then," I said. "Looks like he's made good use of his time."

He scowled down at me. "This is the worst of times!"

What do you know? The kid had learned something. "Buck up," I told him. "Maybe read it a second time for good measure. You'll thank me when you get an A on the test."

He muttered as he wandered back to his bedroom.

Our mission here complete, Brigit and I returned to our car.

Finally, at 3:45 I heard a prophetic *ping* from my phone. The detective had sent a text. *Got some news. Come to the station.*

"Hang on, Brigit!" I called.

My partner had learned from experience that "hang

on" meant she'd better hunker down or the next moment she'd be sliding across the floor. She plopped down and sprawled her legs out for balance.

I whipped a quick U-turn on University, several of the TCU students on the curb watching as I sped past, probably wondering where I was going in such a hurry. In mere minutes, I pulled into the station. I was out of the car in a heartbeat, ordering Brigit to come along. I didn't bother to leash her, not wanting to take the time.

Brigit's nails clicking on the tile behind me, I sprinted down the hall to Bustamente's office and darted inside without stopping at the door to wait for an invitation. Inside sat both Detective Bustamente and Detective Audrey Jackson, my other mentor.

"Did Downey do it?" I asked. "Can I go make an arrest?"

The two exchanged looks and laughed, Detective Jackson's perky dark braids bouncing as she chuckled. "You can get your cuffs ready, Officer Luz. But not for Downey."

My head began to spin. *Huh?*

"Take a seat," Bustamente said, "and I'll tell you what's going on."

I plopped down in the armchair next to Detective Jackson and Brigit sat at my feet.

Bustamente's rolling chair creaked as he leaned back in it. "The tech team determined that the profile was uploaded through the Wi-Fi at the rehab center where Adriana works."

"What!" Why in the world would a woman invite perverts to her door? Willingly and purposely put herself in danger?

"That was my reaction, too," he said. "It doesn't make sense. If she was trying to frame Ryan, there would be much less risky ways to do it." He pointed to Jackson. "I asked Audrey in to get a second opinion, see if she had any insights."

"And?" I said, turning to her.

She raised her palms. "I've got nothing. It sounds crazy to me that she'd have uploaded the profile, but I've seen a lot of crazy over the years. You two need to talk to Adriana." With that, she rose from her seat and stepped over to Brigit, bending over to ruffle the dog's ears. "Hello, there, pup. Have you been a good girl?"

Brigit wagged her tail and gave Detective Jackson a lick on the nose as if to say *Yes! I'm always a good girl.* Before leaving the room, the detective snagged the last piece of fudge from the plastic container on Busta-mente's desk. "Too bad you didn't confiscate all of that marshmallow fluff. I could eat a pound of this stuff."

Once she'd left the room, Bustamente grabbed his jacket and draped it over his arm. "Let's go have a chat with Miss Valdez."

We drove to the rehab center. It was a three-story fa-cility that, according to the signage, handled both inpa-tient and outpatient care. We parked, gave Brigit a second or two to sniff the bushes outside, and checked in at the front desk. When we told the woman we needed to speak with Adriana, her brows reflexively rose in interest. *How long until the office gossip starts to spread?* When the receptionist got her brows back under control, she glanced down at my furry partner, her expression unsure.

"Don't worry," I told her. "I'll keep the dog away from the patients."

The woman picked up her phone and punched three buttons. "Miss Valdez, I've got a Detective Buster Manty and an Officer Louise here to see you."

The woman had butchered our names, but surely Adriana would know who she was referring to.

"Okay," the woman said into the phone. "I will." She returned the receiver to the cradle. "Third floor." She pointed across the way to a bank of elevators. "Room 328."

We thanked her and made our way to an elevator. After waiting for an elderly woman with a cane to exit, we climbed aboard. Though we rode up in silence, I could almost hear the buzz of my nerves.

Would Adriana confess all?

Would we be walking out of here in mere minutes with Adriana in handcuffs?

Would this confounding case finally have a resolution?

The car bobbed and the bell dinged as we came to a stop on the third floor. We exited, consulted the sign mounted on the opposite wall, and headed in the direction the arrow pointed for rooms 315 to 330.

As we walked down the hall, it became clear we were on an inpatient ward where people lived while undergoing long-term treatment. Patients in wheelchairs and others using walkers cooed and called to Brigit. Many of them reached out a hand to pet her. Despite my promise to the receptionist that I'd keep Brigit away from the patients, I didn't have the heart to rush past these people. They probably hadn't seen a dog in a while. Many of them might be missing their own pets while they underwent rehabilitation here.

"Hey, girl!" a white-haired woman with a walker called. She reached down with a gnarled hand to rub Brigit's head. "You sure are a pretty thing. I bet you're smart, too, aren't you?"

"As a whip," I said. Poor choice of words. My mind went back to the leather whips and marshmallow fluff.

"Can she do tricks?" asked a bald man headed our way, his walker tap-tap-tapping on the tile floor as he came along.

"She sure can." I ran through the usual rigmarole with Brigit. *Sit. Shake. Roll over.* In case anyone on the floor was sleeping, I skipped "speak." No sense waking them up. "Here's her coup de grâce." I formed a pretend gun with my index finger and thumb, pointed it at Brigit, and said, "Bang-bang."

She keeled over, falling onto her back with her legs in the air and her tongue hanging out, playing dead. She ought to get a Tony Award for that performance.

The woman let go of her walker and clapped her hands in delight. Bustamente caught the woman as she, too, began to keel over.

"This was such a treat!" she said. "I wish my Roscoe were allowed to come for a visit." She proceeded to pull a photograph out of her pocket. "This is him."

The black poodle in the picture was an absolute doll. "What a handsome boy," I said.

Bustamente discreetly jerked his head toward the end of the hall, encouraging me to wrap things up.

"We have to get back to work now," I told the group who'd gathered around. "Y'all take c-care."

We continued down the hall to room 328. The door

was closed. A hand-lettered sign affixed to it with surgical tape read PLEASE KNOCK BEFORE ENTERING.

The detective put his hand to the door. *Knock-knock*.

A moment later, Adriana opened the door. She poked
her head out and glanced up and down the hall before
hurriedly waving us in and closing the door behind us.

Her office space was tiny but tidy. She worked at
a built-in modular desk with modular shelves lining
the walls. Her window looked out on the parking lot.
Not much of a view. On the corner of her desk was an
industrial-sized pump bottle of hand sanitizer.

She retook her seat and gave the space between me
and the detective a disapproving look. "I wish I'd known
you were coming."

Why? I thought. *So you could bolt?*

She went on. "My boss doesn't like personal visits at
work."

While our visit might seem personal to Adriana, it
was business to us.

Bustamente cut me a look, his eyes flicking to the
cuffs at my waist, telling me to be ready to take her in.
"We'll make it quick," he said. "Miss Valdez, our tech
team was able to trace the profile back through the Internet service provider to determine what system was
used to upload the data."

Her eyes brightened and she seemed to vibrate with
energy, sitting straight up in her rolling chair. Looked
like I wasn't the only eager beaver. "It was Ryan's, wasn't
it? The Wi-Fi at his apartment?"

"No," Bustamente said. "It was not."

Her face clouded in apparent confusion.

"In fact," the detective continued, "the information was entered on the rehab center's system."

Her forehead crinkled and she blinked several times, her head tilting first one way, then the other, like a little bird. She tapped an index finger on her desk. "You're saying he used the system *here* to enter the profile?"

"I'm saying whoever entered the data used this system."

"Wait." She did the blinking-tilting thing again, her eyes narrowing. "You mean someone who works *here* did it?"

"Looks that way," the detective said. He pulled a quartered piece of paper out of his breast pocket, unfolded it, and handed it to her. "Here's their report."

Her eyes scanned the page before she looked up again. "I—I . . ." she stammered. "I can't imagine who it would have been. I mean . . . I—I . . ."

"Miss Valdez," Detective Bustamente said gently. "Be honest with us. Did you enter the profile?"

Her mouth flapped a few times before she ejected from her seat, the rolling chair slamming into the shelves behind her. "No!" she yelled, so loudly the word echoed in the space. If she hadn't wanted to feed the office gossip mill, that scream was not the way to go. "Why in the world would I do something like that?"

Clearly, she was becoming flustered. The detective motioned with his hands for her to sit back down. "Look," he said. "Nothing would surprise us or make us think less of you."

"But I didn't do it!" She looked wildly from his ear to mine to Brigit's, as if hoping one of us would say something, tell her this was all just a bad dream, a mistake, a joke. "I didn't do it!"

"Then how would you explain the fact that the center's Wi-Fi system was used?" he asked.

She shook her head frantically, then stopped and stared at her desk for a few seconds as if racking her brain for a logical answer. A moment later, her head popped up and she threw a hand in the air as if she were in grade school and had the answer to a question. "I know! Or maybe I know. The rehab center uses Interstellar Communications for our Internet and cable. That's the company that Ryan works for. Our system crashed a few weeks ago during a thunderstorm. Our in-house guy couldn't get it back up and it was going to be hours before the service could send a tech out. I thought my boss would be happy if I could help out. I told her that my boyfriend was one of Interstellar's authorized technicians. I called Ryan and he came out right away and got things running."

Bustamente and I looked at each other again. His tight expression told me he was as frustrated as I was. This information could change everything. Just when we thought we'd finally got a break, too.

When Ryan worked on the system, he'd surely had access to whatever codes or passwords were needed to get into the system. And while I knew little about technology, I did know it was possible through various apps and software programs to log into a network remotely. People who worked from home did it all the time, using their company's system even though their physical locations might be miles apart. Heck, the laptops we

Fort Worth PD officers had in our cruisers could connect to the department's main system.

"If you don't believe me," Adriana said, "I can get someone to find the work order and show it to you."

"Do that," Bustamente said.

If there was one thing a rookie cop learned quickly on the job, it was never to take someone automatically at their word, especially if they had skin in the game. Still, I doubted Adriana would have made up this stuff about the service call. It would be too easy to check.

Adriana grabbed her phone and called down to accounting. After telling them what she needed, she was put on hold for a moment. Damned if her face wasn't just a little bit smug.

"Okay," she said into the phone when the person on the other end returned. "Can you e-mail it to me?" She paused a moment. "Okay. Thank you."

She turned to her computer, clicked a few buttons, and maneuvered her mouse. With a flourish, she turned the screen to face us. "There you go."

Sure enough, there on the screen was an Interstellar Communications service report indicating Ryan Downey had performed work to get the system back online after a crash. But did that necessarily mean Ryan had been the one to input the Kinky Cowtown profile? It might not. If nothing else, though, it meant that Adriana could not be definitively identified as the culprit. It also meant we had more work ahead of us.

The detective pointed to the screen. "Can you print that for me?"

"I'd be happy to." She jabbed the buttons on her keypad. A few seconds later, the printer on her desk whirred to life, spitting out the service order. She snatched it from the tray and held it out to the detective as if awarding him a prize.

Bustamente took the report from her, folded it, and tucked it into his pocket. "Thanks for the information, Miss Valdez. We'll let you know if we make any further progress."

She and I exchanged nods before the detective, Brigit, and I left her office.

As we rode back down in the elevator, Bustamente said, "I'm going to speak with their in-house computer guy. See if he can tell me anything more specific."

We checked back in with the receptionist, who made another call and sent us to an office on the first floor. We made our way through a set of swinging doors to a short wing that was at least ten degrees cooler than the other part of the hallway. No doubt this was where the server and other important equipment resided, the lower temperature keeping them cool for best performance. You wouldn't hear me complain. This wing was a welcome respite from the August heat outside.

We found the system administrator in his office. He was a chubby, bearded guy with rectangular glasses. Bustamente handed the guy the printout from our tech department and the man looked it over before consulting his computer. "Nope," he said. "The IP address for the device that was used isn't one of ours. It looks like someone hacked into our system from the outside using their own equipment."

Bustamente cut me a knowing look. Yep, we both

knew who'd have the ability to get into the center's system. *Ryan Downey.* Still, even if we knew it, we'd need to be able to prove it.

"Can you tell who the equipment belongs to?" I asked.

"No," the man said. "There's not a way for me to discern that." He let out a long, loud breath. "Frankly, this scares the shit out of me. We've got all kinds of confidential data on our system. Medical records. Social Security numbers. If the hacker harvested any of that information we could have a major security breach on our hands."

"For what it's worth," Bustamente said, "we don't think that's what happened. We think the system was only used to upload some content to an adult dating site."

"I hope you're right," the guy said, already fiddling around on his computer. "In the meantime, I'm going to have all of the employees change their passwords and take some other precautionary measures."

"Good idea," the detective said. He pulled a business card out of his pocket and laid it on the man's desk, tapping a finger on it. "In case you need to reach me."

"Thanks," the man said without looking away from his computer.

Bustamente and I returned to the cruiser. Once we were seated inside, I turned on the engine, cranked up the AC, and sat back a moment to think. "We know that the computer and phone Ryan turned over to the Fort Worth PD weren't used to access the Kinky Cowtown app, but we don't know what other devices, if any, he had access to." My mind went back to the electronics littering Ryan's floor. He'd had dozens of devices. In fact, hadn't the apartment manager mentioned that Ryan repaired devices on the side? He could have used one of his clients' computers to log into the rehab center's network. I suggested as much to Bustamente.

"I could probably get a search warrant," the detective said, "but it's likely a moot point. If Ryan's the guilty one, he's probably erased any evidence from the device he used or returned it to the client or ditched it in a Dumpster somewhere. Besides, it's still possible, however unlikely, that Adriana was the one who entered the profile. She could've used a device she owned rather than her work computer."

"So where does this leave us?"

"Where?" He said the last thing I wanted to hear. "Right back at square one."

TWENTY-SEVEN
SO MANY HANDS, SO LITTLE TIME

Brigit

Visiting that building had been great! So many people had petted her and stroked her and scratched her. One woman had snuck Brigit a bite of a cookie she'd had in her pocket. Megan hadn't noticed.

If they'd been able to stay longer, the dog might've scored a belly rub. But all's well that ends well. And their visit ended with Megan giving her a liver treat. *Yippee!*

TWENTY-EIGHT

PLAYTIME IS OVER

The Devoted One

The situation had the Devoted One's nerves rankled and offered little satisfaction. These petty acts were child's play. Worse, they hadn't accomplished much, if anything.

Of course the Devoted One realized the cops were keeping a close eye on the two of them. Best to let things settle down a bit, get them to lower their guard. After all, the last thing the Devoted One wanted was to be caught before the goal was achieved.

The goal seemed to be evolving from day to day. Initially, the Devoted One wanted things to be the way they were when the two of them were happy, wanted them to fall back in love, get married, and spend the rest of their lives together. But now? It was hard to say. Sometimes the Devoted One still wanted the love back. But other times the Devoted One only wanted to return the shame and hurt and pain.

How a person could toss love away as if it was garbage

made no sense. Love was a gift. It was meant to be appreciated.

If someone is too stupid to realize that, maybe they're too stupid to live.

TWENTY-NINE
DINNER DATE

Megan

Brigit gave me ample notice of Seth's arrival at my house on Sunday, barking up a storm at the living room window and dashing to the door. I opened it before he even had a chance to knock, finding him ascending to the porch, still wearing his fatigues from reserve duty. *Damn if this guy doesn't make camouflage look sexy.*

I leaned against the jamb. "Hey, soldier."

He reached out a hand to play with a lock of my hair, which was hanging loose, the way he liked it. "I'm shipping out tomorrow," he teased, a sly smile slinking across his face. "Want to show a poor guy one last good time?"

"Nice try," I told him. "But we've got a cookout first."

I leashed up Brigit and led her to Seth's Nova, where we loaded her into the backseat. We drove to the grocery store and took her inside. Though I was wearing a summery dress rather than my police uniform, I'd made sure Brigit had her police vest on and that my badge was in my purse in case anyone gave us any guff about bringing her into the place.

We loaded the cart with all the fixings for a cookout, as well as a six-pack of beer and a bottle of moscato. When Brigit tugged me down the pet food aisle, we added a box of crunchy, bone-shaped dog biscuits to the basket as well. As we passed the small in-house floral shop, I grabbed a potted pink orchid. Maybe a brightly colored plant would help keep the mood bright.

Fully stocked now, we headed to the house where Seth and his mother lived with his grandfather. Their place sat in the Morningside neighborhood, a few blocks east of I-35. Like the home I'd grown up in, theirs was hardly the kind of house one would see featured in *Better Homes & Gardens*, unless it was the before picture in an article about a major remodel. It was a small house that comprised a patchwork of building materials, including gray siding, chipped orange brick, and mismatched shingles. The garage had been enclosed to make more living space. A large live oak shaded the front yard, rendering the space too dark for grass to grow.

We let Brigit out of the back and she hopped down onto the dirt. Seth grabbed the bags, while I rounded up the orchid. I followed Seth to the porch. The hinges gave off a creak as he pulled open the ancient screen door. He put his hand on the knob of the front door but hesitated a moment, as if mustering his strength before opening it.

We walked into a dark living room. The curtains on the front window were closed, only a sliver of sunlight sneaking into the space, illuminating a line of mottled shag carpet that should have been replaced decades ago.

The walls were covered in dark wood paneling. A man who looked like a much older version of Seth sat in a threadbare corduroy recliner, clear tubes running from the oxygen tank beside him up to his nose. He glanced up from the television as we stepped inside, but issued no greeting.

With Blast leading the way, Seth's mother, Lisa, swept into the room, coming over to welcome us. While the dogs tussled playfully at our feet, Lisa took my free hand in both of hers. "So good to see you again, Megan!"

She might have been a lousy mother, but the fact that she'd given birth to Seth at the tender age of fifteen made me cut her quite a bit of slack. She'd still been a child herself at that point. And no matter what had happened in the past, it was clear she was trying to make up for it now, if only Seth would let her. But time is said to heal all wounds, right? I hoped the old adage would prove true.

I gave her a smile. "Good to see you, too, Lisa." I held out the orchid. "This is for you."

Her face broke into a broad smile as she took the plant from me. "It's beautiful! How thoughtful of you. This is the perfect thing to brighten up the room." She placed it on a low bookshelf near the front windows and pulled the curtains open, letting more light into the space. "There. That's better." She turned to her father, Seth's grandfather. "Dad, why don't you introduce yourself?"

She was obviously trying to get the coot to show some manners, but he just as obviously didn't give a rat's ass whether or not he was being cordial. "Why should I introduce myself?" he snapped. "You just called me Dad. She knows who I am."

Even though he'd been less than friendly, I stepped over to his chair and extended my hand. "Nice to meet you."

He eyed my hand and scowled, but took it anyway and gave it one quick shake.

"What would you like me to call you?" I asked.

"My name's Oliver," he grumbled.

Lisa stepped closer. "His friends call him Ollie."

Seth snorted. "What friends?"

The man's head snapped in Seth's direction and he skewered his grandson with a look. "I've got friends. Harry and Leonard from my old regiment."

"And when's the last time you saw them?" Seth asked. "In 2001?"

Something flashed in Oliver's eyes, an emotion that looked like equal parts anger and pain. *Painger.*

Lisa waved her hands as if to dispel the tension. "What did you two pick up for dinner?"

"Burger stuff," Seth said. "We figured we could cook out on the grill."

Oliver's mouth fell open. "We haven't used the grill since—"

"2001," Seth said again. "Last time we cooked out was two months before Grandma died. She roasted corn in the husk. Put a lot of butter and lemon pepper on it. Best corn I've ever tasted."

"You don't have to tell *me* how good it was!" Oliver barked, though despite his tone his expression now bore far more pain than anger. A decade and a half had passed since her death and he still grieved his wife. It was both heartwarming and heartbreaking at the same time.

"Let's go set up," Seth said, continuing with the bags toward the kitchen. His mother and the dogs followed him.

When Oliver turned his attention back to the TV, I said, "Come on outside with us."

"Why should I? I always eat right here in my chair."

"Because your son bought your favorite beer," I said. "Just for you."

When he made no move to get up, I grabbed the handle of his oxygen tank and began to wheel it toward the kitchen.

"Hey!" he hollered after me, grabbing at the air tubes that connected him to the oxygen. "You take that tank and I can't breathe!"

I stopped and shot him a pointed look over my shoulder. "Then you better g-get out of that chair and come with me."

His mouth fell open and he sputtered. "You can't talk to me that way in my own home!"

"Quit being stubborn and I won't have to." I motioned for him to follow me. "C'mon. It'll be fun."

He frowned and muttered a few choice words under his breath, but he seemed to realize I wouldn't take no for an answer. He pushed himself up out of the chair and trailed along behind me.

We made our way through a bright orange kitchen that would've felt right at home on the set of *The Brady Bunch*, and exited a sliding glass door onto the back patio. Seth and Lisa looked over, seemingly surprised to see Oliver coming along with me.

Seth's grandfather plopped himself down in a rusty aluminum lawn chair. "Can I have my air back now? Or is that too much to ask?"

I rolled the tank over and positioned it next to him. "There you go."

He cast me a scathing look and turned to Seth. "Your girl is bossy."

"I know," Seth agreed, sending a discreet grin my way. "But at least she's a looker."

Oliver didn't say much more while Seth fired up the grill and cooked the burgers and Lisa and I prepared plates with heaping helpings of sides. The dogs chased each other around and wrangled in the dry grass of the backyard, occasionally circling by to check on the progress of the burgers and drool in anticipation. When everything was ready, Lisa handed a plate to Oliver and she, Seth, and I took our seats.

We dug into the food. While the three of them seemed content to eat in silence, a quiet family meal was absolutely foreign to me. The table at the Luz home might be noisy, but it was a healthy noise. This silence was straight-up dysfunctional.

Looks like it's up to me to keep the conversation going.

I stuck with light topics. The weather. Texas Rangers baseball. The Lollipop Bandit. Oliver said little, but at least he was no longer being nasty. The dogs made the rounds among us, begging for scraps with a *woof* or a paw on the knee. I noticed Oliver was generous with Blast and Brigit, sharing at least half of his burger with them. He couldn't be all bad then, could he?

After we ate, Lisa and I carried the dishes inside to

the sink and stored the leftovers in the fridge, while Seth scraped the grill and his grandfather sat outside, finishing his bottle of beer.

Lisa put the plug in the sink and began to fill it with hot water, adding a squeeze of dish soap. As the sink filled and the bubbles rose, she glanced out the window that overlooked the backyard, her gaze taking in her father and her son. "I can't believe you got my father to come outside. He lives in that recliner, even sleeps in it some nights." She turned and looked at me now, her eyes misty. "You've been really good for Seth, Megan. You might be good for all of us."

I found myself too choked up to respond. Before I would have been able to anyway, the dogs came to the glass door and barked, wanting in. I slid the door open and they aimed right for the water bowl, lapping up water like they'd never get enough.

When it was time for Seth to take me and Brigit home, I gave Lisa a hug. "It was great to see you again."

She hugged me tight. "You, too."

I stepped over to the recliner, where Oliver had once again planted himself.

He looked up at me. "I'm not a hugger."

I held up my hands in surrender. "I won't force one on you." No sense pushing too hard too fast. I reached out and gave his arm a soft squeeze. Oliver tensed at my touch, going rigid as steel, as if it had been a long time since he'd received any physical affection. He'd be a tough nut to crack, but I was determined to do whatever I could to break through his shell.

I released him and stepped back. "I hope to see you again soon."

He didn't return the sentiment, but he didn't scold me for touching him, either. I'd take that as progress.

More than two weeks passed without incident. Not a single call had come in from Ryan or Adriana. The security patrolman phoned me once to say he'd seen a blond woman leave Ryan's unit at a very late hour, but it could very well have been Danielle. I swung by but saw nothing suspicious. Ryan's car and work truck were both in the parking lot, and the lights were out in his apartment.

Yep, like the Lollipop Bandit, the two seemed to be lying low. Maybe whichever one of them was pulling the stupid stunts had got everything out of their system and decided to turn their attention elsewhere. A big part of me hoped that would be the case. Another part of me wondered whether I'd ever feel a sense of closure if the stalking simply stopped and no arrest was ever made. When a serial killer hasn't murdered anyone in a while, law enforcement never knew what it meant. Had the killer died? Moved away? Suffered a debilitating injury or health condition that prevented the killer from committing another murder? Or was he or she working behind the scenes, plotting and planning an even more heinous crime?

Not knowing was unsettling.

It was near the end of August now, and I was working the swing shift this week. Swing shift wasn't so bad. It started at 4 P.M. and ran until 1 A.M. That gave me the daytime to run errands, do chores at the house, or train with Brigit. I'd done errands and chores yesterday, so today I chose training.

K-9s had critical skills for certain situations and were a vital tool in law enforcement. Nonetheless, those skills were not put to constant use, which made training important to keep the K-9 team up to speed when the need arose. Today, Brigit and I were at Forest Park, playing hide-and-seek with a bag of weed I'd checked out of evidence. Seth had the day off, so he and Blast had come along with us. While having another dog in the midst was a distraction for Brigit, it was also helpful. Police K-9s had to learn to work and focus despite distractions.

The sky was overcast today, but you'd get no complaints from us. The clouds kept the sun at bay, and the temperature was a bearable 86 degrees rather than the usual upper nineties or low one hundreds.

While Seth held on to Brigit's leash, I ventured into the wooded area, looking for a place to hide the dope. My stomach involuntarily clenched as I walked past the spot where I'd found a dead body a few months ago. To say the man's face had been pulverized would be an understatement. The image was the type of thing nightmares were made of, and would be forever seared into my memory.

Forcing myself to move on, I found a tree with a low branch and used it to hoist myself higher up. I tucked the bag of weed into a crook about nine feet high and dropped back to the ground. Lest Brigit simply track my steps to this spot, I hurriedly ran back and forth and round and round in the general area to mix things up before exiting the woods farther down and circling back to Seth and the dogs.

"You're up, girl!" I told her. I issued the order for her to scent for drugs.

She lifted her snout into the air and worked her nose, her nostrils twitching. *Sniff-sniff.* With the rest of us following along, she set off, sometimes stopping and lifting her nose again, then taking off in a slightly different direction. She ventured into the woods, her nose continuing to quiver. With her head lifted high, she appeared to be prancing as she trotted along. But while she might look as if she were playing around, she was actually hard at work.

She sped up as the scent grew stronger. She sniffed and sniffed and eventually circled the tree where I'd planted the weed, rising up on one leg on the trunk to verify that, yep, the drugs were up the tree. With one final sniff she plunked her butt down on the ground and looked up into the tree, issuing her passive alert.

I grabbed the limb and pulled myself up, snagging the bag of weed. "Good girl!" I told Brigit, giving her an energetic scratch and a couple of liver treats. Though he'd done nothing to earn it, other than being a sweetie, Blast got a liver treat, too.

A trio of teenage boys wandered by, throwing sticks and rocks. One of them looked at the bag in my hand, "Is that weed?"

I was dressed in civilian clothes, but I could make an arrest if needed. "You looking to score?"

He looked me up and down, then glanced over at Brigit, apparently putting two and two together and realizing I could be a cop. Any offer to buy the drug from me would land his butt in booking. He was smarter than he looked. "No, man!" he said. "I'm not trying to make a buy. I was just curious, that's all."

I gave him a pointed look and a suspicious *mm-hm.* "You sure about that?"

The boys muttered among themselves and hurried on.

Once they were gone, Seth chuckled. "I think you scared 'em."

"I *hope* I scared them. They've got no business with weed."

After having Brigit find the drugs two more times, we moved on to tracking exercises. Seth hid on the far side of the swimming pool. Brigit got on his trail and found him in no time. Next he hid at the far end of the zoo's parking lot. She found him there, too. The three boys came around again to watch. If they were dabbling in drugs, maybe seeing how interesting police work could be would turn them around, entice them to be on the right side of law enforcement. "Want to join in?" I asked them.

"Hell, yeah!" their leader cried.

"Okay," I told him. "You've got two minutes to go somewhere and hide. My dog will come find you."

Seth gave them an "on your mark, get set, go!" The boys took off running into the woods. I watched the timer app on my phone. When the two minutes were up and the alert sounded, I gave Brigit the command to trail the disturbance.

I followed along after her as she tracked the boys, her nose to the ground. She snuffled around, at one point sniffing around the base of a tree and putting a paw up on it as she sniffed the air around its lower limbs. I'd bet dollars to doughnuts the boys had climbed the tree in an attempt to throw her off. She lowered her head and found their trail again, trotting along at a good clip with me trotting after her.

She found the boys hunkered down behind a berm on the bank of the Trinity River. When she found them, she looked up at me as if to say, *Treat me, Megan.*

"You got one smart dog, lady!" one of the boys said.

"Thanks," I replied on Brigit's behalf, giving her another liver treat.

The boys asked if they could give her a treat, too. I handed each of them one treat. They tossed them into the air, laughing as she rose onto her hind legs to catch them and gobble them down.

After we'd trained for a couple of hours, we were hot and sweaty and sunbaked and nearly done for. Brigit's and Blast's ears perked up and they looked to the parking lot. It was another few seconds before my inferior human ears heard tinny music. A white truck with a snow cone painted on the side pulled to the curb. People streamed over to get a cold treat.

"I could go for a snow cone," Seth said. "How about you?"

I sure could. Hot as I was, I wouldn't mind a couple scoops of ice to stick in my bra, as well.

We walked over to the truck and read over the numerous flavor options listed on the menu. When it was our turn, I stepped up to the window. "Blue raspberry, please."

The server at the window turned to Seth. "What about you?"

"Give me a cherry snow cone," Seth said. "I like the classics."

When the man noticed the dogs wagging their tails down below, he threw in two plain balls of ice for free. The dogs had fun rolling the balls around with their noses and crunching them up with their teeth.

Brigit and I parted ways with Seth and Blast around 3 P.M. That gave me just enough time to shower and dress for my shift.

My fluffy partner and I cruised around W1, circling through the Mistletoe Heights neighborhood, rolling on through Berkeley Place, continuing on to University Park. We slowly cruised the medical district, keeping a keen eye out for a man in scrubs armed with a grape Tootsie Roll Pop. *Nothing*. Had the Lollipop Bandit given up his life of crime? Or had he simply been more careful when he snagged the suckers and thus avoided being spotted committing his crimes?

Around five, rush hour began and the streets got busier. A fender-bender on Berry took up half an hour, as I wrote a report and directed oncoming traffic around the cars. A driver checking out the accident inadvertently swerved too close and nearly sideswiped me.

"Watch it!" I yelled after him.

Once the tow trucks had hauled off the cars, Brigit and I set back out on the streets. While Texas Christian University had its own police department, I decided to take a cruise through the campus and revisit some of the spots from a recent undercover drug case I'd worked there. Over there was the dorm I'd lived in. Beyond that was the library where I'd pretended to study while actually spying on the students I suspected could be dealing Molly. Another turn and I was driving past the common area where the students had snagged free nachos after Essie Espinoza, an aspiring senatorial candidate, had given a rousing speech. *Good times.*

I pulled into a spot reserved for law enforcement so Brigit could take a potty break in one of the grassy areas. After she'd relieved herself, a group of students came over to say hello. Brigit wagged her tail as they approached.

"Are you two the cops who broke up the Molly ring?" asked a boy in a ball cap featuring the university's horned frog mascot.

"Yep," I said. "That's us." *Living legends.*

"Can I get a picture with you?"

"Sure."

He handed his phone to one of the other students to take the pic. I stepped into place next to him and ordered Brigit to sit at our feet.

Click.

"Can I get one, too?" another student asked.

"Of c-course."

We spent the next couple of minutes taking pictures with the students. While I certainly didn't go into police work to become some type of celebrity, I had to admit it was nice to feel appreciated. Of course I knew the students would have been unlikely to recognize me without Brigit by my side and that she was the true star of the show. But I was fine with being her human sidekick.

We bade good-bye to the kids and headed back to our cruiser. On the way, a familiar voice called our names. "Megan! Brigit!"

We turned to see a boy with dark curls, his hand raised in greeting. *Hunter.* He lived in the same dorm where Brigit and I had lived when working undercover on the drug case. If I'd been five years younger and un-attached, I could've had a huge crush on the kid. He was cute, sweet, and smart, not to mention a dog lover. Everything a girl could want in a boyfriend.

I gave him a smile as he approached, while Brigit greeted him with a wagging tail and a happy *woof!* "How's it going, Hunter?"

He returned my smile and shrugged. "Can't complain. A little less exciting without you two around, though."

Aww. Darn if I didn't feel my cheeks heat up. "Everyone behaving themselves at the dorm?"

"Heck, yeah," he said. "There are rumors that another undercover cop is living there. Nobody knows who it might be." He arched a brow. "Care to share any inside information?"

I knew there was nobody from Fort Worth PD currently working undercover at TCU, but might as well let the students think it anyway. Anything that kept them from doing stupid, dangerous things, right? "Sorry, Hunter. My lips are sealed."

At the mention of my lips, his gaze flickered to my mouth before returning to my eyes. "I better run," he said. "I've got a study session for an exam. It was great seeing you."

"Right back at ya."

As he turned and walked away, my inner twenty-year-old coed heaved a sappy sigh.

Having stretched our legs, Brigit and I returned to the cruiser. As we exited the TCU campus, my cell phone rang. It was Adriana.

"Ryan's following me!" she shrieked.

"Where are you?"

"In my car," she said. "I'm heading north on McCart, almost to Park Hill."

I punched the gas but didn't turn on my lights or siren. The siren and lights would only warn Ryan I was coming, give him a chance to perform an evasive maneuver. So far, I hadn't been able to catch either Adriana or Ryan in the act of committing a crime, which was the primary reason I'd been unable to make an arrest. There hadn't been enough concrete evidence against either of them to prove which one was the stalker. Now, I had the chance to catch Ryan red-handed. I'd always suspected he was the guilty party. That is, when I wasn't suspecting it was Adriana.

"Is he in his work truck or the Camaro?" I asked.

"His work truck."

"Is he right behind you?"

"No, he's two or three cars back," she said. "I think he's trying not to be noticed."

"I'm on my way. Stay on the line and tell me each move you make."

"Okay. I'm turning left on Park Hill now."

"Where are you headed?" I asked.

"I was on my way to the grocery store, but now I'm afraid to stop. I don't know what he might do if I get out of my car."

I didn't know, either. She was much safer if she kept moving until I arrived on the scene. "Just keep driving. I'll get him."

I sped east on McPherson, hooked a left to go north on Green Avenue, and intercepted the two there. Adriana's beige Accent rolled by just as I reached the corner. She turned her head my way and raised her fingers from the steering wheel to let me know she'd seen me, but she kept driving. Not ten seconds later, Ryan drove past in his truck. He was so focused on the road ahead he failed to notice me. *Dumbass.*

I pulled out behind him and turned on my lights. *Do you see me now?*

His head angled upward as he checked his rearview mirror and spotted me behind him. His brake lights came on and he slowed, pulling over to the right and coming to a stop.

"I'm pulling him over," I told Adriana as I eased to the curb behind his truck. "You go on. I'll call you back later."

I left Brigit in the car with the windows down as I exited and strolled up to Ryan's window.

"Hey, Officer Luz," he said. "Was I speeding or something?"

I gave him a pointed look. "You know exactly what you were doing, Ryan. And so do I."

He looked away before turning back to me, his face hard. "So you know I was going to meet Adriana?"

Meet? "That's not exactly how I'd put it. You were following her."

"She's up there somewhere?"

"Yes," I said. "You followed her on three different turns."

He raised his hands off the steering wheel in innocence. "I don't know what to tell you. I didn't realize she was ahead of me. All I know is she went to Toby's day camp today and told him to tell me that if I wanted my

Wonder Woman #1 comic book I should meet her at a Mexican restaurant we used to go to."

"Is that true?" I asked. "Or are you just making up a story because I caught you here?"

"It's true!" He frowned, fuming, his face turning red with rage. "That comic's worth a shitload of money, and you police have done jack shit about getting it back for me! I didn't want to see that crazy bitch ever again, but I want my comic book! You can't blame me for agreeing to meet her."

Once again I couldn't prove the guy was lying to me. Heck, I didn't even know if he was, in fact, lying. Maybe he was telling the truth. *This case is really chapping my ass.*

I pulled out my cell phone. "What's your brother's number? I want to talk to Toby. See if he backs up your story."

Ryan smirked. "He will."

As Ryan rattled off his brother's cell number, I dialed it on my phone. When an adult male answered, I identified myself and said, "May I speak with Toby, please?"

"He's playing in his room. Give me a second."

I waited for a brief moment before Toby came on the line. "Hello?"

"Hi, Toby," I said, trying to sound as pleasant as possible. "This is Megan Luz. I'm the police officer who came to your uncle's door with my dog a while back. Remember us?"

"Mm-hm. Your dog is fluffy."

"She sure is. Hey, can you tell me what happened at day camp today?"

"It was fun!" he said brightly. "We did scooter races in the gym and they gave us Popsicles."

While I was glad he'd had a good time, this information was not exactly what I'd been looking for. "Did anyone come to see you at camp?"

"No."

"No?" I glanced over at Ryan, raising accusatory brows. "So nobody said anything to you about your uncle Ryan and his comic book?"

"A girl did."

My accusatory brows fell back into place. "A girl? But she didn't come to see you at camp?"

"She was across the street," he said, which evidently to his young mind meant she had not come to camp. *Interrogating kids is hard!*

Rather than ask Toby more questions he might misinterpret, I decided to let him take the lead. "Tell me what happened with this girl."

"Okay," he said. "When it's pickup time we get to go out and play on the playground until our parents come to get us. There was a girl across the street and she called my name. I went to the fence and she said for me to tell my uncle Ryan she had his comic book and to meet her at their taco place at seven o'clock. She made me say it back to her three times to make sure I got it right. When my dad picked me up I told him, and then my dad called Uncle Ryan and told him, too."

Either the kid was telling the truth, or Ryan's brother had been pulled into this mess, along with his son. Children would say just about anything their parents told them to. I'd learned that pretty early on. *Child:*

Daddy's not home. Me: So that's not his foot sticking out from under your bed? Poor kids, caught in the middle, trying to do what was right but not knowing what that was. But would Ryan go so far as to implicate his brother and nephew in a stalking scheme? It seemed a little far-fetched.

"What did the girl look like?" I asked Toby.

"She had long yellow hair," he said.

Had it been Adriana in a wig? The same wig she might have used to try to gain access to Ryan's apartment? "What kind of clothes was she wearing?"

"I don't remember."

"Anything else you can tell me about her? Did you see her car, maybe? Or where she went after she talked to you?"

"I don't 'member anything else," he said.

"Okay. Thanks, Toby. Bye-bye, sweetie." I ended the call and turned to Ryan. "I'm going to give you the benefit of the doubt and let you go for now, but I'm going to talk to the people at the Southside Rec Center, check their security cameras, see if they back up your story."

Ryan's eyes narrowed. "How'd you know where Toby went to day camp?"

"You shared a picture of him on your Facebook page."

Ryan's brows rose. "You looked at my Facebook page?"

"I did what any competent investigator would do," I said. "You made your posts public." *In other words, you've got nobody to blame but yourself if you feel like your privacy has been violated.*

He shook his head, but he seemed to be shaking it at himself. "I should've realized Adriana would look at my page, too. That must've been how she figured out where Toby would be."

"Change your settings," I suggested. "In the meantime, go on home and stay put for the night."

He scowled. "You gonna tell Adriana the same thing?"

"I will. But don't you even think about going to her place to try to get that comic book. She may not even have it."

He turned red with rage again and huffed. "This is ridiculous! You keep acting like I'm the bad guy when it's her! *She's* the one who tried to choke *me*, remember? I'm the one with the protective order."

I raised a conciliatory palm. "Look, all I want is for you to be careful, okay? The two of you are toxic to each other. Maybe you should think about moving to another part of town, avoiding the places you two used to go."

"That's not a bad idea," he said on an exhale, resignation in his voice. "My rent's going up anyway."

Good. Maybe he'd move farther away and the two of them would never cross paths again.

I returned to my cruiser and drove to the Southside Recreation Center. I let Brigit take a quick tinkle and sniff around the grounds while my eyes scanned the building for outdoor security cameras. *Aha!* One was discreetly mounted under the eaves and was aimed out over the playground area. *Good.* Maybe I'd finally get some irrefutable evidence of wrongdoing here and get to put this case to rest once and for all. Of course, with the way my luck had been going lately, the camera would be another phony like the one at the party supply store.

I led Brigit inside and checked in with the receptionist, who paged the evening supervisor. When he stepped up to the desk, I introduced myself and my partner. "Could we take a look at the security camera footage from this afternoon? There was an alleged incident on the playground that I'm looking into."

He looked taken aback. "I haven't heard about any incident. Did a child get hurt?"

"No. It's nothing that would bring liability on the center. One of the day campers told me a woman spoke to him when he was on the playground at the end of the day. She's a person of interest in one of my cases. I want to see if the camera picked her up."

He looked relieved, but only slightly. Surely it was disconcerting to know a potential criminal suspect had been lurking about the center he was responsible for. "Come back to my office and we can take a look."

A few minutes later, Brigit was sniffing around the baseboards in the man's office while he and I huddled behind his desk, forwarding through video footage. As I watched, a group of about fifteen children from the day camp program streamed out onto the playground, each heading for their favorite play equipment. While two other kids elbowed each other as both tried to be first on the monkey bars, Toby ran for the swings. Watching him swing back and forth at six times speed was dizzying. When he'd had his fill of the swing, he leaped off and climbed onto the playscape, zipping down the slide headfirst at warp speed.

The man frowned. "The counselors are supposed to make sure they don't do that. They could get a concussion."

The two counselors, both of whom were girls who appeared to be in their teens, sat at a picnic table, absorbed in their cell phones, paying little attention to their charges.

The man grunted. "Those two will be watching this footage tomorrow."

A moment later, Toby turned his head to look at something off screen.

I flapped my hand at the screen. "There! Can you slow it down now?"

The man grabbed his mouse and clicked on the icon that controlled the speed, slowing it down to actual time. As we watched, Toby walked over to the edge of the playground and stopped at the plastic edging that ran around it, holding in the wood chips used to soften the ground in the event a child fell. He stood there for a moment, staring through the wrought-iron fence at something off camera and saying nothing. A few seconds later, his lips began to move. Though I didn't read lips and couldn't tell exactly what he was saying, it appeared from the shape of his mouth that he'd repeated the same thing three times, exactly like he'd told me the woman had instructed him to do. As this exchange took place, the counselors never once looked up. They'd be useless in helping me identify the woman.

"Are there any cameras that would show who the boy is speaking with?"

"Sorry," the man said. "Looks like she was across the street. The cameras only show the rec center property. People don't like it when security cameras record anything on their private property, especially if the cameras are operated by a government facility. Big Brother and all that."

I thanked the man and led Brigit outside and across the street, aiming for the point where it appeared Toby had been looking. Two kids, one on a skateboard and another on a bike, sped past on the sidewalk, while a woman with a baby in a stroller approached from down the block. There was no telling how many people might have gone down this sidewalk since Toby had spoken with the blonde hours earlier. Still, it was worth a try.

I issued Brigit the order for her to trail. She sniffed around for a moment, looked up at me as if to say there was no fresh disturbance, and tried again. Eventually she began to walk slowly in one direction, as if she'd found a weak scent. She led me down a residential side street before stopping and plunking herself down on her hindquarters. If she'd been tracking the blonde, and I wasn't entirely sure she had been, this must have been the point where the woman got into her car. I looked around. Unfortunately, there were no security cameras in sight.

None of the windows on the two closest houses faced this direction, but I decided to try them anyway. I spoke to the occupants, but none recalled having seen a blond woman on the street or a car parked along the curb whcrc I pointed.

"I keep all the blinds closed in summer," one of the women told me. "Otherwise I can hardly afford my air-conditioning bill."

Sighing, I led Brigit back to the cruiser and opened her enclosure. She hopped in, plopped down, and began mouthing a chew toy. I climbed into the driver's seat and drove to Adriana's house, not at all looking forward to what was sure to be another frustrating conversation for both of us.

I left Brigit in the squad car as I went up to Adriana's door and knocked. I told her what Ryan and Toby had told me, and told her about the security-camera footage at the rec center. "The kid talked to someone. Ryan is convinced it was you."

She gasped. "So you believe *him*? Instead of *me*?"

I fought the urge to scream *I don't know who or what to believe!* It was all I could do not to grab her by the shoulders and try to shake the truth out of her. "What I believe, Miss Valdez, is that both of you need to do your best to steer clear of each other."

She harrumphed. "Thanks a lot."

How the hell did I end up in the middle of this lovers' squabble? "Look," I said. "I'm glad you called me tonight and I'll do what I can to keep you safe. But you've got to help me help you, okay? Avoid anyplace you two used to go, anywhere he might be. Do everything you can to stay away from the guy."

She sighed but said, "Okay. I will."

Finally, someone being reasonable. Hallelujah!

Thursday night, I cruised W1, making several rounds by Adriana's house and Ryan's apartment. While Adriana's car was parked in her driveway, both Ryan's Camaro and work truck had been gone all evening. Where was he? Was he out on a date with Danielle? Maybe another woman? Out with the guys watching a sports game somewhere? And if he was driving one of his vehicles, who was driving the other?

My mind continued to mull over the possibilities. Ryan could be behind everything that had happened. Statistically speaking, he was the more likely culprit. He didn't seem to have a good sense of boundaries when it came to personal interactions and relationships. The blonde at his apartment and the one at the rec center could have been someone he hired in an attempt to frame Adriana. On the other hand, Adriana could just as easily be the guilty one. She was an odd duck, difficult to read. She didn't seem to have many people in her life, so the loss of a relationship might have hit her especially hard. Either way, these stunts seemed like a lot of trouble to go to just to goad someone into a conversation or get back at them. But obsessive people were willing to go to great lengths to achieve their aims.

It was half past midnight when Adriana phoned me again, her voice frantic. "Ryan's following me again! He's right behind me this time!"

"Where are you?"

"Rosedale, heading east. I just passed Jerome Street."

"Stay on the line," I told her as I jammed on the gas. "I'll be there in under a minute."

Given that it was late on a weeknight, there were few cars on the road. I sped up Eighth Avenue and was approaching from the other direction when I saw head-lights ahead. Their movement indicated that the car in the inner lane was trying to force the one in the outer lane over. *Holy shit! Is he trying to run her off the road?*

I turned on my lights and siren and was on them in an instant. I pulled into the oncoming lane, angling my car to force them both to a stop, and grabbed the mic for my public address system. "Get out of your car with your hands up! Now!"

He did as he was told, though he made a point of rev-ving his engine first. *VROOOOOM!*

Sheesh. Grow up, you arrogant imbecile.

He climbed out of his car, leaving the engine running and the driver's door open. *Is he going to try to get back in and take off? Maybe run me over in the process?* No way would I get out of my cruiser until another officer was on the scene to help me.

I grabbed my radio to call dispatch. "Backup needed." I gave my location. Picking my cell phone back up, I said, "Stay in your car, Adriana." Keeping a close eye on Ryan, I sat back to wait.

Squinting into my headlights, Ryan turned his raised hands palms up. "Is that you, Officer Luz?" he called.

I pressed the button on the mic. "Yes."

With his hands still raised, he pointed the right one in the direction of Adriana's car. "She followed me! She was trying to run me off the road! I was only trying to defend myself!"

I hadn't seen the entire interaction between the two of them, but nonetheless, I wasn't buying it. Even if she'd been the one following him, he could've turned left to evade her or made a U-turn to get away.

In less than a minute, Officer Spalding pulled up behind the two cars. Now that my backup was here, I climbed out of my car.

As I walked up to Ryan, he began to lower his arms.

"Keep 'em up!" I barked.

"But it's starting to hurt!"

"Try bending your elbows a little."

After turning off the Camaro and removing the keys from the ignition, I stepped aside and, in a lowered voice, gave Spalding a quick update. "You remember when I called you a few weeks ago about the brick incident? These two were the ones involved. There have been multiple incidents since then. Detective Bustamente and I have been working the case, but we can't tell who's at fault, or whether one of them might be trying to frame the other. It's a huge mess. This is the second time Ms. Valdez has called me this week about being followed by Mr. Downey. I don't know how the whole thing started, but I saw him swerve and try to force her off the road."

Spalding, being a man of muscles and not words, lifted his chin in acknowledgment.

"Would you keep an eye on him while I speak with Ms. Valdez and search his car?"

He replied with another chin lift and stepped into position a few feet away from Ryan, his hands near his belt, sending the clear message *Try anything and I'll put a bullet in your kneecap.*

I circled around to Adriana's car. Her driver's side fender was less than two inches from Ryan's cockeyed

Camaro. It was a miracle the two hadn't collided. With so little space between the cars, I had to move to the passenger window to get close enough to speak with her.

She rolled the glass down when she saw me peering in. She was dressed in a pair of khaki shorts, an off-white T-shirt, and white flip-flops. The woman seemed to have a serious aversion to color. She wore no makeup and, though her hair was brushed, it was clear it had not been recently styled. Her face was tight with anxiety, her eyes filled with unshed tears, her lips quivery. Her hands gripped her steering wheel as if hanging on for dear life. I noticed her shoulders trembling, too. Needless to say, she was terrified. I also noticed that the inside of her car was immaculate. No loose change, hair bands, or crumpled fast-food napkins in the console. No travel mug or water bottle forgotten in the cup holder. No leftover parking receipts on the dash. Adriana was the queen of the neatniks.

"What happened?" I asked.

"Ryan tried to kill me!" She broke down into an all-out cry, covering her face with her hands and sobbing into them.

I gave her some time to get her emotions out. When she seemed to have calmed a bit, I asked, "Can you tell me how you two ended up out here?"

She sniffled and grabbed a tissue from her purse, which was beige, of course.

"I woke up about an hour ago not feeling well." She sniffled and dabbed at her nose. "I have a horrible migraine. I get them every once in a while. I didn't realize until I looked in my bathroom drawer that I was out of Excedrin. There's no way I'd be able to sleep without it, so I threw on some clothes and left to go to the twenty-four-hour pharmacy. I was on my way when I realized Ryan was following me again."

"So he followed you from your house?"

"I don't think so. I didn't see any headlights behind me until I'd been driving for a couple of minutes. He pulled up beside me at a light and honked his horn to get my attention. When I looked over, he was—" She spewed another quick sob before finishing her sentence. "He was pointing a gun at me!"

Holy shit.

I'd been afraid things would escalate, and they certainly had. Knowing Ryan had a gun made me glad I'd called for backup and hadn't gotten out of my car until Spalding arrived. If I'd done otherwise, I might have been smoked.

"Stay in your car," I told her. "I'm going to talk to him."

I went back around the cars and stood in front of Ryan. "Got a weapon on you?"

"No."

I looked him up and down but saw no suspicious bulges. "Adriana said you pointed a gun at her when you were stopped at a traffic light."

At that, Spalding arched a brow and unsnapped his police holster, giving himself easier access to his weapon should he need it.

"Adriana's a fucking liar!" Ryan cried. "Besides, how could she even see into my car? It's got tinted windows."

I glanced over at his car. The windows were dark, probably the darkest legal shade a person could have on their vehicle. But that didn't mean anything. "She could have seen into your car if you had the window down."

"I didn't!" he insisted. "My windows were up!"

While Spalding watched, I patted Ryan down. He was clean. "You can put your arms down now," I told him.

He lowered them and rubbed first one shoulder, then the other.

"Tell me what was happening out here."

"Adriana came after me," he said. "I took Danielle out to a movie tonight, and after I dropped her off at her place I realized I was being followed. I'm pretty sure Adriana has followed us before but I could never be sure. Every time I slowed down to see if it was her she'd turn off. Tonight, she pulled up next to me at a light and unrolled her window and started screaming that I was a cheater and a liar and didn't deserve to live. When the light turned green and I tried to drive away from her, she kept swerving over like she was trying to hit me."

I gave him a pointed look. "Looked to me like that's what you were doing to her."

"Well, yeah!" he scoffed. "In self-defense!"

Self-defense? "You weren't blocked in by the curb. You could've peeled off."

He said nothing for a second or two before responding with, "I guess I didn't think of that."

Spalding and I exchanged glances that said neither of us was buying Ryan's story. Still, people who were in a panic often did things that weren't reasonable. It was impossible to think straight when your pulse rate had skyrocketed. This could be a real problem for officers in high-stress situations. For that reason, we'd been taught tactical combat breathing at the police academy. Seth had learned the same techniques in the army.

"I'm going to search your car," I told Ryan.

"You can't do that!" He took a step toward me but Spalding put a hand on his chest to stop him.

"I've got probable cause," I told him. "Anything you want to tell me about?"

He said nothing, but the fiery glare in his eyes was so hot it was a wonder it didn't melt me on the spot.

I climbed into the driver's seat and lowered the visor. *Nothing there.* A plastic bottle of Dr Pepper rested in the cup holder, twenty-seven cents in the ashtray. The glove compartment contained the usual registration and insurance papers, as well as the Camaro's owner's manual and a tire gauge. Nothing under either of the front floor mats. I opened the hinged top of the console.

Bingo!

Inside was a small black handgun. It was loaded with a full magazine. I left the gun in the console and climbed back out of the car. "What's the handgun for?"

"Protection!" he yelped. He jerked his head to indicate Adriana. "She keeps trying to get me in trouble. I don't know what that crazy bitch is going to do next!"

Adriana had rolled down her window and heard Ryan's words. "I'm not crazy, you bastard!" she shrieked. "You're the one who's crazy!" She threw her door open to try to get out but with only inches between her car and Ryan's all she succeeded in doing was bashing her door into the side of Ryan's Camaro. *Bam!*

Spalding arched another brow, this time a discreet

one aimed at Adriana that said *You sure you're not crazy?*

Ryan's face exploded in rage. "Watch my car, you stupid bitch!" He tried to take another step, but Spalding put a splayed hand on Ryan's chest and held him back again.

Adriana shoved the door into Ryan's car again. *Bam!*

"Cut it out right now!" I advised Adriana. "Or you'll be in trouble here, too."

We'd have to call another car for transport if we ended up having to take both of them in. If we put the two in the back of Spalding's car together, they were likely to kill each other.

She let loose another sob. "Sorry!" she cried. "I'm just very upset!"

"Take a deep breath," I told her. "Like you do in Pilates."

She nodded, closed both her door and her eyes, and inhaled a long breath.

I turned my attention back to Ryan and his gun. It wasn't illegal for him to own a gun, and under the Texas Motorist Protection Act, a person could carry a loaded handgun in their vehicle, even without a concealed-carry permit, so long as the weapon was out of sight and the person was not engaged in criminal activity. So, my next question was, *Is Ryan engaged in criminal activity here?* In other words, was he stalking Adriana? And if he wasn't, if he was innocent here, why hadn't he told me about the gun?

I turned back to the car and leaned the driver's seat forward. There was nothing in the floorboard behind the seat. Behind the passenger seat, however, there was a plastic bag with the bright orange Home Depot logo on it. I grabbed the bag and pulled it out of the car, setting it on the hood to take a look inside.

My gut clenched and I gasped.

Whoa.

Inside the bag were a roll of duct tape, a package of zip ties, a box cutter, and a bandana, all the necessary tools for an abduction. Heck, someone could package these items together and sell it as a Kidnapper Combo Pack.

"Spalding. Check this out." I pulled out my flashlight and shined it about the items on the hood so my fellow officer could get a better look.

After he took a look at the bag's contents, my co-worker's gaze went from the hood to Ryan. He issued a derisive snort. "A person could do some evil shit with that stuff."

I turned back to Ryan. "Want to tell me what you were planning to do with these things?" *Some of that aforementioned evil shit, perhaps?*

"It's for work," he said. "I use the zip ties and duct tape to keep all the cords gathered and out of the way."

I had expected him to stammer and hesitate and give himself away. I hadn't expected a quick and plausible explanation. Still, while his explanation was plausible, was it an honest explanation, too? Or was it a bold-faced lie? Maybe he'd had the foresight to have a reasonable excuse locked and loaded. "What about the bandana?"

"They come in handy," he said. "For cleaning up and setting my tools on and stuff."

Again, plausible. Still, that gun had thrown me for a loop. I mean, I carried one every day on the job, and sometimes I even took it with me when I was off duty. But when I'd been a civilian I'd never felt the need to own one. Then again, I'd never been involved in a tumultuous relationship. All of my breakups had been relatively clean, involving only a few margaritas or a decadent bar of dark chocolate to get me through. And, hell. Here in Texas guns were nearly as common as cell phones. Seemed almost everyone had one.

"When did you buy the gun?" I asked Ryan. If he'd had it a while, I'd be less suspicious. If he'd bought it recently, it could indicate he'd been planning to take Adriana out tonight.

"Yesterday."

Hmm. "Do you own other guns?" I asked.

"No."

"If you didn't point it at Adriana, then how would she know you had it with you?"

He raised his shoulders nearly to his ears. "Hell if I know! Maybe she followed me to the gun store last night."

That explanation was much more doubtful than his earlier ones. I spoke to Spalding now. "I'm going to have Brigit take a look. See if we missed anything." Of course my partner "looked" with her nose.

Ryan pierced me with his gaze. "If you're talking about drugs, she's not going to find anything. I don't mess with that kind of shit."

"That's a wise decision." *If it's true.* His aggressive behavior could be the result of any number of drugs for which aggression was a side effect. Meth. Crack. Spice, which was a synthetic form of marijuana. Ryan certainly had the skinny build of a drug user. Then again, his behavior tonight could just be anger. His eyes didn't look glazed or dilated, and his speech, though kazoolike, wasn't unusually slow or slurred. Still, better make sure I'd covered all the angles.

I retrieved Brigit from the cruiser and led her over to the Camaro, instructing her to search for drugs. She sniffed around the exterior, paying close attention to the wheel wells, but gave no alert. Inside, she sniffed the floor mats and seats, paying an unusual amount of attention to the gear shift. But in the end she found nothing. "Good job, girl." I gave her a liver treat and a quick scratch under the chin as compensation and returned her to the car.

"Told you she wouldn't find anything," Ryan snapped, his face and voice smug.

I twisted everything around in my head, turning the facts inside out and backward, trying to look at things from every direction. At worst, Ryan had planned to abduct and possibly kill Adriana tonight. At best, he'd driven recklessly, endangering her and others on the road. But maybe she had followed him, maybe she'd tried to run him off the road first, like he'd said. Maybe she was the one at fault here.

Blurgh. I couldn't make up my damn mind! And since I couldn't make up my mind, I decided to consult my second-best decision-making organ. My gut.

My gut said to book him. I hoped my gut wasn't only saying this because it was tired of all the indecision.

I turned to Spalding. He cocked his head in question.

I took a deep breath, hoping I wasn't making the wrong call here, arresting an innocent man who'd been tormented by his crazy ex-girlfriend. I was tempted to mentally run through *eenie, meenie, minie, mo,* or challenge him to a game of rock-paper-scissors. *C'mon, Megan. Be decisive! Your gut said book him, so book him!* I gave Spalding a nod. "Take him in."

Spalding gave me a chin lift in return. "Good call, Luz."

THIRTY
GNAW KNOB

Brigit

The dog would never understand why humans used cow flesh for things like shoes and purses and couches and car knobs. Cow flesh was food! Didn't they know that? She'd smelled cowhide in the car and had to fight the urge to gnaw on the knob it was covered in. She had a feeling Megan wouldn't be too happy with her if she had.

Brigit had also smelled fear pheromones in the car and on the man who'd been driving it. He reeked of them. He must have been terrified. Brigit didn't know what he'd been scared of, but whatever it was had made him fear for his life.

Brigit had smelled other interesting things, too. The familiar scent of the woman who lived at the possum house. She'd smelled her when Megan pulled the woman over in her car. But she'd also scented faint traces of the woman when Megan had taken her to the playground with the cedar chips on the ground. The woman had been across the street a few hours before they'd arrived.

She'd sensed the information would have been important to Megan, but she didn't know exactly how to tell her partner what she smelled. Since she was a mere human, Megan's skills were limited. Though she understood some of the things Brigit tried to communicate to her, she wasn't entirely fluent in dog.

Shortly after they'd searched the car, the two ended their shift and went back home. Brigit could tell something was bothering Megan. Her partner kept tossing and turning in the bed, making it impossible for Brigit to sleep. She finally climbed down from the bed and went to sleep on the sofa in the living room. She found Zoe sprawled across the center of it, her arms and legs stretched out as far as they would go.

Move over, cat. We're sharing the couch tonight.

THIRTY-ONE
COPS AND SLOBBERS

Adriana Valdez, the Devoted One

It had taken everything in her not to burst out laughing when that stupid cop slapped cuffs on Ryan. *That's what you get for leaving me, you bastard!*

That dumb dog had just stood in its cage in the back of the police car, wagging its tail and drooling like an idiot. What anyone saw in the creatures she'd never know. The hairy thing had shed all over her house. She'd swept and vacuumed a dozen times but was still finding stray fur here and there. *Oh, well.* A fur ball or two was a small price to pay to see Ryan being hauled away in the back of a squad car.

She wondered what he was thinking now as he sat in his jail cell, if he was sorry he'd pulled the prank with the marshmallow fluff. She couldn't really blame him for wanting to get back at her. If anyone had tried to frame her for breaking their window and had tried to sneak into her house, she'd have wanted to even the score, too. Nevertheless, he'd added fuel to the fire, given her all the more reason to make sure he got what was coming to him.

He'd get it all right.

She'd make sure of it.

THIRTY-TWO
UNDER THE HOOD

Megan

I woke Friday morning around nine. That is, I "woke" if you could even say I'd been asleep. My mind had been working all night and I hadn't slept worth a crap. I rolled onto my back and stared up at my ceiling, pondering things I'd already pondered to death.

I knew Ryan had been stupid to drive so recklessly, and had nearly caused an accident with Adriana. But people in a panic didn't act rationally. If Adriana had indeed been swerving at him, he might have freaked out. And how would I react if an ex had been harassing me? Had followed me home from a date? If I were honest, I could see how my Irish temper might have gotten the best of me. I might have wanted to give the ex a little scare, to show that I wasn't frightened, to give him a taste of his own medicine. I might've temporarily lost my mind and engaged in a game of vehicular chicken. Heck, road rage was all too common for a reason. And even though I was normally a rational, reasonable person, I had lost my cool and Tasered Derek that time. I couldn't expect suspects to have more restraint than I had myself, could I?

Ugh.

On the other hand, there was the gun, of course. Still, while the duct tape and zip ties had freaked me out and added a nefarious feel to the whole thing, maybe I'd read too much into them. If Adriana was the one causing problems, if she were trying to frame Ryan by throwing bricks and uploading profiles of herself to sex sites, Ryan would have every right to feel threatened, to feel the need to protect and defend himself.

Another aspect that didn't sit well with me was how the two of them had ended up on the road together. I'd driven by Adriana's place several times last night. Ryan's, too. While his car had not been at his apartment, I hadn't seen it near Adriana's place, either. Surely if he were keeping watch on her I would have spotted him lying in wait, right?

Weighed down with questions and anxiety, I rolled out of bed and left the bedroom in search of Brigit. She normally slept on the bed with me, but she'd been gone when I woke up. I found her dozing on the futon. "Need to go out, girl?" I asked.

She didn't even bother opening her eyes, merely turning over to her other side to face away from me.

"Well, good morning to you, too!"

I went into the kitchen to start a pot of coffee, leaving it to brew while I went to the bathroom to take a shower and get dressed. I returned a half hour later and poured myself a travel mug, adding a healthy dose of organic soy milk. Brigit padded into the kitchen, her eyes droopy. She wasn't too tired to demand her breakfast, though. *Woof-woof!*

I filled a bowl with a can of wet food. She wolfed it down in a matter of seconds and went to the back door, giving me her *"if you don't let me out in three seconds I'll piddle on the floor"* look.

"You don't need to give me that look," I told her. "I know the drill." I stepped over, turned the knob, and pushed the door open.

I took my coffee to the window and watched as she went outside. She engaged in a brief spat with that same stupid squirrel that taunted her every day—*what a jackass*—and popped a squat in the back corner. Once her load had been lightened, she trotted back into the center of the yard, flopped over onto her back, and rolled around, letting Mother Nature scratch her back. After a minute or so, she was sufficiently itch-free. She stood, shook the dried grass and leaves from her fur, and headed back to the door.

Frankie rounded the corner of the kitchen in her rumpled pajamas. Zoe chased after her, grabbing at her heels. You had to admire the cat's ambition, trying to take down something fifteen times her size.

"Do I smell coffee?" Frankie asked.

"You do." I grabbed a mug out of the cabinet and handed it to her. "Give me ten more minutes and you'll smell cinnamon-raisin oatmeal, too."

She slid into a seat at the kitchen table and Zoe hopped up onto her lap. I whipped up two quick bowls of oatmeal and set one in front of Frankie, the other in my usual spot. Given that first responders worked odd, inconsistent shifts, Frankie and I—like Seth and I—had been like ships passing in the night the last week or so. Eating breakfast together would give us a chance to catch up.

"You settling in at work?" I asked as I scooped up a bite of the steaming oatmeal.

"Yep," she said. "They've put me in the regular rotations for cleaning duty, so I think that means the hazing is over."

"That's good."

"I'm on cooking duty next week. I've never cooked for eight people before."

They might put her back on cleaning duty once she'd cooked for them. She wasn't exactly Rachael Ray. Her philosophy was to coat everything in ranch dressing to make it palatable.

I stirred my oatmeal, seeking a raisin. "I'll e-mail you my spinach enchilada recipe. It's easy and loaded with carbs for energy." No doubt it took a lot of energy to fight fires and run up and down ladders.

"Thanks." She took a sip of her coffee. "You wanna come to our bout tomorrow? We're going up against the Shreveport She Devils."

"Count me in. Gabby, too. She's been dying to see you in action." I always enjoyed watching Frankie and the other members of the Fort Worth Whoop Ass team play Roller Derby, even if I did cringe on occasion and cover my eyes when a player wiped out in spectacular fashion. Hitting that rink at such high speed had to hurt.

She scooped up a spoonful of oatmeal and blew on it to cool it off. "What's going on in that stalker case?"

I gave her an update. "I'm not sure which one of them

is the actual stalker," I said, "but I felt like it was time to make a move. And since I saw Ryan swerve at Adriana and found the gun and other stuff in Ryan's car, well . . ." I shrugged and issued a weary sigh.

Frankie chewed her oatmeal thoughtfully and swallowed. "So if you could figure out who followed who last night, that could help you figure things out."

"Yeah."

"What about traffic cameras?" she asked. "Maybe they picked something up."

"There aren't any in the area where they were."

"Security cameras, then?"

I shook my head. "Those aren't usually mounted to t-take in street traffic. They're normally aimed at the parking lots. Besides, the cameras would only catch a snippet of time. Unless we got really lucky and found a video that showed one of them initially setting out after the other, they're not likely to tell us much."

Video footage that caught only part of an event often didn't tell a complete story. This fact was one of the arguments for body cameras for police officers.

Undeterred by me shooting down all her ideas so far, Frankie spooned up another mouthful of oatmeal and held it aloft. "You said this Ryan guy is a techie, right? He installs Internet and cable? Maybe he tracked Adriana with some kind of gadget."

"Hey. You may be on to something now." While I hadn't spotted Ryan's car near Adriana's house, that didn't mean he wasn't preparing to pounce. Maybe Ryan had been lying in wait electronically. "He could have installed some type of GPS or tracking app on Adriana's phone when they were still dating."

Surely she'd taken her phone with her when she'd left for the pharmacy last night. Cell phones were like underwear. Nobody left their home without it. Well, some did, I supposed. But they shouldn't. And I'm talking both undies and cell phones.

Frankie ate the bite of oatmeal and circled her spoon in the air. "You can also get those magnetic tracking thingies that stick to the bottom of a car. I saw one used in a television show once."

True. There were as many gadgets to spy on people as there were gadgets to protect a person's privacy. Security devices, and devices that trumped other security devices, were a big business in America. Everyone seemed to want to know everything about everyone else, but they wanted to control what others knew about them.

When we finished breakfast, I slapped on some makeup, brushed my teeth, and headed to the W1 station in my Smart Car. I'd bought the thing before I'd been partnered with Brigit. Its excellent gas mileage and easy-to-park compact size had made sense at the time. Of course, I didn't know I'd soon be responsible for a furry dog that weighed nearly as much as I did. Had I known, I'd have opted for a hybrid SUV.

I parked and took Brigit inside with me, heading down the hall to Detective Bustamente's office. He was sitting at his desk, staring straight ahead, repeatedly riffling a stack of sticky notes. *Rrrrriffle. Rrrrriffle.* He looked up as I took the liberty of stepping into his office without waiting for an invitation.

"You thinking about the stalker case?" I asked.

"I am." He tossed the sticky pad on his desk. "I heard what happened last night."

"Do you think I made the right call? Bringing Ryan in?"

"I do."

"That's a relief."

"It might be a relief, but it's also a moot point. The assistant DA disagrees with us."

"What?" I groaned and flopped down into one of his chairs. Brigit, in turn, flopped down at my feet.

"Downey bonded out already," the detective said, "and his defense attorney has raised a stink. They say we're going after the victim. He's threatened to make fools of us. The assistant DA that's been assigned the case is balking."

I was familiar with many of the ADAs and none were wimps. A menacing defense attorney would only fuel their determination to get a conviction, not make them back down. They did like to keep their stats up, though, and they didn't like to waste time and resources on cases they weren't likely to win, especially when their caseloads were extremely heavy. Couldn't much blame them for that. Given the questionable evidence against Ryan, it wasn't entirely a surprise the DA wasn't excited about moving ahead.

I leaned forward in the chair. "What if we could show that Ryan had tracked Adriana? That he'd used a GPS device on her car or put some type of tracking device on her phone? Do you think that would change things?"

"It might," Bustamente said, "or it might not. One on her car would certainly be suspicious. But if there was something on her phone, some type of app, for instance, who's to say she didn't put it there?"

Damn it. He's right. "Should I check her car? Just in case?"

"Can't hurt," he said. "I've got a bad feeling about those two. Whoever is causing problems isn't getting over it."

"If it's Ryan," I said, "maybe his arrest will make him think twice about doing something else. If it's Adriana, maybe she'll consider his arrest to be the chunk of flesh she needs to be satisfied."

"I hope you're right, Officer Luz," he said. "But I'm afraid that might be wishful thinking."

Brigit and I bade him good-bye, hopped into our cruiser, and headed over to the rehab center. I found Adriana's car parked in the employee section behind the building. I parked in an empty spot nearby and climbed out, bringing my Maglite with me.

I lay down on my back next to her car and shined my flashlight around. There were all kinds of metal in all sorts of shapes. I had no idea what I was looking for. *What does a GPS device even look like?* I could be staring right at the thing and not even know it.

I sat up, pulled my phone from my pocket, and ran a search on the Internet. Dozens of different devices came up. Some of the models could be secreted in a glove compartment or ashtray, or under a seat, tracking the vehicle's whereabouts for later access. That type of device would be of no use in this instance, as it did not provide immediate information. I scrolled down, reading the specs on other devices, looking for models that gave real-time information. While some had limited battery life and would have to be removed and recharged on a regular basis, my common sense told me that if Ryan had installed such a device, he would have chosen one with a long battery life so that he wouldn't risk being caught removing or later reattaching the device.

I slid the phone back into my pocket. With the images in mind, I lay back once again and shined my flashlight around. Still, I saw nothing. *Hmm.*

My cell phone pinged in my pocket. I pulled it out again. The readout indicated it was Adriana on the line.

I jabbed the button to accept the call. "Hello, Miss Valdez."

"What are you doing?" she asked. "I can see you from my window."

I looked up to the third floor and saw her standing at her window. Even at this distance, I could tell she wasn't making direct eye contact. As always, she was dressed in something drab. *What does she have against color? Had she once fallen in a puddle while looking up at a rainbow?* I raised a hand and she raised hers in return.

"I'm looking to see if Ryan might have attached a GPS device to your car so he could track your location."

"Oh my God!" she gushed on a shaky breath. "I didn't even think of that."

"It's also possible he might have put one on your phone," I said. "Most people carry their phones with them at all times—"

"So if someone knows where a person's phone is, they know where the person is?"

"Exactly."

"I always have my phone with me," she said. "Especially now, with all this weird stuff going on."

"Did you ever give him your password for the app store?"

"Not that I remember," she said, "but I couldn't swear to it. He used my phone once or twice when his was out in his car or in another room or whatever. He synched our calendars, too, but I was able to unsynch them after we broke up. I don't want him knowing what I'm doing, obviously."

"Has your phone been doing anything unusual?" I asked. "Do you run out of data faster than normal? Or does the battery wear down more quickly than it used to?"

"Gosh," she said, "I can't say. I mean, I haven't noticed that happening, but I really haven't been paying much attention, either. Should I call my provider and see if I can get a report on my data usage or something?"

"You should definitely find out for your own protection. Maybe visit your provider's store and have one of their people take a look at the phone. But as far as the case is concerned, even if there was some type of tracking installed on your phone, the prosecutor will say it will be impossible to prove who downloaded the app."

When Adriana spoke again, she sounded miffed. "I thought prosecutors were supposed to be on the victim's side."

"They are," I said. "But part of that is thinking like a criminal defense attorney, considering what arguments would be made on the defendant's behalf. That helps them better build their cases and keep from putting victims through traumatic court proceedings they aren't likely to win."

"I get it," she said. "I don't *like* it, but I get it. Are you having any luck with my car?"

"Not really." I thought things over for a moment. While I knew little about cars, I knew someone who knew a lot about them. *Seth.* Maybe I should have him come take a look, see if he could find a tracking device. "Do you mind if I have someone else come take a look?"

"That's fine with me. If Ryan put something on my car I'd really like to know."

We ended the call and I phoned Seth. He had the day off and I caught him at home. "Want to help me out?"

"In exchange for . . . ?" He waited for me to fill in the blank.

"My eternal gratitude."

"Gratitude?" He gave me a *pffft*. "I was thinking more along the lines of another back rub."

"You got it." Heck, he didn't have to ask me twice. I loved touching his broad, strong shoulders.

He arrived in his Nova fifteen minutes later with Blast in the backseat. He parked next to my cruiser and our dogs greeted each other through the open windows with tail wags and barks.

Woof-woof!

Arf!

I handed him my flashlight and he did the same thing I'd done earlier, lying down on his back next to the car.

"I don't see anything over here," he said after looking under the driver's side. He repeated the routine on the passenger side. "Don't see anything over here, either." He checked the undercarriage from both the front and back, too. "Nothing." He stood back and cocked his head in thought. "Any chance it could be in the engine?"

Who knows? "Let's find out."

I dialed Adriana's cell phone. When she answered I told her that there didn't appear to be anything under the car. "We'd like to check under the hood. Can you unlock your car so we can pop it open?"

"All right."

A moment later, we saw her at the window, pointing her key fob at her car. The headlights flashed and we heard a click as the door locks released. I opened the passenger door and gave a thumbs-up to Adriana.

As I slid into the driver's seat, Seth ducked his head inside the car. "I don't think I've ever seen a car this clean. Not one that wasn't brand-new and on a sales lot."

"Adriana's a little—"

"Uptight?" he supplied for me.

"Yeah. I guess you could say that."

"I'm glad you're not that way," he said.

"Hey!" I said. "I'm clean." It was true. I wasn't a germaphobe like Adriana, and I didn't shelve all my books by height, but I kept things reasonably sanitary and neat. It wasn't difficult when you only owned little more than the bare essentials. Of course everything I owned sported a stray strand or two of dog hair. It was impossible to be immaculate with a dog around.

I tugged on the release for the hood.

Pop.

Seth circled back to the front of the car and raised the hood. I climbed out, closed the door, and stepped up next to him. He leaned in, shining the flashlight between the parts. While I could identify the battery and the reservoir for the windshield wiper fluid, I had no idea what all of the other parts were for.

"Aha!" Seth said a moment later. "There's something that's not supposed to be there."

He shined the light on a small black rectangle hidden along the front. It looked very similar to the devices I'd seen in the photographs.

I exhaled sharply in relief. I had little doubt Ryan had put this device in Adriana's car. I'd been right to arrest him. With any luck, this piece of evidence would mark the end of this investigation and the beginning of a new life, free from harassment, for Adriana. I fought the urge to shout *hip-hip-hooray!*

I snapped several pics of the device in place as well as one of Seth flexing his bicep, despite the fact that it was his mental muscle, not his physical muscle, that he'd been using. After returning my phone to my pocket, I donned latex gloves and plucked the device from the metal, having to wiggle it a little to break the magnetic bond. It was ironic, I thought, that Ryan had put something magnetic in her car. Magnets were drawn together when they were opposites, just like Adriana and Ryan seemed to be opposites. I dropped the GPS into an evidence bag, sealed it, and tugged off the gloves, wiping my hands on my pants to remove the excess powder.

After Seth closed the hood, my phone rang again. It was Adriana. "I saw you pull something out and put it in a bag. You found a GPS, didn't you?" Her voice was high and slightly frantic. "Ryan was tracking me?"

"We did find a device," I said. "But it's out now. Try not to worry, okay? I'll take it to our crime scene techs and see if they can find prints on it." Now that Ryan had been booked, we'd have prints to compare them to so that we could know for certain if they were his. "You might also want to apply for a protective order yourself. There are forms online that you can download."

"I'll do that," she said. "Thanks, Officer Luz. Please thank the guy with you, too. Who is he, by the way? Maybe I should come down in person."

Lest she have designs on my man, I merely said, "He's an associate. No need to come down. We have to roll." With a quick promise to let her know the results of the fingerprint search, I ended the call.

I returned to the station, where I passed the GPS device on to the crime scene techs for analysis. "If you find any prints," I told them, "see if they match a man by the name of Ryan Downey. He was booked last night."

"Downey," the tech said as he took the baggie from me. "Got it."

We picked up lunch on the way back to my house, where I treated Seth to that back rub he'd bargained for. After all, that's what relationships are about, right? Give-and-take.

THIRTY-THREE
SQUIRREL SNACK

Brigit

There he is, she communicated silently to Blast in her canine way.

The two of them were hunkered down beside the doghouse in the backyard, hidden from view. That stupid squirrel had come down from the tree to scavenge for pecans on the lawn. He didn't realize the dogs were in the yard. Well, he was about to find out. *The hard way.*

Brigit slowly rose to a crouch, her neck stretched, her head extended out in front of her. Every muscle in her body was tensed. Blast did the same. Now that she was in the ready position, Brigit's mouth began to water. She hadn't ever caught a squirrel, but she could imagine what it would taste like. Probably chicken.

Ready? she conveyed to Blast.

Get set.

GO!

The two bolted out from behind the doghouse and tore their way across the lawn, kicking up grass and dirt behind them. The squirrel turned their way, dropped his nut, and streamed across the yard, a small brown blur.

He reached the base of the tree and sprang up it. Brigit leaped after him and snapped her teeth hard. *Snap!* Beside her, Blast did the same. *Snap!*

Dang. They'd just missed him. All they had to show for their efforts were a few pieces of squirrel fur on their tongues.

It was probably just as well, Brigit thought. If she ever caught and ate that squirrel, the backyard wouldn't be nearly as much fun. But if she couldn't have the squirrel, she could at least have his nut. She picked the pecan up from the ground and crunched it between her teeth, the squirrel scolding her all the while. *Chit-chit-chit!*

THIRTY-FOUR
EVER AFTER

Adriana

"Happily ever after" was nothing more than a fairy tale, a myth, a lie. A fantasy, just like the stories in comic books.

Her and Ryan's love story would not have a happy ending, either.

But there was still a chapter or two left to write before the end.

THIRTY-FIVE

ORDER IN THE COURT

Megan

Friday morning we finally got a break in the lollipop theft investigation. A few minutes after ten, Brigit and I were cruising past John Peter Smith Hospital when I saw a man with short, sandy hair walking up the sidewalk from the opposite direction. He had a medical mask hanging around his neck and what appeared to be a surgical cap tucked into the pocket of his green scrubs. He also had a white sucker stick protruding from his mouth.

Is this him? Is this the Lollipop Bandit?

My heart pulsed double time as I pulled to the curb and unrolled the passenger window. "Excuse me, sir?"

He cast a glance my way and froze in his tracks, his eyes wide and wary.

I gestured to the stick in his mouth. "By any chance is that a grape Tootsie Pop in your mouth?"

He shook his head emphatically but said nothing.

I raised a finger. "Stay right there."

He waited on the sidewalk while I climbed out of

the cruiser and walked over to him. His lips were pursed so tight around the lollipop stick it was a wonder the thing didn't snap in two. The wild look in his blue eyes told me he might be thinking of swallowing the evidence and was contemplating the potential health consequences.

I gestured to his mouth. "Mind showing me your sucker?"

He shook his head.

"No you don't mind?" I asked. "Or no you aren't going to show it to me?"

He opened his mouth as little as possible when he spoke, but it was still enough for me to see that his tongue and lips bore a purple tinge. "I don't have to tell you anything."

"That's true," I replied. "Your purple tongue just spoke for you."

His eyes flashed in alarm as I pulled my handcuffs from my belt.

"Where'd you steal the suckers from today?" I asked.

He opened his mouth as if to respond, said, "I . . . uh . . . ." and turned to take off running. *Sheesh.* Petty theft of candy would be a Class C misdemeanor, punishable only by a fine, but now he could add resisting arrest to his charges. Resisting arrest was a Class A crime, punishable by up to a year of jail time.

Though I might be able to catch the fleeing thief myself, it was always best to be prepared, just in case. As quickly as I could, I yanked open the back door of the cruiser and let Brigit out of her enclosure. I issued her the order to stay with me as I took off after the man, who had a one-block lead on me.

"Stop!" I hollered after him. Not sure why I bothered. Nobody who'd ever taken off on me had experienced a sudden change of heart.

He ran past the hospital and continued onto St. Joseph Court, which circled behind an adjacent medical building. My feet and heart were pounding, my ears flooded with the sound of blood rushing through my veins. Knowing I couldn't keep up this pace much longer, I deployed my partner to go after the guy. She'd get the man, and quick. Brigit's nails scrabbled on the asphalt as she took off in pursuit.

When the street ended at a parking lot, the man darted between the building and the train tracks, running along a row of trees that had been planted there. Brigit was gaining on the man when I realized a train was gaining on us, a northbound freight train roaring up the track to our right. *Clickety-clack. Clickety-clack. Clickety-clack.*

I glanced back and saw the engine coming under the Allen Street overpass. My heart leaped into my throat and I turned to holler to Brigit, to call her back to safety. No way in hell would I risk her life to catch some petty thief!

Though I yelled as loud as I could, Brigit didn't hear me over the sounds of the train. Her legs ate up the ground ahead as she hurtled after the man.

The train sped past me now, kicking up dirt and pea gravel, and a warm rush of air.

"Brigit!" I screamed again, so loud it seared my vocal chords. "Come back!"

Still she didn't hear me, running after the Lollipop Bandit with everything she had. Brigit reached the man just as the train reached the two of them. The man swerved to the right, directly in front of the train. I gasped, sucking in dust, as the conductor laid on the horn. *WAAAAAAH!*

"No!" I cried, as much to God as the dog. *Dear Lord! Please don't let Brigit follow him! She'll get hit by the train, too!* I fell to my knees next to the track, gulping air in terror, white sparks erupting like fireworks at the edge of my vision.

Brigit snapped her teeth at the thief's scrub shirt in one last attempt to catch him, but instead veered off to the left, loping in a half-circle to head back my way.

My first and foremost thought was, *THANK YOU, GOD!*

My second thought was, *The Lollipop Bandit is dead. Holy crap!*

When Brigit ran up I grabbed her in a bear hug, inadvertently tackling her to the ground. I'd never been happier to see the furry beast, and I didn't want her to get anywhere close to the train again. She didn't seem to mind my embrace. She wagged her tail and wriggled playfully under me as the train continued on. I supposed it would take it a while to stop with all of the weight and momentum it had going. I could only imagine the gruesome gore that would be waiting for us.

As the last car went past, I released Brigit and sat back, wiping the tears from my cheeks. She sat up, too. *Wait. What's that in her teeth?*

I reached out and pulled a white laminated identification card from her mouth. It was an ID tag featuring a photograph of the Lollipop Bandit, as well as information identifying him as Gregory Higginbotham, M.D.

At least now we know whose remains we'll be scraping off the tracks. I could hardly believe a doctor would risk his life to avoid arrest for such a small crime. But people did irrational things when they were frightened. I saw it all the time.

I looked down the tracks, surprised to see the train continuing on its way out of sight. *The conductor's not going to stop?* He'd obviously seen Dr. Higginbotham run in front of the engine or he wouldn't have blasted the horn. It wasn't unusual for people driving cars to be involved in a hit-and-run. But a train? It didn't seem to make sense. Then again, maybe another train was on its way and the conductor planned to stop somewhere safe down the tracks.

I clipped Brigit's leash onto her collar and stood. Taking a deep breath to prepare myself, I raised my head and ran my eyes down the track, looking for a mass of bloody flesh that had once been Dr. Higginbotham. But my eyes saw nothing on the track other than a flattened copper penny gleaming in the sun.

What the—?

Leading Brigit, I jogged up the track. Had his body been carried away by the train? Maybe thrown to the side?

My eyes searched and scanned the surroundings but saw nothing. No fingers, toes, or limbs in the brush. No ears or nose. No severed head lying aside the tracks, a purple-stained tongue lolling out of it. My partner and I walked a full half mile of track but saw not a single drop of blood or body part.

I looked across to the other side of the tracks. "He made it across, didn't he?" *Lucky bastard.* I supposed that I was lucky, too, though. Law enforcement officers had to make judgment calls, weigh the benefits of catching a suspect against the potential costs. Cops who pursued small-time criminals with deadly results often found themselves the subjects of internal investigations and lawsuits. The last thing I wanted was to garner the attention of the ACLU, especially now that they had millions upon millions of dollars in their coffers thanks to a deluge of recent donations inspired by the president's executive orders. Heck, some of those dollars had once been mine. I was all for civil rights and liberties, but I much preferred to remain on the organization's mailing list rather than their shit list, thank you very much.

I led Brigit back to the approximate place where the elusive doctor had run in front of the train and issued the order for her to trail him. She put her nose to the ground and snuffled around a bit before heading over the tracks. I jogged along behind her, keeping a tight hold on the leash.

She led me over several more sets of tracks until we reached a brushy area. Behind the brush was a fence. Brigit led me up to the fence and stood on her back legs, her front paws extended up on the boards, her nose scenting the air at the top of the fence. She looked back at me, communicating without words. *This is where he hopped over.*

"Good girl!" I said, giving her a liver treat. I put my hands on the top of the fence and pulled myself up to take a look over it. Without anything to leverage my feet on, I could only get a quick glimpse, but it told me the man was no longer in the barren yard. He must've escaped out the front gate. I pulled myself up for another quick look at the house, taking mental note of its features. *Light blue. White shutters. Light gray shingles on the roof.*

We stepped back and I scanned the fence in both directions, looking for a break that Brigit and I might squeeze through. Unfortunately, I saw none. *Dang!*

We hurried back to the cruiser, climbed in, and drove around to the neighborhood the Lollipop Bandit had escaped into. When I spotted a house painted light blue with white shutters, I pulled to a stop and retrieved Brigit. Leading her over to the gate, I again issued the order for her to trail the escaped thief.

She performed her usual preliminary sniff test, and headed off through the yard into that of the house next door. We continued on down Arizona Avenue, passing East Morphy Street, until we reached Magnolia Avenue, a major thoroughfare that ran north of the JPS hospital complex.

We'd begun to make our way west on Magnolia when my shoulder-mounted radio came to life. "Officer Luz, you and Brigit are requested for a vehicle search on I-30 between Jennings and Main."

I let loose a frustrated breath. My partner and I were so close to nabbing the Lollipop Bandit! But I supposed there was no telling how far he'd continued to run. We could be tracking him for another hour or more. He might have even retrieved his car and driven off. Who knows? But what we did know was his name. There'd be no hiding from us now.

We returned to the cruiser and headed north, merging onto I-30. I could see Officer Hinojosa with a car pulled over up ahead. A black, high-end SUV with lots of chrome, the kind often driven by successful drug dealers. Really, if they didn't want to stand out, they should drive minivans. Standing beside the car with his palms on the back of his head was a white guy with short hair and a full, bushy beard in the same tannish-gold color as much of Brigit's fur.

I put on my flashing lights and blinker and eased to a stop in front of the SUV, backing up to block the vehicle in case the suspect should get the dumb idea to try to flee in it. Keeping an eye on the guy, who was cutting me every which way with his sharp gaze, I let Brigit out of her enclosure. I walked her over to the car.

My eyes met Hinojosa's, asking a silent question. He angled his head toward the driver's window, which was open. I stepped closer and took a quick glimpse inside. I saw nothing that would give rise to probable cause. No drugs. No drug paraphernalia. No rolls of cash. What I did see was a scented cardboard pine tree hanging from the rearview mirror and four of those special automotive air fresheners that clipped on to each of the air-conditioning vents. My first intake of breath and I nearly became high on pine and lavender fumes.

Nobody needed this much scent in their car. Not unless they were trying to mask another smell. Fresh bud, perhaps?

Hinojosa chimed in. "He says someone got sick in his car and that's why he's got all those air fresheners."

I looked back into the SUV, eyeing the floor mats. Looked clean to me. So did the leather seats.

I opened the door and removed each of the air fresheners. No sense overwhelming Brigit's nose or making her job any more difficult than it had to be. I stepped back and gave Brigit the order to sniff for drugs.

She began at the driver's seat, sniffing around the padded seat, the seat back, and the floor. *No alert.* I opened the back door and she repeated the process, working her way up and down. *No alert.* The same thing happened when I led her around the front of the car so that she could sniff the passenger side. But when I led her back to the door of the cargo bay, she took one sniff near the handle and immediately sat, giving her passive alert.

"There's something back here," I told Hinojosa as I opened the door. While nothing was immediately visible, all it took was me lifting the carpeting to find multiple bricks of marijuana in clear wrap tucked in around the spare tire and jack. I turned to my partner. "Good job, Brigit." She'd earned two liver treats for her efforts.

Brigit followed me as I picked up one of the bricks and carried it over to Hinojosa. I handed it to him. "There's a half-dozen more of them back there."

The glare the man locked on me was so heated it was a wonder my skin didn't catch fire. He began shuffling back and forth on his feet and clenching his fists, his eyes darting from me to my partner. *Yep, he's going to blow.*

He charged at Brigit and cocked his leg back to kick her, but I was faster. I whipped out my baton and flicked my wrist to extend it. *Snap!* Before he could land his kick, I'd smacked his calf aside with a solid *whap!*

Nobody hurts my dog.

The dealer screamed in agony and grabbed his lower

leg, hopping around next to the cars on one foot. Pass-ersby probably thought we were performing an unusu-ally difficult sobriety test on the guy.

Brigit and I kept watch while Hinojosa grabbed the man, cuffed him, and loaded him into the back of his cruiser, beard and all.

"Thanks for your help, Luz," my fellow officer said.

As if she knew she was deserving of some sign of ap-preciation and praise, Brigit bent in half, backed toward Hinojosa, and looked up at him.

He looked down at the dog. "What the heck is she doing?"

"She wants you to scratch her butt."

He chuckled. "All right, girl. You got it." He reached down and scratched the sweet spot at the base of her tail. She lifted her snout and closed her eyes in bliss.

I raised a hand in good-bye. "See ya." With that, Bri-git and I loaded ourselves back into our squad car. *One down, one to go.*

I whipped out my cell phone and ran a search on the Internet for Dr. Gregory Higginbotham. According to my search, he was a pulmonary specialist with admitting privileges at both Cook Children's Hospital and JPS. His medical office sat on Oleander Street, about equi-distant between the two facilities. He was part of a practice that included two other pulmonologists.

I started the engine and turned back to Brigit. "Let's pay the doctor a little office visit, shall we?"

I drove to his office, taking a spot near the edge of the parking lot where he'd be less likely to spot us ap-proaching. I attached Brigit's leash and we stepped inside. The waiting room was heavily populated. An adolescent boy in the corner sat wheezing alongside his mother, who was rubbing his back. A middle-aged man took a puff from an inhaler. An elderly woman coughed so hard it was a wonder her lungs didn't collapse.

The receptionist looked up from behind the counter, her eyes moving from me, to Brigit, and back to me again. "May I help you?" she asked as we approached.

"I need to see Dr. Higginbotham. As soon as possible."

"Would you like an appointment?"

"No. It's not medical related. It's a police matter."

Curiosity sparked in her eyes. "He's handling rounds at JPS today," she said. "With all the ozone alerts we've had lately we're seeing a lot of severe asthma cases. He'll be back here in the morning."

I thanked her for the information and turned to go.

As I stepped away, she craned her neck and called after me. "Can I let him know your name and why you stopped by?"

Though her voice was cordial and professional, I suspected her reasons for asking were more out of nosiness than any desire to keep her boss informed. I turned back as I reached the door. "No need," I told her, forcing myself to sound casual. "I'll catch up with him another time."

I'll catch up with him all right. In just a few minutes, at the hospital.

We drove the few blocks to JPS. I parked in the outdoor lot and led Brigit inside. We checked in at the desk in the main lobby. "I have a personal matter I need to discuss with Dr. Gregory Higginbotham. Could you page him for me?"

"Certainly." The receptionist picked up a telephone

receiver, consulted a chart posted at her desk, and dialed his pager. "I'll let you know when he calls."

I leaned in and whispered. "Don't tell him there's a police officer here to see him. Tell him it's a patient with a question, okay?"

She stared at me a moment as she mentally processed my request, and nodded nervously.

I stepped aside to get out of the way, but remained close enough to overhear the calls the woman took. When a call came in a few minutes later, she turned my way and waved her hand to indicate it was Dr. Higginbotham on the line. "There's a patient here to see you. She says she has a question." She paused for a moment. "I think she said her name was . . ." She glanced around, as if looking for inspiration. She found some on her desk, where an African violet rested in a small pot. "Violet. Violet Potter."

Nice improvising. I gave her a thumbs-up.

"Okay," she said. "I'll tell her." She hung up the phone. "He'll be right down."

And we'll be ready for him.

Brigit and I took up places against the wall next to the swinging doors that led from the hospital into the reception area. No sense letting him spot us through the window and attempt to escape out another entrance.

A minute or so later, the man we'd chased earlier in the day came through the doors. He glanced left and right ahead of him, but failed to notice me and Brigit behind him. He stopped at the reception desk. "Where's Miss Potter?"

I walked up behind him and tapped him on the shoulder. "Here I am."

When he turned, the smile on his face turned into a gape and his eyes bulged. Before he could bolt, I reached out and grabbed his bicep. Below me, Brigit issued a warning growl. *Grrrrr.* "Don't even think about it," I whispered.

"How'd you—"

I held up his badge, which bore two puncture marks from Brigit's teeth.

He groaned. "I was wondering where that went."

I looked at his chest to see that he was wearing what appeared to be a recently minted replacement. After ordering him to turn around and affixing the cuffs to his wrists, I turned to the receptionist. "Get me someone from the hospital security team, please."

She nodded and picked up her phone. "We need a security guard to reception," she said into the receiver.

I squeezed my shoulder radio and called for transport. I also let Dr. Higginbotham make a call to one of the other doctors in his practice to let him know he'd need to put an early end to his golf game and cover the remaining rounds.

While we waited for security and transport to arrive, Brigit and I stood guard over the doctor. He stared at the tile floor in an attempt to hide his face from the patients and other medical workers going in and out of the facility. There were whispers and murmurs among the staff, people wondering what was going on. *They'll figure it out soon enough.*

Shortly after security arrived, transport also arrived in the form of Summer and Derek Mackey. They must have been close by. While Summer waited in the cruiser in the drop-off area outside, Derek came into the building, walked up to the doctor, and looked him up and down. "What's the charge? He kill someone or something?"

"Misdemeanor theft and resisting arrest."

Derek scoffed. "What did he steal?"

"Grape Tootsie Pops."

He looked from me to the doctor. "No shit?"

"No feces at all."

Derek scoffed. "Now I've seen everything."

As Derek led Dr. Higginbotham out to his cruiser, I turned to the security guard and asked to search the doctor's locker. He led me to a dressing room for male staff at the end of the hallway, made sure those inside were decent, and allowed me to enter. He opened Dr. Higginbotham's locker with a master key. Sure enough, I found a dozen grape suckers inside. Also a number of stethoscopes, blood pressure cuffs, thermometers, and other medical supplies and equipment, many of which bore the names of other doctors or nurses.

The security guard whistled when he saw the stash of stolen property. "This guy's got a real problem."

Maybe now he'd get help for it.

By the end of the day Friday, the crime scene techs had called me with confirmation. Unfortunately, it was confirmation that the GPS device had no prints on it. Whoever had put it in Adriana's car had been careful to wipe the device clean. Still, even without prints, it seemed clear, to me at least, that Ryan must have put it there. He seemed to be the only person with both a motive to do so and access to Adriana's car. When he began to sense that their relationship was failing, he could've snuck her keys out of her purse and planted the device.

I spoke with Detective Bustamente before heading out for my swing shift. "What did the prosecutor say? Does this change anything?"

"He said it might. He called the defense attorney to see if he wanted to work out a plea deal based on this new evidence. You'll never guess what he came back with."

"What?"

"He said after hearing about the device Ryan went out and checked his car. He claims he found one under his hood, too. Ryan brought it to his attorney's office and the two of them drove his car here. Our tech guys removed it."

"Was it the same model as the one in Adriana's car? Or different?"

"Yep. They were the same."

That likely meant the same person placed both of them. *But who?*

"Any prints on it?" I asked.

"Nope," Bustamente replied. "It was clean."

"So the evidence is inconclusive."

"Yep. The DA said he'd try to get Downey to agree to a lesser charge, but if they don't come to some kind of agreement soon he's going to move on. He doesn't think there's enough evidence to get a conviction on any bigger charges."

In other words, Ryan Downey would get away with just the citation I'd written him for reckless driving. I closed my eyes for a few seconds before releasing an elongated breath. "This has been an extremely frustrating investigation."

Bustamente opened a drawer, pulled out a plastic

container, and held it out to me. "Here. Have a piece of fudge. My wife made a fresh batch."

I fished out a piece, said good-bye to Bustamente, and ate the fudge on the go. *Dang, that's some fine fudge.*

On my way out the door, I was stopped by Melinda as I passed her sitting behind the front counter. Melinda was a bleached blonde in her forties, and she served a dozen or more roles around the station. She was the receptionist, office manager, and assistant to Captain Leone, who ran the station. She was also the keeper of keys to the supply cabinet and many little secrets about all of us officers. But while she'd gladly give you the keys if you could justify your need for yet another ballpoint pen or notepad, she wouldn't share secrets to spare her life. Nope, definitely not a gossip.

She held out a thin manila envelope. "This just came in for you."

I took the envelope from her, opened it, and pulled out the single sheet of paper inside. It was a subpoena issued by the lawyer Adriana had hired and it required me to be in family law court at 8:00 Monday morning. I would've voluntarily agreed to attend the hearing on her protective order, but I knew lawyers liked to make everything official, so I took no offense at the legal summons.

"Thanks, Melinda." I folded the document and tucked it into my breast pocket.

"You were quite popular today." She reached over to her stacked bins on the counter and pulled out another envelope. "This came for you, too."

I opened the second envelope to find a virtually identical subpoena, though this one had been sent by

Ryan's attorney. Looked like everybody wanted a piece of me.

I drove by Adriana's place to give her the news about the GPS. We spoke on her porch.

"There were no prints on the GPS in your car, and Ryan claims to have found a device in his car, too."

"That's ridiculous!" she cried. "He probably put it there!"

I shrugged my shoulders and shook my head. "I really don't know what to tell you at this point."

"What does this mean for me?" she asked. "Is Ryan going to get off scot-free?"

"The DA's trying to work out a plea deal."

"A plea deal?" Her mouth gaped. "The guy threatens me with a gun and tries to run me off the road and they're going to give him a plea deal?" She covered her face with her hands, as if unwilling to face this decision. "I'm going to end up dead, Officer Luz. I just know it."

My stomach turned and twisted inside me, pangs of guilt cutting through as if my organs were being processed through her Cuisinart. "Is there somewhere else you can stay for a while?" I asked her. "Maybe with a friend?"

"I'm not particularly social," she said. "I'm friendly enough with people at work but there's nobody I'd feel comfortable staying with."

"What about a vacation?" I asked. "Maybe you could go visit your parents for a few days, let things settle down."

"Ryan and I spent a week in Austin in July," she said, "and I took two days earlier this year for my cousin's wedding. I've only got three vacation days left and I wanted to use them at Christmas."

"How about a hotel?"

"I could afford a night or two, maybe," she said. "But dietitians don't make a lot of money, and staying in a hotel isn't going to solve anything. I'd have to come home sometime. Then what?"

At that point, I was out of ideas.

"We'll continue the patrols," I assured her. "If he keeps this up, we'll catch him sooner or later."

Her face hardened. "No offense, Officer Luz. But that doesn't make me feel better." She said nothing more before turning and going back into her house.

I stared at her closed door. Was there anything more I could be doing to help her feel safe? I thought and thought and thought, but I couldn't come up with a damn thing.

Woof? Brigit barked from the cruiser. Funny, even though it was only a sound and not a word, I could tell it was a question. She was probably wondering why I was standing there staring off into space. Hell, I was wondering the same thing. It was an exercise in futility.

As I poured food into Brigit's bowl Saturday morning, I noticed we were running low. Once she'd crunched down her kibble and I'd polished off a bowl of equally noisy granola, I loaded her into the car to head to the pet-supply store.

To our delight, a local pet-rescue group was holding an adoption day on the front sidewalk. Cages and portable enclosures were lined up along the walkway. Brigit woofed and wagged her tail as we rolled by, searching for a parking spot.

On our way into the store, Brigit insisted on introducing herself to each of the dogs, which ranged in age from a trio of three-month-old boxer-mix puppies to a middle-aged collie to a twelve-year-old senior Scottish terrier. While Brigit and the dogs made canine small talk, I struck up a conversation with one of the volunteers who was holding an adorable fluffy dog who was mostly gray with touches of brown on her face. When the dog looked up at me with her bright brown eyes and wagged her tail I felt my heart melt.

I reached out a hand to ruffle the dog's ears. "Who's this cutie?"

"This is Maya," the woman said. "Maya's mother was a miniature Doberman pinscher and her father was a Maltese. She was my surprise Christmas present a few years ago. My husband claimed he didn't think we had time for a puppy, but then I found her in a box under the tree Christmas morning. We've been inseparable since." She went on to tell me that Maya's addition to their family had not only brought her endless joy, but had also led her to an acute awareness of animal-welfare issues. The overpopulation problem. Puppy mills. Dogs left chained and unattended in yards for long, lonely days. "Now I foster dogs who are up for adoption. Maya is wonderful about welcoming them into our home. She's calm and sweet and never jealous or resentful."

"Pretty and sweet, huh?" I angled my head to indicate Brigit, who'd grabbed the end of a colorful rope hanging from the mouth of a pit bull for an impromptu game of tug-of-war. "My dog's a stubborn pain in the butt with a squirrel obsession. Want to trade?" I was only joking, of course. I was as crazy about Brigit as this woman clearly was about her precious little Maya.

We shared a chuckle before I rounded up Brigit to go inside. "Good luck with the adoption day."

"Thanks!"

I led Brigit inside where we filled a cart with a forty-pound bag of her favorite food and a nylon chew toy, as well as a catnip-filled mouse toy for Zoe. Three boxes of liver treats made their way into the basket, too. Brigit sure had been running through them lately. Of course she'd earned every one. I also grabbed a bottle of peach-scented flea shampoo. Nobody needed to know that particular purchase was for myself.

On our way out of the store, we were met with squeals of delight from two young boys whose parents had just given them the green light to adopt one of the boxer pups. Both the dog and the boys would have years of fun ahead of them, as well as new best friends. I gave Maya a final scratch under the chin. *Yep, she's irresistible.* "Bye, sweetie pie."

She wagged her tail and gave me and Brigit an *arf* in good-bye.

That afternoon, I left Brigit home with Zoe while Frankie, Zach, my sister Gabby, and I went to Frankie's Roller Derby bout. Seth was working today, so he couldn't come along. As I watched the women skate round and round and round the rink, I thought how similar it was to the stalking investigation. The case had me and Detective Bustamente going around in circles and seemingly had no end. Hell, at least in Derby they could keep score. I had no idea what the score was where Adriana Valdez and Ryan Downey were concerned. Only the two of them truly knew which of them had won each of their battles. The brick through the window. The woman with the red balloons. The sex-site profile. The visit to Toby at day camp. The car chase.

Frankie skated at warp speed, blowing by us in a blue-haired blur as we stood at the rail cheering her on. "Frank-ee! Frank-ee!"

Gabby pumped a fist in the air as she chanted along with us. She turned to me. "This looks like fun! Maybe I should give Roller Derby a try."

Just then, another skater cut Frankie off and the two of them locked skates, wiping out, and slid across the polished wood, slamming into the half wall that surrounded the rink. Next to me, Gabby cringed. "Ouch! That had to hurt!"

Despite that fact, Frankie somehow made the fall look graceful, rising back up to her feet in a seamless motion.

I nudged Gabby with my elbow. "Still thinking you'll give it a try?"

"Maybe I should give it some more thought first."

We shared a laugh.

Zach turned to me. "I'm really glad you asked Seth to set up me and Frankie. I've never met any woman like her before."

"You'll never meet another one like her, either."

Frankie was certainly unique. Fearless and ferocious, but with a soft and tender side, too.

"I worry about her," he said. "You know, with the new job and all. Firefighting is such a dangerous profession."

"Tell me about it," I said. Not only was Seth a firefighter, but he served on the bomb squad, as well. The job came with a lot of risks. But the two of them had willingly accepted those risks, and if we wanted to be part of their lives, we had to accept them, too, even if it meant developing ulcers in the process. Besides, I supposed the risks of my job had given Seth a sleepless night on occasion.

We turned our attention back to the track. Frankie's teammate Raven skated by, her dark hair pulled back in jaunty pigtails, the lights glinting off the multiple piercings in her ears. Mia, a petite Asian woman, followed her, looking both fierce and feminine in her pink skates and lacy fingerless gloves.

It was an exciting bout. The Fort Worth Whoop Ass and Shreveport She Devils were evenly matched, and the score went back and forth. As soon as the Whoop Ass got a lead, the She Devils would come from behind, score, and get ahead. But at the end of the bout the Whoop Ass emerged both bruised and victorious, the final score 161 to 158.

The teams exchanged sportswomanlike high fives on the track, rolling past each other in a procession before skating off. Zach, Gabby, and I exchanged our own high fives with Frankie as she skated over to us, sweaty and exhausted, but happy with the win. "That was a tough one!"

"You pulled it off, though," I said. "Good job."

After dropping Gabby back at my parents' place, the rest of us returned to the house. Frankie spent a few minutes showering and freshening up before she and Zach took off for a dinner date, leaving me behind with only Brigit and Zoe for company. With Seth on a shift at the fire station, I'd be dateless tonight. *Sigh*.

I fixed myself an organic peanut butter sandwich on whole-wheat bread, making a second for Brigit. She and I curled up on the couch together to watch television.

After a half hour or so I realized that I was lonely, *dammit*. I'd always been a bit of a loner, a maverick who did just fine on her own. Not that I hadn't had friends. But because of my childhood stutter I'd often kept both quiet and to myself. Even as my stutter abated as I grew older, I found the old habits hard to break. I'd attended events with groups of kids from band while in high school, and in college there had always been groups from the dorm to hang out with, but I'd never grown particularly attached to anyone. Now, though, I realized I'd grown attached to both Seth and Frankie, in different ways, of course, and for different reasons. But I had to admit I felt very lonesome here without one or the other of them to keep me company.

I looked over at Brigit, feeling a twinge of guilt. While I loved having her as a partner, there were some roles she simply couldn't fulfill in my life. It dawned on me that she likely felt the same way. Maybe it was time to get another dog to keep her company when I wasn't around, to be her friend in a way that only another canine could. Of course if Seth moved in, like he seemed to be doing even though he wasn't acknowledging it, we might soon be sharing the house with him and Blast on a regular basis.

Despite my loneliness tonight, I wasn't sure I was ready for that. Moving in together would be a big step, not to mention that I already had Frankie to think about.

Oh, well. None of these things had to be decided to-night.

It also dawned on me that Adriana must feel lonely like this a lot. Even if she was an introvert, everybody needed someone, even if only on occasion. With Ryan out of her life now, even if it had been her choice, she must be feeling this same type of emptiness and heart-ache. On top of that feeling, she had the fear that Ryan might be out to kill her. I could only imagine how awful it would be to live with that kind of thing hang-ing over you. I hoped my fellow officers who were out on patrol tonight were keeping an eagle eye on her place.

The following week I was back on the night shift. *Ugh.* The only good thing about it was that it would give me the chance to keep close tabs on both Adriana's house and Ryan's apartment. While I knew the other cops in W1 wanted to keep everyone safe under our watch, the sit-uation between these two was personal to me given how involved I'd been. I couldn't help but think that I'd pay a little more attention than anyone else, be the most likely to notice something that was awry.

But first things first. And first thing Monday morn-ing I had to appear in family law court. I'd been sub-poenaed by Adriana's attorney to testify on her behalf in the hearing on her protective order. Of course Ryan and his attorney had come to fight the order. If the judge granted the order, Ryan would no longer be allowed to possess a gun. Besides, these types of things could follow a person for life. It wasn't something to be taken lightly.

Family law court had to be one of the most depressing places on earth, the portal to hell. It was where dreams of happily-ever-afters were crushed, where once-loving relationships were officially and finally severed, where children were legally—and sometimes physically—torn from one parent and given to another. The place was a maelstrom of rage, grief, disappointment, and despair. In other words, it sucked. Big-time.

When Brigit and I walked into the crowded room, the effect of all those people and their negative emotions were suffocating. I had to pause for a moment to mentally adjust. As we stopped, Brigit's tags jingled. The people turned to see what had caused the noise and spotted my partner.

I'd been in family law court before, but that was before I'd been partnered with Brigit. As it turned out, a furry, friendly dog was like a breath of fresh air in the room. People who'd been scowling or holding tissue to their crying eyes before now smiled and pointed at Brigit, telling their children to look at the "doggie."

We made our way slowly up the aisle, stopping to let everyone who wanted to pet Brigit have a chance. By the time we made it to a seat on the second row, she'd had dozens of hands on her and a couple of Cheerios were stuck to her fur, but she'd enjoyed every second of it. She also enjoyed licking the Cheerios from her back. I admired my partner for many reasons, but her ability to be not only fierce and formidable, but also sweet and loving, was definitely one of them. Some police dogs couldn't be trusted to be touched and hugged, but Brigit ate that stuff up. She was an incredibly intelligent animal, with good instincts. Hell, sometimes I thought she was smarter and had better instincts than me. I know the same thought crossed her mind on occasion, too. The disdainful looks she sometimes sent me said it all. *Oh, you poor, stupid human. What would you do without me?* Fortunately, she forgave my faults and failures.

I slid onto a bench to await instruction, Brigit lying on the floor at my feet. Both Adriana and Ryan were already seated at opposing tables at the front of the room. Adriana had sucked it up and hired an attorney this time. She'd been smart to do so. Only fools tried to represent themselves. The two stared straight ahead, not casting so much as a glance in the direction of the other, probably on the advice of their attorneys. Still, Adriana's shrunken posture said how uncomfortable she felt to be here. Ryan, on the other hand, sat up tall and rigid in his seat, seemingly both confident and angry at the same time.

While the male judge looked down on her, passive and expressionless, Adriana's attorney stated their request for a protective order and, in support thereof, began to run through the events of the past few weeks.

"A brick was thrown through my client's bedroom window," she said. "Given that my client has no conflicts with anyone else, we believe Mr. Downey had to be behind the incident."

Ryan's attorney leaped to his feet. "Your Honor, Mr. Downey was not arrested for the incident and there is no solid proof he committed that act of vandalism. To say he threw the brick is pure conjecture and speculation."

Given that conjecture and speculation were synonyms, I thought the attorney's words were redundant and repetitive, but who am I to judge? The judge was to judge, not me.

The judge looked from Ryan's attorney back to Adriana's. "Go on, please."

"The brick was only the first of a series of stalking incidents, which became progressively more threatening and dangerous." She looked back to where I sat in the gallery. "Your Honor, I'd like to call Officer Megan Luz to the stand, please. She's the officer who responded to the various calls and is familiar with the police department's investigation."

The judge waved me up. "Come on up, Officer Luz."

I led Brigit over to the witness stand, where I raised my hand like a dutiful Girl Scout. Brigit looked up at me and raised her paw, too.

"Do you promise to tell the truth," the bailiff asked, "the whole truth, and nothing but the truth?"

Truth. What an elusive concept. When you only knew parts of the truth, those parts could be misleading and taken out of context. If only I had complete knowledge of what the hell was going on between Adriana and Ryan and who was at fault. Then I could set the record straight, enforce the law. But I knew that even if the facts I had were incomplete, it was all the court had to go on. I was the only unbiased witness here.

I answered the bailiff's question. "I do."

As if she, too, were swearing to tell the truth, Bright let out a bark. *Woof-woof!*

The bailiff reached down and ruffled her ears.

Adriana's attorney launched into a line of questions for me. "You collected a pair of shoes and a brick from outside Mr. Downey's apartment the night my client's window was broken, correct?"

"I did."

"And the Fort Worth PD's crime scene lab determined that Mr. Downey's shoes had been used to make the prints on the patio behind the house leased by Ms. Valdez."

"That is correct." Of course, they weren't certain the prints had been made naturally, or whether they'd been faked. My gaze reflexively went to Ryan's attorney, anticipating that he would raise the issue.

As expected, he leaped from his seat with an objection. "No arrest was made after that incident, Your Honor. In fact, the crime scene team concluded it was probable the prints had been manufactured."

"Possible," I corrected him. "Not probable."

The judge looked down and admonished me. "Only speak in response to a question, Officer Luz."

"Yes, Your Honor."

The judge looked at Adriana's attorney. "Continue."

She eyed me and asked another question. "The brick you collected from Mr. Downey's apartment was the same brand and type as the one that had been thrown through Ms. Valdez's window, correct?"

"Yes, ma'am."

When she moved on to the next incident, the judge said, "Let's take these events one by one, okay? Otherwise I'm going to have a hard time keeping it all straight." When the two attorneys murmured in agreement, he looked to Ryan's counsel. "You got anything else you want to ask about the broken-window incident?"

He stood. "I do." He gestured at Brigit. "Did you have your dog track that night?"

"I did," I said. "She sniffed around but seemed to only go to the side fence and around the yard and kitchen door."

"So that meant whoever had thrown the brick came from inside the house," he said.

It was a statement, not a question, but I knew in this instance the judge would want me to correct the attorney. "Not necessarily," I replied. "The person could have gone over the fence into the adjacent yard. Unfortunately, the neighboring gate was locked. I shined my flashlight over the fence but didn't see anyone."

"No arrests were made in relation to the broken window; isn't that true, Officer Luz?" he asked.

"That's correct."

Ryan's attorney indicated he had no further questions about the window and sat down.

Adriana's attorney glanced back at the courtroom full of families and addressed the judge. "Your Honor, could you ask the parents to cover their children's ears for just a moment?"

"This ought to be good." He banged his gavel to get the attention of everyone in the gallery. *Bam-bam.* "Cover your kids' ears or take them outside," he instructed. "We've got some adult content to discuss."

Once the parents had either cupped their hands over their kids' ears or shuffled them out the door, he waved his gavel at Adriana's attorney to indicate she could continue.

"We believe Mr. Downey is behind a later incident in which a profile of Ms. Valdez was entered into a cell phone app known as Kinky Cowtown."

The judge's brows lifted. "Did you say *Kinky Cowtown*?"

The two male bailiffs exchanged glances from either side of the room, both of them fighting grins.

"I did, sir," Adriana's attorney continued. "It's a site people use to find sexual partners who live in the area. A photo of Ms. Valdez was uploaded to the site along with her address and a request that men who responded bring both a leather whip and marshmallow whip."

The bailiff on the right couldn't take it. He snorted in an attempt to rein in a guffaw, but tried to cover his blunder with a cough. I supposed I might find the situation humorous, too, if I hadn't seen firsthand how terrified Adriana had been when creep after creep had come to her house looking to hook up with her.

Again, Ryan's attorney argued that there was no proof Ryan had committed the crime. "In fact," he said, "the tech specialists with the Fort Worth Police Department determined that the profile had been uploaded via the server at the rehabilitation center where Ms. Valdez works. Isn't that right, Officer Luz?"

"That is correct," I replied.

Adriana's attorney pointed out that Ryan had accessed the rehab center's Wi-Fi system at a previous time and could have retained the information he'd need to log into it remotely.

Ryan's attorney scoffed. "That seems awfully far-fetched, wouldn't you agree, Officer Luz?"

Hell, I didn't know if it was far-fetched or not. I barely understood how the technology would work.

Before I could respond, Adriana's attorney objected. "He's asking for an opinion, not facts, Your Honor."

The judge agreed the question was objectionable and didn't require me to answer it.

Over the next half hour, the two went back and forth over every event, pulling me metaphorically back and forth between them as if engaged in a game of legal tug-of-war. Yes, I'd questioned Adriana regarding the woman with the balloons who'd come to Ryan's complex and attempted to gain access to his apartment. No, I had not arrested her afterward. No, I hadn't arrested Ryan the first time Adriana had called about him following her. Yes, I'd seen Ryan swerve toward Adriana's car in his Camaro. Yes, I'd found a loaded gun, ammunition, zip ties, and duct tape in his car. Yes, the gun was within his reach. Yes, I'd decided to have him arrested that particular night. Yes, I'd found a GPS device affixed to Adriana's engine. No, prints were not found on the device.

Adriana's attorney mentioned that charges were still pending against Ryan relating to the night of the car chase. "He's likely to be found guilty of various charges," she said, "including assault. He should've been charged with attempted murder, if you ask me."

"Well, we didn't ask you!" snapped Ryan's attorney.

The judge raised his gavel in warning. "Speak to me, not each other. I'll not tolerate rude behavior in my courtroom." He pointed the gavel at Ryan's attorney to let him know he now had the floor.

"The prosecutor offered a plea deal. Six months' probation for attempted vehicular assault." The attorney forced a chuckle. "They obviously know they can't prove anything more. We're not planning on accepting the offer. They'll end up dropping the case."

"They don't know that," Adriana's attorney said sharply. While her eyes were on the judge, it was clear her comment was directed at Ryan's lawyer.

The judge let this one slide and instead turned to me. "Has the police department closed the investigation?"

"We're not actively pursuing other suspects or witnesses," I told him, "but we're planning to continue having extra patrols drive by both of their residences."

"For how long?"

As long as it takes. "Indefinitely."

The judge sat back, the handle of his gavel in one hand, the head in the other, as he contemplated his decision. Still hunched, Adriana leaned forward in her seat, her face pained and pensive. Ryan's face, on the other hand, looked slightly smug.

His smugness didn't last long.

The judge looked my way. "The gun he had in his car is still in the possession of the police department, right?"

"Yes," I said. "It's in the evidence locker along with the ammunition, zip ties, duct tape, box cutter, and bandana."

The judge turned away and gave Ryan a pointed look. "Do you own another gun, Mr. Downey?"

"Yes," he replied. "I bought another one over the weekend."

Wow. He hadn't wasted any time replacing the weapon we'd seized, had he?

The judge said, "I'm granting the protective order. Mr. Downey, be aware this means you cannot possess a gun until such time as the order is revoked." He banged his gavel once to indicate the finality of his decision. "Officer Luz, I order you to take custody of Mr. Downey's weapon."

Ryan's mouth gaped and he turned to his attorney. "What the hell?" he shrieked.

The attorney quickly silenced him, and whispered in his ear. I wasn't sure what he said to Ryan, but whatever it was didn't seem to sit well. He shoved his chair under the table after they stood, taking his anger out on the furniture.

I nodded to Adriana and her attorney as I followed Ryan and his lawyer out of the courtroom and across the street to the parking garage where he'd left his car. We took the steps up to the second floor. Ryan wore no smirk now. In fact, his countenance bore more than a little trepidation. Was he scared of how the protective order might affect his life? Or was he scared of Adriana? How I wished I could get inside his head and find out!

As we approached the Camaro, I asked, "Is the gun in the console like the one you had the other night?"

"Yeah," Ryan said softly, sounding a little choked up.

"You unlock the doors," I said. "I'll get the gun." No way in hell would I let him reach in for it. He might turn around and blast me in the face. That would be a closed-casket funeral.

He stood back several feet with his attorney and aimed his fob at the car. *Bleep-bleep. Click.*

I instructed Brigit to sit. Keeping one eye on Ryan, I opened the car and, as quickly as I could, grabbed his gun and the new box of ammo he'd purchased.

He looked at me, his expression troubled. "If she comes after me, and I can't defend myself, it'll be all your fault, Officer Luz."

Oh hell no. He wasn't going to lay responsibility for his or Adriana's actions on me. "All I did was tell the truth."

"You don't know the truth!"

"Then tell me."

"Dammit!" he screamed, bringing his fists down on the trunk of his car. "I've tried!"

His attorney looked at me. "I think it's best you leave now."

I thought that was best, too.

THIRTY-SIX
AWAITING ORDERS

Brigit

The man was yelling and had hit the car. Brigit knew this was the type of behavior that often came before Megan ordered her to take someone down. She could also smell his adrenaline. He was angry, that was for sure. She stood at the ready, one eye on the man, one eye on her partner.

As it turned out, Megan didn't tell her to take down the man. Instead, she told Brigit to "come on." As Megan walked away, Brigit stepped into place beside her. She cast a final look back over her furry shoulder.

The man's eyes locked on hers in challenge.

You really want to go there, buddy? When Brigit silently curled back her lip and showed her teeth, the man pulled his head back, his eyes dilating in fright. *Yeah, that's what I thought.*

THIRTY-SEVEN
ROCK, PAPER, SCISSORS

Adriana

The protective orders between the two of them were meaningless. A mere piece of paper, a few words signed by a judge, wouldn't stop what had been set in motion. Paper might beat rock, but it didn't beat scissors, and it sure as hell wouldn't beat her.

THIRTY-EIGHT
WHAT A PARE

Megan

While Adriana's protective order gave police the right to arrest Ryan if he violated it, the awful truth was that it was merely a piece of paper. It wouldn't stop him from violence if he was intent on committing it. I could only hope he wasn't. Maybe the order would prove to be a tipping point, make him realize he needed to back off and move on, maybe see a therapist or counselor to deal with his emotions.

He behaved himself all week. I hoped that was a good sign, that his anger had abated rather than festered and grown during those days.

Shortly after eleven on Friday night, dispatch came over the airwaves. "Officers needed on Vickery at Stage West Theater. We have reports of a female suspect causing property damage. Civilians have restrained the suspect."

Many times, people were hesitant to get involved in stopping a crime or apprehending a criminal, and with good reason. Criminals could turn on them, sometimes with deadly consequences. But sometimes people stepped up, risking their own safety. Looked like there'd been a hero or two taking in the play tonight.

I grabbed my microphone and pushed the button. "Officers Luz and Brigit on our way."

I took a right on Hemphill Street and hooked a left onto Vickery. A block and a half later, and we'd arrived at Stage West. The theater had been founded by Jerry Russell, an accomplished actor and father to Wendy Davis, a politician who'd served on the Fort Worth City Council and in the Texas Senate. She'd risen to national fame when she'd filibustered for eleven hours on the final day of the legislative session against a bill that imposed restrictions on women's access to reproductive health care. Though the bill later passed, the stand Wendy took, in a pair of pink running shoes, had nonetheless made her a living legend. And when the Supreme Court later ruled the law unconstitutional, she was vindicated, even though she'd lost a bid for governor in the interim. Interestingly, the theater's current offering was *Ann*, a play based on the life of Ann Richards, another brassy female Democratic politician who was also a legend in Texas. Like they say, well-behaved women rarely make history. They also rarely get a Broadway play written about them.

People were filtering out of the theater, the show having apparently just ended. As I drove up, two women waved their arms to get my attention. "Over here!" one of them called.

I quickly parked and retrieved Brigit from the back of my car, clipping her lead onto her collar.

The women who'd called to me scurried over. "When

we were leaving the theater, we spotted a woman scratching up our car. Our dates ran over and tackled her."

As they led the way, I strode over with them. "Is it someone you know?"

"No," she said. "None of us have ever seen her before."

I found their dates hunkered down between two cars, both of which had been scratched to pieces, the paint cut through to the metal underneath. The two men were situated at either end of a blond woman who lay facedown on the asphalt between the cars. One of the men had dropped down over her legs to try to hold them, while the other had sat on her back to hold her arms. She struggled against the men, grunting and groaning as she exerted and strained to raise herself up. Her efforts were futile. Not only did the men outweigh her by at least four times, they had gravity on their side.

I caught the men's eyes. "Keep a hold on her until I secure the area, okay?"

They both nodded.

"Stop struggling!" I ordered the woman. "Now! Or I'll deploy my dog!" I gave Brigit a hand signal and she let loose with her most ferocious growl and a warning bark. *RUFF!*

Still facedown, the woman went stock-still.

A knife lay on the asphalt, just inches from the woman's hand. She must have dropped it when she'd been tackled. Holding Brigit close, I circled between the adjacent car to the right and bent down to take a closer look at the weapon. It appeared to be a paring knife. The blade, which was around four inches in length, bore the

words WÜSTHOF CLASSIC. The black handle was con-
toured, with three stainless steel circles in a row and a
red square with a three-tined fork logo. It was an unusually fancy tool for an act of vandalism that could
have been accomplished with a set of keys or a simple
pocketknife. Had the woman also planned to peel and
mince a human victim, too?

Lest she somehow regain possession of the blade, I
used my toe to push it back a few feet. Time to find out
who this woman is and why she'd taken it upon herself
to go all Etch A Sketch on these vehicles.

"Ma'am, you need to—"

Before I could speak to the woman, an outraged
squeal erupted nearby and a kazoolike male voice
yelled, "What the fuck?!"

Wait a second. That voice sounds familiar.

The two women who'd flagged me down stood at the
rear of the vehicles. They looked to their left, where the
voice had come from.

The one who had spoken with me earlier called out
to the man. "She got our cars, too!"

There was a third car in the mix? *Great.* I hadn't noticed the vehicle parked to the left; my focus had been
on the suspect.

The male voice came again. "At least your tires
weren't slashed, too!"

Slashed tires? The damage must have been more ex-
tensive than I'd realized at first glance.

A second later, a man stepped up next to the women.
Ryan. His car had been keyed, too? And his tires cut?

His head jerked back in surprise. "Officer Luz?"

A brown-haired girl in a sexy pink satin slip dress

stepped up next to him and put a hand on his shoulder. "You know this cop, Ryan?"

Uh-oh.

Was the woman at my feet Danielle, the one I'd spoken with after the unknown blonde had shown up at Ryan's place with the gift and balloons and tried to sweet-talk her way in? Had she lied to me about her involvement? Had she realized he'd been on a date with another girl tonight and come here seeking revenge in a Carrie Underwood "Before He Cheats" kind of way?

I glanced down at the woman, whose face was still hidden under the curtain of blond hair. I couldn't tell if it was Danielle. But there was one way to find out.

I crouched down near her head. "Ma'am, in just a moment I'm going to ask these men to release you. When they do, you need to roll over onto your back and keep your hands over your head. Understand me? Any funny business and you'll get bit."

Brigit barked again. *RRUF!*

The woman didn't speak, but her head moved up and down as she nodded in agreement.

I motioned for the men to release the woman. When they did, she continued to lie facedown for a moment or two, but finally, and slowly, rolled over onto her back.

Adriana.

Ryan's mouth gaped. "You bitch!"

When he stormed forward, I held up a hand. "Touch her and you're in trouble, too."

He threw his hands in the air. "When will you get it, Officer Luz? *She's* the problem! She's always been the problem! All I've done is try to protect myself!"

His date gave him a confused, sideways glance. "What's going on?"

He cast her an annoyed glance. "I'll fill you in later. There's too much to tell."

I wondered what had happened with Ryan and Danielle. Had she called things off? It seemed likely. She hadn't seemed that into him.

Turning my attention back to Adriana, I instructed her to sit up and put her hands behind her. "Wrists together. Now."

Her shoulders shook with sobs, but she did as she was told. I slid the cuffs onto her wrists and told her to remain sitting. Pushing the button on my shoulder-mounted radio, I said, "Transport needed at Stage West Theater. Single suspect."

Ryan ranted, raved, and paced until Summer and Derek arrived a few minutes later. I gave them the scoop.

"Oh, honey," Summer said to Adriana, shaking her head. "No man is worth all this trouble."

Derek yanked Adriana to her feet and stowed her in the back of their cruiser. Considering his work done, he slid back into the passenger seat, grabbed an enormous fountain drink from the cup holder, and sucked on the straw. *Slurrrrp!*

While Adriana hung her head in the back of Summer's squad car, Summer and I took a few minutes to interview the witnesses and victims, assess the damage, and take photos. Ryan's Camaro bore the brunt of Adriana's knife assault. It looked as if it had been attacked by a pride of angry lions. Numerous deep gouges ran the length of the side, with dozens of shorter, shallower vertical scratches along the way. All four tires had been cut and rested in deflated rubber puddles under his car. While the two adjacent cars on the right had also been damaged, it seemed clear to me that Ryan's car was the real target and Adriana had only scratched the other cars to make the attack seem random and keep suspicion off herself. She obviously hadn't expected to be caught in the act. *So much for that, huh?*

When we finished, I told the group of victims that I'd input my police report immediately so that they could have it available for insurance purposes as soon as possible.

The two couples thanked me, shook my hand, and drove away.

Ryan, however, looked as if he was ready to explode. "That bitch is going to kill me one day! I told you as much! But *nooo!* You didn't think she was dangerous." He scoffed before leaning into my face and giving me a pointed look. "What do you think now?"

What did I think now? I thought that it was damn hard to read some people. I thought that Adriana had been immensely stupid to do what she did. But most of all, I thought that I needed a damn vacation.

An hour and a half later, Detective Bustamente and I were seated in a conference room across from Adriana, who was still shackled but with her hands in front of her now.

"I want you to look me in the eye and tell me the truth, Adriana," I said. "Who was behind each of the events? Was it you?"

"No!" she cried. "You have to believe me!"

Bustamente, who was always the epitome of calm,

raised his hands from the table. "Why? Why should we believe you? You just did something very impetuous tonight and violated the law. Give us a reason to think you're telling us the truth."

Her voice was shrill and shaky. "Because I am!"

"You're going to have to do better than that," he said. "Help us understand. What were you thinking tonight?"

She paused for a few beats, her chest heaving, before she took a couple of deep breaths and spoke. "I know I shouldn't have done what I did," she said. "But I just couldn't take it anymore. The pressure, the constant worry. It was too much. I guess I . . . snapped."

"You got the protective order against him," I said. "I took away his gun. You had the advantage now."

"What advantage?" she cried. "After you took away his gun that first time he just went out and bought another. He's probably bought another one by now!"

Bustamente and I exchanged glances. She could very well be right. The protective order against Ryan was in the system and a gun seller required to run a background check should find it and refuse the sale. Unfortunately, there were myriad ways to work around the regulations. No background checks were required on gun sales between private citizens, for instance. Ryan could have attended any of the dozen or so gun shows being constantly held in the state. Heck, the Will Rogers Center hosted gun shows on a regular basis, some big, some small. One of the oddest sights I'd ever seen was when the center was simultaneously hosting a gun show and a ballet recital. Little girls in pink tutus were dancing and leaping their way through the parking lot while hunters and gun enthusiasts dressed in camouflage pulled rifles and pistols and shotguns out of their trunks.

Adriana released a shuddering breath. "That car means more to Ryan than anything else. I wanted to hit him where it hurts. Just once. Before the inevitable happens."

"What's 'the inevitable'?" I asked.

She looked up and fully met my gaze for the first time ever. "Ryan killing me."

THIRTY-NINE
PILLOW TALK

Brigit

When Brigit and Megan returned home after their all-night shift, the dog was more than ready for a nice snooze. It seemed Megan, though, was not. Once again she tossed and turned in the bed, making it impossible for Brigit to rest.

But Brigit wasn't in the mood to go sleep on the sofa like she had last time. The couch was comfy enough, but it wasn't as soft and warm as the bed. Besides, the sofa was in the living room at the front of the house, and Brigit's sleep would be distracted by the noise from outside. Cars driving by on the street. Delivery trucks. People walking by on the sidewalk. The mailman.

No, it was Megan's turn to sleep on the sofa.

The next time her partner shook her awake, Brigit put all four of her paws on Megan's back and pushed as hard as she could. *Get out of the bed.*

Megan cut Brigit an irritated look over her shoulder. "You're not the boss, you know."

While Brigit wasn't entirely sure of the meaning of

Megan's words, the tone was clear. Still, so long as Megan left the bed Brigit didn't much care if her partner was angry with her. She wanted some shut-eye. She stretched her legs out and pushed again.

Finally, Megan took the hint. With a sharp breath, she threw back the covers, climbed out of bed, and marched out of the room.

Brigit took advantage of the space by climbing on top of the covers and using her front paws to scrunch them up under her for maximum fluffiness and comfort. When she got the sheets and spread just right, she flopped back down on them and settled her head on the pillow.

Aaahhhh . . .

FORTY
GIVE-AND-TAKE

Adriana

Relationships were about give-and-take.

She had given Ryan so much.

Her time.

Her affection.

Her love.

All Ryan had done was take, take, take, and in return he'd given her nothing but shit.

Well, those days were over now. And soon, *his* days would be over.

FORTY-ONE
A MATCH MADE IN HELL

Megan

I was back on nights in mid-September. After scratching up the cars and slashing Ryan's tires, Adriana had been charged with felony criminal mischief and violating the protective order Ryan had against her. But given that she had no prior record and that it appeared Ryan's actions might have led to her "losing it," the prosecutor went easy on her and worked out a plea deal under which she pled guilty to a misdemeanor and agreed to perform twenty hours of community service at a soup kitchen. I hoped they'd keep her away from the knives.

There was no moon tonight and an abundance of clouds that blocked out all starlight. The sky and earth were exceptionally opaque, as if trying to hide their darkest secrets. Forest Park was nearly invisible in the blackness.

Brigit seemed to sense the odd, ominous quality of the night, too. I'd left the windows down so she could get some fresh air, and she stood at the mesh, sniffing the breeze, her furry brow furrowed as if she smelled trouble coming our way.

As I drove out of the park and onto the dimly lit streets, I wondered if, or when, Ryan's and Adriana's prophecies might come true and one of them would kill the other. But who would be the killer and who would end up in a body bag? I still had no idea.

Despite Detective Bustamente's assurances that I'd done all I could, that some cases would always go unsolved, that many questions would go forever unanswered, I had a difficult time accepting what felt like a failure to me. I'd let someone be victimized, let another get away with it. I still wasn't sure who was the real victim and who was the real perpetrator where Adriana and Ryan were concerned.

And it's eating me alive.

A soft *thunk* sounded as Brigit flopped down onto the platform of her enclosure to chew on a toy. It dawned on me that for both of us, work time and playtime had essentially melded into one. She often got to nap or play while working, and I often spent what should be my personal free time mulling over pending investigations.

We rolled up Hulen, approaching Ryan's apartment complex. While nothing had happened between him or Adriana in a few weeks now, I turned in out of habit. As I circled through the shadowy lot, white reverse lights illuminated on his Camaro across the way. Looked like he was going somewhere. Odd, given that it was midweek and after two A.M.

Had he put another GPS device on Adriana's car or tracked her in some other way? Was she having another migraine, maybe heading to the pharmacy for more headache medicine? Or was he going to his brother and sister-in-law's house to help them with Toby? Maybe something had happened, an emergency, and they needed an immediate sitter to watch the tyke. I had no idea what was going on. I could only surmise that, given that Ryan was in his Camaro rather than his truck, it seemed unlikely he was going to help with some type of urgent communications outage.

I decided to follow him. If he was the stalker, maybe I'd finally catch him in the act and get that closure I so desperately sought. If he wasn't, maybe I'd catch him going to the convenience store for an emergency roll of toilet paper or condoms. For all I knew he had Danielle up in his apartment, or maybe the brown-haired girl from the theater.

He turned out of the parking lot and I followed several seconds behind him, leaving enough space between us that it would be difficult for him to discern that the vehicle behind him was a police cruiser.

I eyed my partner in the rearview mirror. "What do you think he's up to, Brig?"

She wagged her tail in response, but continued to gnaw the nylon bone I'd bought her a few weeks ago. She found the toy more interesting than speculating on Ryan's destination and motive for this late-night excursion.

I followed him as he turned right at a red light. *Hmm.* He was headed in the general direction of Adriana's place, but we were still too far away for me to say for certain that's where he was going. There were lots of places he could stop between here and there, lots of places where he might turn and take a freeway instead of the surface streets.

He sped up, exceeding the speed limit by at least fifteen miles per hour. Still, I was more interested in where he was going than in giving him a ticket. If I could finally catch him doing something big and illegal I could put this frustrating investigation to rest.

A couple minutes, three more turns, and one blatant failure to stop for a stop sign later and I knew without a doubt he was headed to Adriana's house. *How?* Because he'd careened onto her street and I could see his red brake lights illuminating up ahead and hear the screech as his car skidded to a stop in front of her house.

What the hell was he doing here? Not only did he have a protective order against this woman, but she had one against him, too. He'd also claimed to be afraid Adriana would kill him. Had that been bullshit? Both I and Detective Bustamente had warned him against having any interactions with her. *Dammit! Why don't people do what judges and cops and common sense tell them to?!?*

I punched the gas, but Ryan was faster. He bolted from his car and stormed up the steps. I caught a glimpse of Adriana in a short white nightgown before she closed the door behind him.

What the hell just happened?

Are they reconciling, after all the shit one of them has put the other through?

It wouldn't be the first time a couple had been at each other's throats one instant and bumping uglies the next. It wouldn't be the last time, either.

I hopped out of my car and yanked open the door to Brigit's enclosure, not even taking the time to shut it before giving her the order to stay by my side. The two of us stormed up to the porch. As I approached, my nose caught the acrid scent of petroleum. Brigit scented it, too, her black nose twitching in the air. *Holy shit! Is that gasoline?*

My mind barely had time to form the thought, when *WHOOSH!*

I heard the sound of the fire igniting the same instant I saw the flames light up through a gap in the curtains on the front window. Instinctively, I grabbed the door handle but it wouldn't turn. It was locked. I pounded on the door with both fists. "Adriana! Ryan!"

There was no answer.

I pressed the button on my shoulder-mounted radio. "We need a fire truck immediately!" I screamed into the mic, following with Adriana's address. "There's a fire in the house and two people inside! It smells like gasoline!"

The dispatcher's voice came back as I ran down the steps. "Fire and ambulance units are on the way."

I ran to the window and tried to see inside. All I could see were red-hot flames. No doubt they were licking at those perfectly arranged bookshelves, the paper providing perfect kindling for the fire.

The smell of gasoline was strong by the window, too. Had Adriana set this fire? Or had Ryan poured gasoline out here earlier, then concocted some ploy to convince her to let him into the house so he could burn it down?

I banged my fists on the window. "Adriana! Ryan!"

There was no response. I wasn't sure what to do.

Despite everything that had happened, I didn't want either of them to get injured or die. But I didn't want me or Brigit to get injured or die, either. And my partner and I weren't equipped to fight a fire.

Or were we?

I grabbed the closest oleander bush and wrangled it aside, my eyes desperately seeking a faucet and hose.

Nothing.

I grabbed the second bush and pushed the limbs aside so I could see. There was a faucet but no hose.

Dammit!

I ran to the side gate and bolted through it, Brigit loping after me. There had to be a second faucet back here somewhere, right? And a hose? Sure! Adriana must use them to water her garden, right?

As Brigit and I ran around the back corner I came face-to-face with Adriana. The clouds broke and a glint of starlight reflected off the Cuisinart cradled in her arms just before momentum carried me forward to collide with her. Our skulls met with a *smack!* The impact knocked her back on her ass on her patio, and the Cuisinart flew out of her arms, smashing into a dozen pieces on the patio. What looked like sparklers flared at the edges of my vision and I fell to my knees on the concrete. *Thump.* Damn, that hurt!

It took only a moment for our heads to clear and, when they did, Adriana looked at me, her eyes wild with surprise. "What are you doing here?"

Really? That's how a person reacts when their house is up in flames?

No, I realized a moment later. *It's not.*

I knew with absolute certainty then that Adriana had set this fire and that she'd lured Ryan to her house to kill him. My conclusion must have been written on my face because the next thing she did was reach out with a bright pink stun gun. *Finally! Some color!* Before I could slap her arm away she gave me a solid *zzzap!*

The jolt seared me to my very core. I slumped over, unable to control a single muscle, falling sideways onto the concrete, my cheekbone hitting the cement with a teeth-rattling *smack*! My mind screamed to Brigit to watch out, but I couldn't make my mouth cooperate. But while my body wouldn't work, my mind did. *If that woman hurts Brigit, I will kill her in the most painful way possible. I'll take my baton and shove it down her throat until it comes out that tight little ass of hers.*

After that thought processed, I realized just how much danger Brigit and I were in. This woman had just set fire to a house with a person inside it. She'd have no qualms offing a police officer or a dog, too.

Fear flooded my immobile body. I was helpless. I couldn't do anything for myself or my partner.

Luckily, Brigit had a mind of her own. While I usually found this trait to be annoying, it served both of us well tonight. Rather than await orders from her disabled handler—*me*—she made her own decision. And that decision was, *I'm going to take down the bitch who hurt my partner.*

When Adriana reached toward her with the stun gun, Brigit ducked in the nick of time and grabbed Adriana's wrist in her teeth, chomping down with all her might. The woman screamed at the top of her lungs and dropped the stun gun onto the patio, where it hit with a loud *clack* and immediately broke into two pieces among the shards of the food processor. My mind might be rattled, but it was coherent enough to think, *There goes the warranty.*

Adriana whipped her arm back and forth, but with an enormous dog like Brigit hanging from it, she couldn't shake it free. "Let go!" she shrieked. "Let go!"

Yeah. Not gonna happen.

Adriana used her free arm to leverage herself to her feet and tried to run, dragging Brigit along with her. As the two wrangled their way down the side of the house, my limbs finally began to cooperate again and I pushed myself up on all fours.

The sound of sirens coming up the street seemed like the song of angels. *Hallelujah!*

Using a garden gnome for leverage, I got to my feet, a little wobbly still, but at least upright again. *Thanks, little guy.* I yanked my baton from my belt, flicked my wrist, and it opened with its usual decisive *SNAP*!

I lumbered after Adriana and Brigit, putting one hand against the outer wall of the house to stabilize myself. I could feel the heat coming from inside. I passed the door that led from the kitchen to the outside. Through the square pane of glass, I saw the café curtains catch fire, the flames eating their way up the fabric.

As I made my way out of the gate to the front yard, I found Adriana lying facedown on the grass with Brigit sitting on top of her, the woman's arm still clutched in her teeth. I also found a fire truck pulling to a stop in the street. Frankie leaped out of one side of the cab, while Seth leaped out of the other.

"Megan?" they cried in unison.

"Ryan's inside!" I waved my baton at the house. The fire had breached the ceiling and roof. While it was too dark for me to actually see the smoke billowing out, the fact that a wide swath of the neighborhood and sky were obscured told me there was a lot of it and it was thick. I ran up to Adriana and brought my baton down on the grass next to her face. *Whap!* "Where is he?" I shrieked. "Where's Ryan?"

Her shoulders began to heave with sobs. "Last I saw him"—she gasped for air between sobs —"he was on the kitchen floor."

"Did you zap him?"

"Yes."

My mind flicked back to the burning café curtains. It would be nothing short of a miracle if the fire hadn't killed Ryan yet. Hell, he'd probably already succumbed to smoke inhalation. But there was always a chance, right?

"He's in the kitchen!" I hollered to Frankie, who was bolting for the door. "It's the second room!"

Two men used a battering ram to break through the locked front door. *Bam! Bam! Bam!* When the hole was big enough, Frankie ducked through with a mask over her face, disappearing into the cloud of smoke like a magician with a death wish.

My heart contracted so hard in my chest it threatened to implode. *Would this be the last time I'd see my friend alive?*

I wish I knew, because if it was I would beat Adriana to death with my baton right here on her lawn. I wouldn't even care if a judge ordered the prison wardens to lock me up and throw away the key. It would be worth it.

While I stood guard over Adriana and Brigit continued to hold her arm in her grip, Seth and the other firefighters scurried about their truck and the yard. In seconds he had a hose in his hand and a steady stream of water aimed into the house. I closed my eyes and prayed it wasn't too late for Frankie and Ryan. *Please, God! Frankie's a good person and the best human friend I've ever had. Don't take her away. She doesn't deserve to die! And Ryan . . . well God, you tell me. I still haven't figured this all out.*

Over the sounds of the fire engine, the forceful spray of the water, and the shouts of the firefighters, another sound came. A sickening sound. A creaking sound.

CREEEEEAK.

I watched in horror as the roof caved in, slowly at first and then gaining momentum. *BAM!* It fell in completely, leaving behind a jagged, gaping hole trimmed with broken two-by-fours, torn pink insulation, and shingles. *Dear God! Has Frankie been crushed to death inside?*

My mind went woozy, unable to entertain the thought, and I found myself gulping air in a panic. *Uh-uh-uh!* The hyperventilation caused my vision to narrow until all I could see was Brigit's troubled brown eyes watching me. She whimpered, worried.

"Megan!"

Hallelujah! Frankie's voice was like birdsong in spring. Despite my having skipped that Wednesday mass in favor of wine, the Almighty had not only heard my prayer, He'd also answered it. I turned to see Frankie stumbling along the side of the house I'd just stumbled along. Her mask hung down in front of her, no longer on her face. Slanted across her back was a prone Ryan, and sticking out of his back was the long metal handle of the meat fork I'd seen in Adriana's dish drainer the first time I'd come to her house.

Yeek.

After reflexively crossing myself—*Catholic rituals die hard*—I ordered Brigit to continue to guard Adriana while I rushed over to help Frankie. I reached her just as her strength gave out. She collapsed to the ground with Ryan on top of her. In his hand was the *Wonder Woman #1* comic, enclosed in a protective plastic sleeve. Looked like he'd been right about Adriana. She had, in fact, taken his prized comic book.

"What do I do?" I cried to Frankie. *Please don't make me pull out that meat fork.*

"Get the paramedics over here!" she coughed out.

I ran back to the front of the house and waved my arms over my head as I shouted to the ambulance crew. "Over here! Over here! We've got injuries!"

Seth turned my way. "Did she find Ryan?"

"Yes! They're out!"

His face and posture relaxed in relief and he closed his eyes for a split second. I had a sneaking suspicion he was silently thanking God, too. These types of emergencies tended to make believers out of even the biggest skeptics.

In minutes, the paramedics had oxygen masks on both Ryan and Frankie and were loading Ryan into the back of the ambulance. He was unconscious, his clothing was singed, and one leg appeared badly burned and bloody, but at least he was still breathing on his own. There was a chance he could survive. If he did, he was sure to need all kinds of work on the leg, skin grafts and the like, but maybe the doctors could save it.

Frankie climbed into an ambulance, too. My eyes met hers over her mask and I raised a hand in encouragement and support as the doors of the second ambulance swung shut on her. As the vehicle pulled away from the curb, the driver activated the siren.

Neighbors had swarmed out of their houses and gathered in a driveway across the street to watch the activity. As I turned back to the house, I noticed the comic book lying on the grass. I ran over and snatched it up before it could be soaked by the hose or trampled by the firefighters.

Returning to Adriana and Brigit, I ordered Brigit off the woman, but instructed her to continue to stand guard. When Brigit released her hold, blood ran from Adriana's arm and Brigit's jowls. It wasn't Brigit's fault. If Adriana hadn't struggled, she wouldn't have been injured so badly. Before I could wipe the blood from Brigit's mouth, she licked it off herself. The sight made my stomach seize. *Ehhhh.*

I radioed for another ambulance for Adriana, as well as backup that could keep an eye on her in the ambulance and hospital until she was released into the custody of the Fort Worth Police Department to be booked and charged. Her bite wounds were deep, but given that she'd just attempted to murder her ex-boyfriend, she had no right to complain.

Minutes later, Summer and Derek Mackey arrived.

Summer pulled her cruiser to the curb across the street and the two of them climbed out.

Summer, being the sweet person that she was, rushed over, her eyes bright with concern. "My gosh, Megan! What happened here? Are you all right?"

Derek, living up to his nickname of "the Big Dick," sauntered up. He eyed me and nudged Adriana with his toe. "Party get out of hand?"

Both of us chose to ignore him.

To Summer, I said, "I spotted Ryan Downey leaving his apartment and followed him here. Before I could get to the door the house went up in flames. Adriana ran out with a stun gun and zapped me."

"Ha!" Derek barked, slapping his thigh in delight. "You got shocked? Hoo-ah! That's some poetic justice right there." He skewered me with his glare. "Doesn't feel so good, does it, Luz?"

I supposed I deserved that. Getting zapped by the stun gun had been no fun at all, and the Taser I'd used on Derek packed even more punch. But just because I deserved his verbal spanking didn't mean I would take it graciously. "Shut up, Derek."

He merely cackled in response. Adriana had made his day.

I gestured to the woman. "She's got some bite wounds that'll need treatment. One of you will need to accompany her in the ambulance and keep watch on her at the hospital until she's released into custody."

"I'll do it," Mackey said.

His offer didn't surprise me. He was a brave guy, but he was also a lazy one. He'd probably much rather sit around a hospital drinking sodas and playing games on his phone than patrolling the streets of Fort Worth.

He looked down at Adriana. "Let's move, Little Match Girl."

When he made no move to help her up, she used her good arm to push herself up to a stand. As she turned to walk to the ambulance, she took one last look at the house.

I couldn't help myself. "Say good-bye to your security deposit."

She sent me a heated glower that packed nearly as many volts as her stun gun. Seemed eye contact was no problem for her now. I only hoped that she didn't spend her time in jail plotting vengeance against me and Brigit.

When the last of the flames fizzled, Adriana's house stood smoldering, a huge black hole in the roof, its front door smashed in, and its floors flooded. Evidently alerted by a neighbor, the owner of the house drove up and climbed out of his car to assess the damage.

"My goodness!" The gray-haired man shook his head in disbelief. "What the hell happened here?"

"A bad breakup," I said, "some stalking, a little bit of arson, and a whole lot of attempted murder."

The next few days brought many developments and some information that finally helped us see things clearly.

Adriana was treated for the bite wounds and prescribed an antibiotic to prevent infection. A physical therapist ran her through some tests and determined Brigit's bite had resulted in no permanent injury, though Adriana would likely have bite scars for the rest of her life, a little souvenir from the night she'd gone bat-shit. Perhaps they'd serve as a constant reminder not to cross a K-9 or her partner.

She was released into the custody of the Fort Worth PD and charged with a variety of offenses ranging from attempted murder and battery to arson and stalking. The judge denied bail and ordered Adriana to undergo therapy to treat her mental health issues.

After a psychological evaluation and consultation with her defense attorney, Adriana determined it was in her best interests to come clean and hope that her diagnosis as one who suffered from a personality disorder might get her a reduced sentence. At the behest of both her attorney and her therapist, she admitted that she'd attacked Ryan at his truck weeks ago, causing the scratch marks on his neck. Her claims that he'd been into kinky sex were made up. Though he had a healthy sexual appetite, his desires were not the things pornos were made of.

She admitted that she'd stolen the brick and shoes from Ryan's front porch, and had used them to break her window and fake the footprint on her patio. She also admitted that she'd been the woman with the gift bag and balloons who'd tried to gain access to Ryan's apartment. She'd seen Danielle's picture on Ryan's Facebook page, and had dressed to look like her in the hopes it would throw off suspicion if the plan didn't work. She'd hoped to get inside and wait for Ryan to come home, then attempt a reconciliation. A stupid plan, at best.

What man would want to reconcile with a woman who'd snuck into his house uninvited and disguised? How could he ever trust her?

She admitted that she'd placed the GPS units on both his car and her own. She'd placed the one on his car first so that she could track his comings and goings. She then realized that she'd look guilty if the device were found on his car, so she'd placed one on her own as well, to confuse the issue. She said she'd been surprised I'd thought to look for the devices. She hadn't thought I was all that smart. *Grr. I showed her, didn't I?*

She also admitted to stealing Ryan's *Wonder Woman #1* comic book and using it to lure him to her house the night of the fire. She'd phoned him from an untraceable burner phone and told him if he wanted it back he needed to come to her house immediately or she was going to put the comic in her food processor and julienne the busty superheroine on maximum speed until Wonder Woman was nothing more than red, white, and blue confetti.

Ryan was less forthcoming, but an electronic device we recovered told the tale he wouldn't. After seeing the story of Adriana and Ryan on the news, a call came in from one of Interstellar Communications' customers who'd recently had Ryan at their house to install new service. When they'd gone to use their new promotional tablet, they'd been surprised to discover a photo of a pretty young Latina woman on the device. Being an older couple with no great knowledge of electronics, they'd assumed the photo was a placeholder or sample, akin to the glossy paper photos placed in physical frames at stores. But when they'd seen Adriana's and Ryan's pictures on the evening news, they recognized Ryan as their installer and Adriana as the woman in the photo on their tablet.

Ryan had evidently used the promotional tablet, his technical know-how, and Adriana's credentials to remotely log in to the rehab center's Wi-Fi and upload the profile of Adriana to Kinky Cowtown. While he'd wiped the remote login from the browser history and deleted the remote desktop app, he'd forgotten about the picture. *Dumbass.* Still, I could hardly blame him for pulling the stunt. Few people wouldn't consider retribution against someone who had tried to frame them the way Adriana had tried to frame Ryan, and had tried to get access to their home to do who knows what. The assistant district attorney evidently felt the same way, that Adriana had got what she had coming to her, and declined to file charges against Ryan. A judge also revoked the protective order Adriana had gotten against him.

Ryan was treated for smoke inhalation and burns. Luckily for him, the meat fork had missed all of his vital organs. Once the fire had been fully extinguished, another gun was found on the floor of Adriana's kitchen. He'd brought it with him when coming to retrieve his comic book. But, again, it was hard to blame him for feeling the need to protect himself. His former lover had indeed become a crazy ex-girlfriend.

The investigation was finally over and the case was closed. Though I wished we could have figured things out sooner, I knew both Adriana and Ryan had been careful and crafty so as to not be discovered. Detective Bustamente said any stalking case that didn't end with a dead body was a victory, and congratulated me on saving Ryan's life. He also insisted I take that vacation I'd been dreaming about.

He didn't have to tell me twice.

FORTY-TWO
VACATION

Brigit

The dog wasn't quite sure where Megan had taken them. The sign they'd passed that read WELCOME TO GALVESTON ISLAND meant nothing to her. She couldn't read. She only knew that the place smelled like fish and salt and had big water that crashed onto the sand and that she was having a ball! A beach ball!

While Megan and Seth lay baking in the sun, Brigit and Blast ran up and down the beach chasing the seagulls. The dog knew her chances of catching one of the birds was small, but she didn't care. It was still fun. What wasn't fun was the crab who'd pinched her nose when she'd gone to sniff him. She'd swung her snout and flung that nasty creature right back into the bay.

Another day, she and Blast found a dead fish in the dunes. It smelled disgustingly wonderful, so they took turns rolling on it. Megan and Seth didn't even make them take baths afterward, just encouraged them to romp in the waves, which the dogs had fun doing anyway.

They even went for a ride on a boat. At first, Brigit and Blast slid around the deck as the boat pitched from side to side, but eventually they got their sea legs—all four of them.

When Megan and Seth packed up all their things and loaded Brigit and Blast into the backseat of Seth's car, Brigit knew the vacation was over. As the motion of the car moving up the highway lulled her to sleep, Brigit wondered what lay ahead for them when they returned to work. Would they get to play chase? Take down a bad guy?

The only thing she knew for sure is that a new adventure always awaited them.

Look for these other *tails* of romance
and K-9 suspense from Diane Kelly

PAW ENFORCEMENT

PAW AND ORDER

UPHOLDING THE PAW
(an e-original novella)

LAYING DOWN THE PAW

AGAINST THE PAW

ABOVE THE PAW

From St. Martin's Paperbacks

. . . and don't miss the hilarious Tara Holloway novels!

Death, Taxes, and a French Manicure

Death, Taxes, and a Skinny No-Whip Latte

Death, Taxes, and Extra-Hold Hairspray

Death, Taxes, and a Sequined Clutch
(an e-original novella)

Death, Taxes, and Peach Sangria

Death, Taxes, and Hot Pink Leg Warmers

Death, Taxes, and Green Tea Ice Cream

Death, Taxes, and Mistletoe Mayhem
(an e-original novella)

Death, Taxes, and Silver Spurs

Death, Taxes, and Cheap Sunglasses

Death, Taxes, and a Chocolate Cannoli

Death, Taxes, and a Satin Garter

Death, Taxes, and Sweet Potato Fries

From St. Martin's Paperbacks